DARE TO LOVE

THE HOLLINGER SERIES
BOOK ONE

TRISHA FUENTES

Published by
Ardent Artist Books
www.ardentartistbooks.com

↳ ABOUT US

Ardent Artist Books was established in 2008. We publish modern and historical romances several times a month!

Get Your FREE Download:
Published & Upcoming Books
Visit our website at:
https://bit.ly/3Wva4o0

* * *

↳ WATCH THE BOOK TRAILER

Follow us on YouTube!
https://www.youtube.com/@theardentartist

Like, Subscribe & Comment

CONTENTS

Prologue 1

Chapter 1 11

Chapter 2 17

Chapter 3 31

Chapter 4 37

Chapter 5 49

Chapter 6 59

Chapter 7 65

Chapter 8 73

Chapter 9 85

Chapter 10 95

Chapter 11 101

Chapter 12 109

Chapter 13 117

Chapter 14 125

Chapter 15 133

Chapter 16 141

Chapter 17 149

Chapter 18 159

Chapter 19 165

Chapter 20 175

Chapter 21 181

Chapter 22 191

Chapter 23 197

Chapter 24 203

Chapter 25 211

Chapter 26 219

Chapter 27 227

Chapter 28 235

Chapter 29 241

Chapter 30 251

Chapter 31 261

32. Five Winters Later 271

About Trisha 283

Also by Trisha Fuentes 285

PROLOGUE

ATLANTIC OCEAN, 1798

When Tommy joined his wife in the Great Cabin, he found her frozen at the dressing table, staring at her reflection in the mirror. She looked lost, unnerved, trying to separate her ivory-laced veil from her head. Two steps towards her, and she focused on him coming near. He stood directly behind her, yearning to touch her, wanting to help her, but he too felt unease.

"The ceremony was nice… was it not?" He said, trying to break the tension.

Gwendolyn laid her hands atop the nightstand. "Yes—yes, it was, I have never been to a wedding atop a ship before."

"My ancestors were married on the *Junia*, my father wanted to continue the tradition."

"Yes…I know the stories," she gave out shaken, "…and immediately afterwards, the women in your family darted to the ledge to vomit."

Tommy continued to stare at Gwendolyn in her opalescent satin wedding dress. She looked remarkable, beautiful, like a princess. He turned on his heel and eyed the bed only a few feet away. "We don't have to this night; it can wait until tomorrow, or the next, whenever you are ready. I am not going to force you."

Gwendolyn blinked a few times, on the verge of a panic. "Th—thank you Tommy."

Intimidation still choking him, Tommy blurted out what was really on his mind. "May I...may I ask you something?"

"Yes, of course, what?"

Tommy sat down on a nearby chair next to her and ran his hands down the front of his stockings. "Since we weren't allowed to see each other before the ceremony," he exhaled, "And we haven't spoken in two weeks since your decision, I just want to know...why me? Out of all my brothers, Jordan especially, he is the titled heir, you picked me to be your husband?"

Gwendolyn did not bother to look at him and continued to stare at her reflection in the mirror. On any given day, she would have thought she looked like a queen and welcomed the fantasy. Instead, she blinked out of her stupor and became more at ease eyeing her new husband downside up. "Isn't it obvious? You are my best friend Tommy. We could always talk to one another—tell each other riddles. I have known you since you were born, I could not bring myself to be with Jordan, he is...he is so much older, and strange."

Tommy laughed aloud, glad that the frostiness melted with her humor. "Strange? But all ladies fancy him."

Gwendolyn finally stood up from her seated position and looked shyly down at the ground. "I am sixteen Tommy, what do I know about pleasing a twenty-five year old man?"

Tommy stood up also, ran his fingers through his scalp. "I am sixteen as well, and you are asking me to give you an answer?"

Gwendolyn smiled and felt relieved for some reason, the bizarre tension broken. Gwendolyn raised her eyes to find Tommy's green staring into her brown. Their eyes lock and hold and Gwendolyn felt her pulse race and pushed his body away. "Do not do that."

Tommy sighed, "What now?"

"Look at me that way. You make my heart thump."

Tommy began to grin. "I was not aware of my magic power."

Gwendolyn huffed at his response, "Now you are, so make it stop." She purposely glided over to a smart sitting area full of cherry mahogany. A lavish space which rivaled a mansion ashore, the couple was awarded the Captain's chamber for the evening. With cushions made of gold embroidered fabric transported from India, the cabin encompassed a red plush settee, marbled table tops, a piano, fur rugs, a generous hearth and a zinc-lined bathtub. The bed was fit for a king...and queen. A rich poster bed, so intimidating in size, Gwendolyn felt anxious all over again knowing what was supposed to take place there. She turned to look at Tommy once more. He looked a little odd and out of place in his fancy black togs and continued to stare at her in an undeniable way. Feeling an unfamiliar blush rushing up her fair neck, Gwendolyn turned and looked away.

"So what do we do now?" Tommy relayed, ripping through lengthened silence.

"Unsure," Gwendolyn voiced, plucking a few roses out of a vase that was secured to a wall.

Tommy sat down again and began to pull off his leggings and shoes. One by one, each shoe fell to the floor with a loud clunk.

Startled by the noise, Gwendolyn sharply gazed at him undressing, "I beg your pardon?"

Tommy was tired now. Worn-out from the argument he had earlier with his father, exhausted from the day's activities, drained from all the endless questions he had about their obligatory matrimony. "It is customary to take one's shoes off before entering a bed."

"You are not sleeping here."

"Where am I supposed to sleep tonight, the ocean? Our families are all on the lower decks Gwendolyn. They all think we are in here consummating our union. I cannot sneak off and sleep in the lifeboat outside."

Gwendolyn noted Tommy's tone. "You can rest on that couch over there."

Tommy let go a frustrated grunt and began to put his leggings back on. "Never mind—distance sounds rather good to me right now than be in here with you a minute more."

Gwendolyn started at the sight of her new husband putting on his footwear to parade himself in front of the family only ten minutes after they arrived down below; it could only mean one thing, disaster. It was unheard of for a groom to leave his bride so soon. Her mother told her that she was supposed to *"stay in the room"* for the next three weeks. That all meals were being *"sent down to them,"* that they were on their way to the West Indies on their *"honeymoon"*. What the heck was she supposed to do alone with Tommy for the next three weeks? She was getting claustrophobic just thinking about it. "You are not leaving me, are you?"

Tommy sneered at her; a growl so unbecoming of him, Gwendolyn actually took a step backwards in retreat. "Go—stay, which is it Gwendolyn?"

Gwendolyn grabbed her head in frustration. "Oh, I don't know." But before she could change her mind again, Tommy exited. Gwendolyn crossed her arms across her chest and stomped her foot in frustration as she tried to ignore the strange stab of disappointment suddenly surrounding her heart.

Tommy practically ran down the narrow staircase, skipping steps two-by-two. He was just about to turn the corner unseen when he bumped into his father exiting the dining room with a glass of port in one hand. The quick unexpected bump spattered the scarlet liquid onto his father's flamboyant white evening shirt.

"Going somewhere?"

Tommy froze; his father's stern voice penetrated down to his very core. He was too empowered, too large and way too frightening to figure out. "I'm thirsty; I'm on my way to the galley for some milk."

His Grace, Thomas Albert Hollinger, II, 4th Duke of Norwin and Earl of Wilderbrand was not amused. "Tommy, this family has waited too long to have this marriage come to pass," he proclaimed, taking a sip before carrying on, "With all the boys in this household, along with Lord Drummond's only son, we've waited years for this unification. You know how important it is for this lineage to form an alliance. Our two wharfs in Bristol align one another; our shipping business relies on the very foundation of the Drummond vessels. Gwendolyn's dowry solidified this family's future."

"For the last time father, I don't care about the family business."

His father jabbed him in the shoulder with the drink still in his hand. "You *will* obey me son or I will enforce a consequence even you will not be able to tolerate. Either way, Gwendolyn *will* be compromised and this union will be inevitable."

Tommy shuddered at his father's ominous tone. Would he really do that? "You wouldn't dare, she is innocent."

"Jordan will be happy to oblige," the Duke said matter-of-factly, "I cannot fathom why the little unsullied picked you for a husband when he has far more to offer her."

"I am her best friend," Tommy said under his breath.

"Yes," the Duke chortled, guzzling down the rest of his alcohol. "You two have always been inseparable."

The ship suddenly jolted causing the two men to hold the sides of the narrow hallway for balance. Tommy looked at his father with uncertainty. "What was that?"

"Do not concern yourself; I will go up deck to speak with Captain Porter. Now, go back upstairs this instant and bed your bride."

Tommy stood silent and eyed his father turn on his heel to walk down the hallway towards the Captain's stairs.

When Tommy arrived back in the room, the lamp had lowered and Gwendolyn had fallen asleep. The moon's glow had streamed through the bordering beveled glass windows, illuminating her face to angelic proportions. She looked like a doll with her auburn curls cascading across the pillow. Walking backwards, he tiptoed to the sitting room and began to undress.

How to bed her? He's never thought about it before; she was his best friend, his comrade when he felt lonely. They shared the same interests, identical humor and equivalent competitiveness, in fact; he's never felt more comfortable with another person. But this new phobia of exposing himself to rejection was an all-out riot of nerves. He was used to taking direction from her. And now he had to be assertive to get her to do what was mandatory? After what his father had declared, there was no chance in hell he would ever allow that to happen. He cared for her too deeply... yes, he did care for her...love her...oh, how could he not? Oh, whom was he kidding—he was head over heels in love with Gwendolyn! And now, he was supposed to...how did his brother describe it? *Open her legs and poke her with your stick Tommy...she is going to bleed down there, but give her a hanky, she will be good as new...* Wasn't there more to it? Good God, he had to hurt her on purpose...cause her to bleed? It made him crazy when all she did was skin her knee! He could not believe he had to intentionally afflict her with pain?

Completely nude, Tommy rushed to the bed and silently entered under the covers without waking his bride. He stared at her sleeping for a moment then traced the edge of her chin with his finger. *God, she was...wonderful,* he thought, and leaned over to smell her hair. The enchanting aroma drenched him in a fluttering craving.

She was not asleep, only pretending. Gwendolyn could not wait for him to arrive back to the room, she was even eager. What took him so bloody long? Tommy even slipped under the bed sheet, which was something she never counted on. She thought he would follow her order of sleeping on the couch, but he doesn't? She felt him smelling her hair, caressing her cheek, but why? She could not take the silence any longer and opened up her eyes—his unusual heat was practically burning a hole through her thin nightgown!

Realizing he was completely nude, she immediately rolled away from him. "Tommy, what are you doing?"

Tommy reinforced himself and challenged her stern voice, "We are going to consummate our marriage."

"B—but, you said I could have more time."

Tommy noted Gwendolyn's fright. "I know what I said but I've changed my mind—" he broke off suddenly feeling sick with the vision of his brother touching Gwendolyn. "You're mine now, and as your husband, you have to do what I say..."

The next morning, Gwendolyn and Tommy were woken up abruptly by a thump of books falling from the bookshelves in the sitting room; the *Junia* was being tossed about. Gwendolyn grabbed at Tommy and squeezed his arm. "Did we hit rough waters?"

Tommy sat up and watched the room tip...then topple the opposite way. "Unsure, but I'm going up deck to find out."

Gwendolyn yanked at his arm again, "Don't you dare leave me alone—I'm going with you!"

Both of them jump when pounding fists and the jingling of the doorknob echoed throughout the room.

"Children! Children!"

Tommy quickly pulled up his breeches and ran to the door. Swinging it open, he was faced with the captain's panicky first mate. "Ralph, what is it?"

"Master Tommy, stay in your room something is amiss!"

"Is it a storm, Ralph?"

"Yes," he yelled, running down the hallway, "Stay in your room! I shall return...I shall return—"

The ship tilted sideways and caused Tommy to lose his bearings to a bolted down bench. Looking up from the floor, he pinpointed Gwendolyn who was already out of bed, searching for her shoes.

"The sea was calm last evening."

"We must have sailed right into a monsoon," he joked, trying to lighten up her panic. He then gulped at the sight of her shoving her arms through her coat. "Planning on taking a stroll?"

"My mother—my brother, I want to be with them."

"Ralph said to stay put."

"Are you going to stay here, or are you going to follow me?"

Tommy doesn't even think about it. "Button up your coat then; I don't want my brothers ogling you."

Moments later, loud rumbling sounds of wind being hurled through the planks greeted them at the hatchway. Gwendolyn grabbed hold of Tommy's arm in hesitation. "Do not open the door Tommy, the wind sounds funny."

"I want to see what is happening out there, I don't see my brother's, my mother, yours, where did everyone go?"

"I will stay behind you."

Tommy head out first and swung the door open. Covering their faces with their hands, the strong airstreams of rain hit them like pebbles pitched to the skin. To their shock, all around them was nothing but thick, grey fog; the air was equally icy and unnatural, the sea had taken over and swallowed the ship with every dunk and turn.

Tommy gazed up at the sails. Carrying only her topsails and a small jib in the violent windstorm, the topsails were low enough for easy reefing, but still high enough to catch the wind. *It was purposely done*, Tommy thought, knowing that the *Junia* could hold her course through the fierce storm without overtaxing the masts and rigging. He could not believe no one was on deck; she was completely bare of every officer and ship hand. Captain Porter was nowhere in sight and the helm spun freely round and round.

"Stay here, go back to the room!" Tommy shouted to Gwendolyn, pushing her back through the door.

"I'm not going back without you—I'm scared! Where is everyone?"

Tommy flinched from the further shower and wind that slapped his face like needles. "I don't know!" He shouted again, feeling his heart sink. His brothers should be maintaining the topsails at least. Where did everyone go? The *Junia* was like a specter ship, running itself and then left eerily alone. Tommy took a step forward without Gwendolyn to see if he could spot anyone around the bend; but found no one, nothing. When he turned to grab Gwendolyn's hand, the ship suddenly veered left causing his stance to slip and Tommy's whole body slid down the embankment towards the sheer.

"Tommy!" Gwendolyn screeched, watching him rapidly hitting the side of the mizzenmast in pain.

Tommy grabbed hold of the inert damp column. Reopening his eyes, he distinguished Gwendolyn clear across the span extending out her arms as if she could reach him.

In the corner of his eye, he noticed an airborne rope that was freely waving at his side. Outspread and susceptible, he tried to catch the rope that dangled enticingly in front of his face. Waiving his one free arm— while the other grasp hold in a struggling grip, Tommy finally caught hold of the serpentine cord and made an attempt to wrap it around his torso. But to no purpose, the rope loosened and blew behind him, forcing him to let go of the pole. He tried to snatch the cord another time, but the persistent gale swept him frontward and his body went tumbling down the embankment. Grasping and clinging to anything in order to stay compact, Tommy's heartbeat escalated when noticing a wave of green sea rushing towards him in an alarming rate. He closed his eyes from the visible strike and the breaker swallowed his weightless body up and whisked him over the ledge to his ultimate rest.

Tommy had vanished, gone from the ship?!

Oh God, oh no! Gwendolyn let go of the ratlines and ran towards the sheer. "Tommy!" She yelled out again and again, but it was no use, the murkiness was way too thick—and she was forced to her knees. The ship continued to sway in the opposite direction causing Gwendolyn's fragile body to collapse back into the ropes. With all her might, she grabbed hold of the cords and began her fit of terror. "Where—where are you? *Tommy! No—no—no*, you cannot be dead...you just can't be. Oh God, not my Tommy, not my beautiful husband...Oh God, please... please do not do this to me...don't you dare leave me alone!"

CHAPTER 1

1808 - LONDON, ENGLAND

TEN WINTERS LATER

"$\mathcal{I}$t is a shame your fiancé could not make the trip, Gwendolyn."

Gwendolyn does not bother to look at her friend but continues to stare out the window and the scenery beyond. "Yes, it is I miss him so. He wanted to be with me, but it was necessary for him to attend the rancher's caucus."

"Your fiancé is such a wonderful man," Phyllis Tallymen noted, looking out the stern window. "Considerate and hard-working, he will make a wonderful husband and a good father to Mary."

"Yes," Gwendolyn agreed with a joyful smile. "I insisted she come as well, but you know how stubborn she is in wanting to stay behind with her best friend," she replied, adjusting her bonnet and tying the ribbon. "By the by, I am truly sorry to have dragged you away from your home Phyllis. Although I no longer need a chaperone, I am so grateful for your company...I simply hate to travel alone."

Phyllis smiled at her young friend; "I would do anything for you my dear. Your Great-Aunt was my best friend, and after she passed, I feel it almost necessary to watch over you."

"Thank you Phyllis, you are too kind," Gwendolyn offered, gazing out the window another time.

"I wish we were coming to London under happier circumstances though. The reading of a will is so disheartening."

"I agree...I too am not looking forward to this at all," Gwendolyn decided, feeling cheerless by her Great-Aunt's death.

"Anyhow, haven't been to London since I was a girl, where are we staying?"

Gwendolyn continued to stare outside. The hills had suddenly vanished and unrecognizable structures began to appear. "The Quail Inn," she said with a sigh. Both tall and unfathomable, dirty and breath taking, London appeared to be a metropolis of contemporary convenience. With so many people hurrying about, there were carriages of every stature and notoriety; men on horseback, women, children, dogs, livestock marching upon the streets—a chaos of convolution.

The hack slowed down and came to a complete stop. "Here at last!" Phyllis exclaimed happily. "Three weeks from Kettlewell to London – let me out of this fancy contraption before I vomit again," she demanded, unlatching the coach door and swinging it open.

Gwendolyn was first to be let out by the footman, followed by a queasy Phyllis. Stepping down onto the gravel, Gwendolyn immediately gazed up and around her. To her amazement, they had arrived at a garishly painted courthouse, deeply impressive with French influence and design. Gwendolyn then instructed the hack to wait for them while they finished their business inside.

Gwendolyn had never been so nervous before! In anticipation of what, she had no idea, but her stomach was in knots and her hands could not stop trembling. The two women walked arm-in-arm down the long corridor, peaking through glass windows and halting at the door of their intended goal. An engraved nameplate of "ARCHWALD" on its glass face caused Gwendolyn's pulse to race with further anxiety. She looked down at her hands…they were shaking again. Why should a reading of a will make her so uneasy?

Once inside, a stunted man stood up immediately. "Mrs. Hollinger?" He asked openly, receiving his confirmation when Gwendolyn nodded her head, "So sorry to hear about your Great-Aunt."

Gwendolyn studied her Great-Aunt's solicitor. Mr. Stewart Archwald owned kind eyes, a hefty build and baldheaded. He wore glasses on the edge of his nose that appeared to be too snug a fit and pinched his skin to redness. "Thank you Mr. Archwald," Gwendolyn acknowledged, trying not to laugh at his cheery beak, "She always had kind things to say about you."

Mr. Archwald accepted the praise with dignity, "Thank you Mrs. Hollinger, and may I extend my gratitude to you for making this long journey. If it was not for my brother's hospitality, I would not have been able to use his fine office here in town. Several other wills in London I must recite, so sorry to confess, otherwise, I would have met you in Kettlewell." He then extended out his hand to show her a chair. "Please—please, do sit down," he asked of her, eyeing Phyllis in the background.

"And who is this charming lady?"

Gwendolyn arched her brow and eyed Phyllis, "My friend, Miss Phyllis Tallymen, Mr. Archwald, my Great-Aunt's solicitor."

Mr. Archwald received Phyllis's gloved hand and kissed it respectively, "So nice to meet you Miss Tallymen."

Phyllis Tallymen, fifty-two winters with violet eyes and peppered hair, was spellbound.

Mr. Archwald took his seat and then met eyes with Gwendolyn. This was no country girl; in fact, she was the epitome of classic beauty and imagined she would have made a fine prize for any titled gentry but had been wasted away in the countryside for far too many years. Properly dressed in a cobalt bonnet with ribbon fastenings, she wore a navy blue pelisse over a thin white chemise. Deep russet curls framed a pair of heavily lashed brown eyes that were concentrated and hypnotic. She was absolutely stunning, just stunning, but his inspection of her went on far too long however, and he fidgeted in his chair trying to clear his embarrassment. He gave Phyllis a momentary look before, "Let us proceed, shall we?"

"Mr. Archwald, pardon my interruption, but I want to make sure that my Great-Aunt's cottage will not be sold at auction. If there is anything that can be done, I wish to keep residing there. I do not have much money, but please, kind sir, I have come to love its simplexes and wish to remain its lessee."

"I was hoping you would say that, Mrs. Holl—" he wheezed, pounding his chest repeatedly, coughing up phlegm.

Gwendolyn and Phyllis both leaned away from him in their chairs, the reaction sounded consequently painful. "Mr. Archwald"

"A bit of a cold...so sorry," he coughed again, grabbing the middle of his chest.

"You should see a doctor, sir."

"Yes—yes," he agreed, shuffling papers on his desk. "Now, the cottage is yours Mrs. Hollinger, along with your Great-Aunt's extensive book collection," he pronounced, clearing his throat for the fourth time, "But asked specifically that your daughter receive the zinc and limestone assortment once belonging to your Great-Uncle."

"Oh Mary will love that!" Gwendolyn gushed, gazing at Phyllis apparently immersed by Mr. Archwald's poor health.

Mr. Archwald met eyes with Phyllis and then continued on, "Your Great-Aunt and Uncle were very modest, good-natured folk and they will be greatly missed."

"You are too kind," Gwendolyn smiled, eyeing her companion gazing intently into Mr. Archwald's eyes now. Gwendolyn does a double-take and nudged her friend. "And the cottage?" She asked, incredulous that her friend was now in a deep magnetic trance. "It is free and clear? Why, that's wonderful! Isn't that wonderful Phyllis?"

Phyllis just nodded her head. Gwendolyn rolled her eyes and then focused on Mr. Archwald's pigment, he was blushing now, and his complexion swiftly blended in with his nose—a nice rose-tinted hue. Gwendolyn held back her amusement and heard him clear his throat yet again trying to continue, "She also left you a trust fund."

"A *what?*"

"From what I gather, Mrs. Hollinger, or may I correct myself and properly address you as *Duchess?*"

Having stopped shaking, Gwendolyn allowed the accolade to sink in. It had been a long time since anyone had addressed her formerly; she was not used to it. "You may," she stated softly. "But I must admit it is uncomfortable to hear the title."

"Are you by any chance associated with the Hollinger Commerce Company?"

"The what?" Gwendolyn asked, unsure of what he was asking; and then it hit her, "As I recall, it was a shipping trade, a lineage Mr. Archwald, a company I no longer have association with. Why do you ask, sir?"

Mr. Archwald shook his head, "Never mind, and gossip you know — well, it does not matter, let us proceed, shall we?" He laughed, and then changed the subject. "I have known your Great-Aunt for nearly thirty years and not once had she mentioned that she was related to an Earl."

"By marriage, Mr. Archwald, and they were not on speaking terms," Gwendolyn quickly brought to the forefront. "When my father was younger, my Grandmother and Great-Aunt, her sister, were very close. But when my Grandfather matched my father into an advantageous marriage, his state of affairs changed, thus, drastically separating both influential families. My Great-Aunt vowed never to speak to him again and thus never did when I was brought to her door." She explained, thinking too much about this *'Hollinger Commerce Company'*…who was supervising it?

"Oh, I see…well, from my extensive research into your family, Mrs.—*Duchess*, it was detected that with his sudden demise, the Earl's last will and testament did not reflect his marriage, therefore, not even his descendants. So when your father passed on, all land and resources transferred to the nearest relative, which was your Great-Aunt. Now it makes perfect sense that she did not covet the wealth and that the estate was bequeathed to you."

"How much is left?"

"Your father owed on many notes dear, most of his wealth was liquidated a few winters back. One hundred pounds a year is what you can claim. But there is property that has remained secure. The land and manor are substantial. Why, if you liquidate the property, you would never have to worry about your finances again."

"Gisleham Manor?"

"Yes—" he spat out, trying to clear his gullet, shuffling through further paperwork on his desk. "The property bordering…"

"Wilderbrand Castle," Gwendolyn finished for him, thinking about the Hollinger's once again.

"Yes," Mr. Archwald agreed lying down the document he had in his hands.

Gwendolyn closed her eyes. She had never cared about her father's wealth or preceding capital; she had been living happily all these years without it, but the house…*oh God*, her childhood home, this was a blessing in disguise. It was her place of birth, where she grew up, so many seasons, winters, and summers spent there, fishing, rowing, swimming and ice-skating on its shared lake.

So many memories dashed in and out of her head, she could hardly keep up. It was all so long ago…in a different lifetime…in a distant memory. "The manor…is mine? May I go there now?"

CHAPTER 2

*A*mongst the most memorable estates in Berkshire, Gisleham Manor was a forgotten marvel. Once an imposing chateau in its halcyon days, its gates were rusted and the sod and foliage, overgrown.

With a luxurious water fountain and monumental urn as its focal point, Gisleham Manor had a long low edifice with twelve bays under a high copper roof. Finial-capped cupolas surmounted two square alcove towers that contained rooms. The garden, derived from formal French influence once encompassed a canal, flat parterres, thickets and elaborate hedges.

Opening up the door, the reception hall was engrossed in painted murals; intricate woods with gold-rimmed etchings clouding the interior. Built-in glass display cabinets welcomed Gwendolyn in, while parquet flooring in distinctive shades graced the base to guide her along. Leading out of the scope, was the threshold to the Earl's sizable library, an area where Lord Drummond held most of his business meetings, late night negotiations and one colossal order.

Gwendolyn stood frozen at the entrance of the great library.

Everything was still there, nothing had been moved—just a thin sheath of dust appeared on all the exposed furniture. Green buckskin couches; empire chairs, marble sculptures and powdered silk drapes were even in ideal condition. A fireplace she remembered sitting by when she was younger was still inviting; the rug she used to play on with her cat was still off center. Walking in farther, she stopped cold. Heavy elaborate moldings suspended oil paintings of each member of her departed family. Gwendolyn slowly moved towards them and stood underneath the life-sized portraits.

There they were…a touch away…a tangible sight of loved ones who once adorned her day-to-day life were now twisting her heart in inevitable grief. Her father, Lord Kenneth Drummond, the Earl of Suffolkshire, with all his authority and power displayed by way of his overconfident pose; her mother, the beautiful Mary Drummond, with her rich reddish brown hair done up around her grey-green eyes; and Nathaniel, her older brother, so kind and gentle and then finally…one of her. Strange to see herself so young, cheerful, and unbeknownst of the anguish this young maiden was about to endure. So many years of loneliness the girl would have to overcome, so much pain and longing.

After staring at herself for a few minutes more she finally realized the portrait was not straight and appeared to have been moved. A visible thick base of dust surrounded the rectangle frame, while a triangle of clean surface could be noted from one of its corners. Gwendolyn wondered at it for a moment longer, and then leaned over to reposition her picture back to its original state.

Gwendolyn then ambled over to her father's work area and lightly glided her fingertips across the once polished surface but gathered up a lump of disappointment in dust clumps instead. Wiping off her fingers on her dress, she was in awe that the doublewide desk was still filled with maps, nautical instruments, building plans and models of ships; designs her father had been working on and planned to return to if ill fortune had not been introduced. She then wondered…was everything still there? Her clothes, her dolls, her parents' wardrobe, her brother's bow and arrow collection…had no one step foot in the manor since the tragedy? She was the last of the living Drummond's, she figured; no one really cared or bothered. Walking away from the maritime instruments, she then focused on her father's leather chair.

Standing at the edge of it, Gwendolyn imagined her father sitting there with a superior look on his face. The Earl of Suffolkshire always had to have his way when he was alive. Closing her eyes, Gwendolyn recalled what last happened in the great library. She could still hear her father's thunderous voice echoing throughout the enormous span. One month after her sixteenth birthday, she received the devastating news…

"What!" I yelled, on the verge of panic. "Why didn't anyone tell me?" I ran out into the hallway, my mother caught my shoulders—she said I had to go back inside; I was betrothed to one of the Hollinger brothers since the day I was born, she said simply. The only reason why they did not tell me, she added, was because they wanted me to get acquainted with the boys without restriction. Now that I am older, I understand the value of their decision, but at the time, I was devastated and thought my life had ended. In less than a month, barely enough time to have a dress made, I was to be wed…

The following day I was back in the library, a multifaceted burden weighed heavily upon my shoulders. I had a choice to make, a choice I never got to deliberate. Four separate options, with four different men, all good-looking in their own diverse way were awaiting my verdict.

I paraded in front of the four of them; they were all standing in line, Jordan Hollinger at the front, Tommy at the rear. I walked over to Jordan first and stared into his eyes, only his gaze had lowered and raked up my figure from toe to tip. He was the eldest, probably prepared for this very day and was pretentious because of it. I knew I was supposed to pick him; he was the inheritor of every trophy offered to womankind. All my friends considered Jordan Hollinger the ultimate catch, but his significance made me feel awkward, as a result, made my choice easy. Pitch-black hair encasing light green eyes, comely features, and he knew it, leering at me with a pompous, lewd grin on his face. I hated him simply because he thought everyone loved him, but I did not like him and I would never choose him.

I next stepped over to Philip, a virtual stranger to me, no eye contact when I passed him by. Slightly shorter than Jordan, he was a humorless spectacle-wearing bookworm with a noticeable frown in the middle of his forehead. We had a lot in common, he and I, we both loved to read and I always felt I could ask him for help on complex school subjects, but never did. He was so unapproachable, just too grave, when I found it difficult to nevertheless make him smile. He won't do, not him, ever.

Standing to the rear of him was Andrew, light brown hair, dingy stare... A mean-spirited chap who oftentimes beat up on the rest of his brothers and sometimes, even mine! Enough said, not an option, no, not him.

Then, in the back of all three stood my best friend; a boy who could always give me the giggles, take on a good dare, challenge me in every which way until now. My choice was painless...there was no alternative. No one could replace Tommy Hollinger in my mind... with his arms, chest and long legs swimming in his enormous white cambric shirt and navy breeches. Too shy and not anticipating my deliberation, he was biting his fingernails and looking panic-stricken.

"Your Grace?" I asked quietly, cutting through the tension in the room.

"Yes, Gwendolyn?"

"I may have my pick of any of your sons, is that correct?"

The Duke of Norwin turned to eye my father and raised an eyebrow. "Yes, Gwendolyn, you may have your choice of any of my sons."

By that smug grin on his face he thought I was going to choose his precious prized titled heir!

"Then I pick Tommy."

I remember the gasps coming from everyone, even one from Tommy. I stood idle now, and stared into Tommy's frozen gape. His eyes round like the moon, staring into mine...

. . .

"YOU LOOK AT LITTLE GREEN GWENDOLYN, DO YOU NEED a basin?"

Gwendolyn could not believe her eyes and maybe it was partly her fault as well. Staying in the country far too long, wanting to close those doors to her past forever and neglecting her daughter's rightful future. She should have asked questions years ago, should have faced this past long before, but deep down, did not want to. The pain it usually surfaced was simply too much to bear. Her Great-Aunt had been her solace from hurting and sheltered her for far too many years; it was easier to suppose everyone perished in some unexplained hoax rather than grasp the distressing truth.

Gwendolyn trotted around Phyllis and lifted up her skirts to hi-tail it out of there. She scuttled down the hallway and passed through the large French doors that led out to the courtyard. My mother's cherished part of the house, she remembered, eyeing the vaulted ceilings of the staircase spiraling down towards the square; and from the stone laced court, looking up into the arcades, Gwendolyn viewed the many arched porticos that surrounded the terrace.

Gwendolyn slowed down and remembered finding her mother alone crying one night and instantly brought to mind the conversation she had with her just a few days before the wedding voyage…

"Mother? Why are you crying?" I asked, running over to her and sitting at her feet.

She wrapped her hands around my face and said, "Do you know how lucky you are Gwendolyn?"

I remember looking up at her with tears in my own eyes; she was the most beautiful woman in the world to me. Auburn hair with the most incredible grey-green eyes I have ever seen. "I don't feel lucky."

"I envy you," she said, wiping away her own tears and covering her mouth with a hand.

"Envy me—but why?" I asked, continuing to blubber. "I don't wish to be married."

"Neither did I at your age, but you'll see things differently in a few winters."

"You were under obligation as well?"

She closed her eyes and shut them tight, "My father had an arrangement with the 1st Earl of Suffolkshire. I begged and pleaded with my father, but it was no use."

A deep sense of realism entered my heart. "But...but don't you love father?"

"I like your father very much, Gwendolyn... he has been so good to me, but my heart will always belong to another."

"Another? Another man?"

Smiling through tears, she revealed, "His father was a business associate of mine and when his family came by to visit, he would end up talking to me. Elegant and oh so charming, he took my very breath away; but we were both betrothed and dreadfully aware of our social restrictions. Until one evening, while both our parents were dancing in the ballroom, he took me aside and kissed me. I will never forget that kiss of his, Gwendolyn; there were so many ardors in his embrace, I—I hungered for him after dark. Even on my wedding day, I loved a married man."

My mouth flew open wide and I grabbed at her waist, hugging her near. "Oh mother, I am so sorry."

"I am glad I told you darling, it is a suffering that I have had to bear these many, many winters. That's why I envy you," she voiced, caressing the sides of my face, running her fingers through my hair. "You made the perfect choice, Gwendolyn. Tommy is an affectionate boy and he will make a wonderful husband. I have seen the two of you together; he is so focused on you. You are so fortunate to already be friends with him; it will help when you two are not intimate. Now, close your mouth dear, stop blushing, he is not a complete stranger like your father was to me on our wedding night. I am sure your first time with your husband will be a memorable one."

"Oh mother, I am so scared."

She continued to stroke the side of my cheeks, "Just remember darling, *that when he shows you that he cares, prove your own devotion darling. I know you care for him Gwendolyn, more so than you permit everyone to witness. Allow him to catch you every now and then. Please do not make the same mistakes turning frigid at your husband's touch. So many years wasted I…I forced your father into the arms of a mistress…"*

GWENDOLYN FLEW DOWN THE STAIRS AND RAN INTO THE lawns, halting at the sight of a massive emptied fountain that once held lily pads and numerous frogs. It was no wonder she could still hear the laughter the dew pond generated…

"I am not going to touch it, you touch it," I demanded of Tommy, crossing my arms in front of him in my best commandant stance.

"Quit being such a girl," Tommy ribbed, sticking his whole arm down the side of the moss-filled water.

"I am not a girl; I am an officer in the Royal Navy."

"No, you aren't, you're a scaredy-cat and I dare you to touch that toad."

I twisted my lips and gazed down at the scaly beast. It had titanic eyes and seemed to stare back at me daring me to touch it to prove that it would leap off the side of the lily pad and right into my hair. "If I touch it, you have to hold it," I challenged him, thinking what a better idea would be if we used the toad to scare our governess.

Tommy smiled and puffed up with acceptance. "Deal," he proclaimed, grabbing the toad with both hands and shoving the beast in front of my face. "Wouldn't it be funny if we put this toad in Miss Pinkel's washbasin this evening?"

That brought on a huge smile, wasn't I just thinking the same dastardly thing? "Yes," I said, reaching out to the toad and gliding my finger across its back. It was not so bad; wet and bumpy, anyhow, I could not wait for Tommy to take it upstairs to shock Miss Pinkel! Oh how we loved to play tricks on her, retribution for making us wash down before supper…

. . .

23

WALKING AWAY FROM THE LIMESTONE FOUNTAIN, Gwendolyn reached the rest of the gardens. Once a surplus of envied roses and flower beds, the garden had lost its color, misplaced its fragrances, and won an array of shriveled up plants, fallen trees and dried out leaves. Gwendolyn shook her head at all the waste and could not look at it anymore and began running away from the ruins. Picking up speed, she finally reached the coach house and began her ascent towards it. Eerie friezes of horses' heads above its entrance summoned her in. Once inside, Gwendolyn was shocked to see the Drummond carriages still lined up for usage! *One, two, three, four...four carriages?!* Did she really own such luxuries; so much prosperity at the mercy of disuse. She instantly brought to mind the hired hack she left waiting at the gates. *I will have to let him go,* she thought happily, she now had four luxurious carriages at her disposal. Walking around them, she pinpointed a steel bench and froze at the sight of it instantly remembering the last time it was visited. Slowly walking over to it, she sat down and spread out the fabric to her dress, languidly fingering the benches edge and recollected the tears that were once shed there...

I wanted to talk to Tommy alone, had to get to him before the wedding took place. Maybe we could run away, or better yet, even stowaway on one of my father's ships abroad. I was not allowed to see him though, my mother told me so. We were to be kept apart socially, until the matrimony began.

I ran to the estate as fast as my legs could carry me, halted when I observed Tommy alone with his father. The window was open and I could hear them shouting. Making sure they could not see me, I meshed into the brick wall and threw my ear to the window. Tommy and the Duke of Norwin were debating on something that I could not quite understand.

"You can live anywhere you wish," the Duke proclaimed. "How about India? Madagascar or Africa?" Tommy snapped back, adding fuel to the fire.

"Do not be absurd, son," the Duke sharply replied. "You must live in

London in order to help oversee the trade according to the provisions in the dowry."

"I do not want to be involved, father!" Tommy recited with a cry in his voice. "I hate the maritime business!"

"You will do what I say, and that's an order!"

"But father, for the last time, this isn't suitable," Tommy yelled back at him. "I never wanted Gwendolyn this way…"

Within hearing Tommy's invariable insult, my very heart sunk into my chest. I had never heard him say something so…wounding. I followed my feet as fast as they could take me back to Gisleham, not even caring if I bumped into anything along the way and did not notice Jordan when I walloped into him. I did not realize that I was running so fast for he caught me before I fell backwards, his two strong arms firmly gripping against my forearms aiding me for balance.

"Are you hurt?" He asked, his thumbs unintentionally digging into my shoulders.

"Yes," I said, thinking how much Tommy's rejection really impaired me.

"Where?" He asked, whirling my body around, inspecting my outer physique for any possible injury.

Satisfied that he could not find any blood or broken bone, he finally released his clench from my shoulders and I took a few steps backwards only to watch him take a few steps ahead. Through tear-filled eyes, I tried to look up at him but my view was clouded and uncomfortable; I had never been so close to him before, he smelled of fresh laundered linen and some unknown fragrance that caused my senses to come alive. I remembered thinking how tall he was and broad and perfectly shaped until my eyes leveled to his waistcoat and felt him raise my chin.

"Why the tears?" He asked in a soft unfamiliar voice.

"It does not concern you," I spat back at him still distraught over Tommy.

"Oh, I see," he said letting go a chuckle. I watched him cross his arms across his chest and with tears still gushing down my cheeks he looked straight down into my eyes. I noticed his usual pretentious outward show was no longer visible. He appeared different to me now, more relaxed…

25

almost tender and beguiling. He went to reach for my face but held back his contact. I knew what he wanted to do but I beat him to it and wiped my own tears that were trickling down my face. Making me nervous than ever before, I no longer wanted to be near him and stepped away only to hear "I could have made you happy" at my backside.

Bit by bit, I curved around, my ears still not willing to believe what was just conveyed. "I beg your pardon?"

Coughing first, he let out, "Congratulations again," he quickly rejoined, not smiling.

"That is not what I heard," I let go challenging him.

His green eyes were compelling and gazed deep into mine trying to search for something but when he doesn't find it, moments later he confessed, "It was what was meant."

His bow was quick but poignant and I stood there idle and watched him drudge away. For once he had his head down in defeat but his coattails flipped about with each proud stride he took. He truly was a handsome man and maybe that would have been enough, but the only boy I ever truly cared about was Tommy.

WIPING AWAY THE TEARS THAT QUICKLY STREAKED HER cheeks, Gwendolyn stood up immediately and scampered out of the coach house. Wandering around aimlessly now, Gwendolyn covered her mouth in disbelief. So many memories there…so many incredible memories, blissful, tragic, exuberant in their generosity. Running and running, she finally reached the lake and began the endless stretch around it. It was still a blackish blue, like the nighttime sky just after sunset. Leaning back on a large oak one memory bit against her tear filled eyes…

"Why are we hiding up here again, Gwendolyn?" Tommy asked, peering through the branches, trying to see if Mademoiselle de la Motte, their French tutor was still searching for them.

"We are hiding from that weird woman," I remarked simply, sticking out my head to see if I could notice her approach as well. "I do not understand her and she bothers me."

"She is our French tutor, Gwendolyn. We've ditched her twice this week, and once last week. My father's going to skin me alive if I do not learn French."

"Oh, stop being so honorable, wouldn't you rather go swimming? It is so hot today; I just want to swim all day long," I complained, stretching out my legs on the growth of the tree. "I bet you I can dive off that edge over there and make it into the middle."

Tommy gazed down at the water. After looking over towards Gisleham once more, he headed out towards the brink of the tree. "All right, but you have to reach the middle, you cannot cheat like you did last time."

"I did not cheat. I do not cheat, you big nincompoop," I mouthed, crawling on the thin branch, reaching over to the brim. I then jumped out as high as I could and stiffened my body up to dive right in the middle. I remembered the water being refreshingly cool, and instantaneously relaxing my agitation. Dipping my head under the water, blowing bubbles underneath, I looked up at the tree and noticed Tommy springing up on his feet, doing a perfect dive into the lake, missing me by a foot.

Wading my body backwards in the water, Tommy shot up directly and spat in my face on purpose. "I win."

I then splashed water into his. "You did not; you missed me by a horse hair. See," I showed him, having not moved an inch. "This is where I landed."

Tommy rolled his eyes then dipped half his face back into the water. "Gwendolyn, you always do that," he expressed running his hand through his wet hair. "Why can't I ever win? You land in one place, but you swim to another."

"I do not," I shrieked, splashing water into his face once again. Tommy then cupped water in his hands and sloshed liquid into mine. It turned into a competition of spatter when we heard...

"Enfants? Chulledren? Oh là-bas vous êtes! There you are!"

"Oh no!" I screamed, "She found us!"

"Hurry," Tommy shouted, grabbing my shoulder and directing me towards the other side of the lake. "Let's swim back to Wilderbrand, she won't find us there..."

CLOSING HER EYES, GWENDOLYN FINALLY ALLOWED THE tears to worsen. With so much inundating her, she fell to her knees, gripping her stomach in heart-breaking agony. Maybe it was healthful she was there. Maybe it was meant to be...to let go, to finally release those haunting memoirs of her childhood...and about *him*. Burying her head within her lap, Gwendolyn let loose her lingering misery. Hurling the rest of her body to the ground, she allowed her head to rest on a soft patch of grass; reopening her eyes, she looked up at the blue sky and spotted a hawk in the distance searching for mice. Gwendolyn felt her eyes close for the last time and continued her liberation. It was good to be there... good to cry...good to move forward...move on...to start a new life...with another man...create new memories...close those doors to her past...forever.

Continuing to weep in the middle of an overgrown field, Gwendolyn unexpectedly felt the thunderous sounds of hooves slowly emerging. Sitting up within the saw grass, she witnessed an approaching horse rapidly startling her. She barely got out of the way as it circled around and galloped near.

Repositioning her stance Gwendolyn could not help but notice the woman atop a glorious black mount. The female was stunning, with exquisite blonde curls encasing her bright blue eyes. Her burgundy velour riding dress showed iridescent gloss and shades of purple from the sunlight, her men's top hat engrossed roses and trailing muslin. She was poised and graceful, and when she finally calmed down her horse, Gwendolyn felt intimidated not only by her beauty, but the woman's continued scrutiny of her own examination.

"Who are you? You are trespassing Madame."

Gwendolyn was taken-back. *Who was she? And why was she speaking to her in a manner as if to challenge her?* "I beg your pardon?"

"This is a gated estate Madame, a private household. What business do you have here?" The female asked, dismounting her horse and dusting down her outfit.

Gwendolyn wiped the remaining tears away from her eyes, straitened her attitude then stared into the woman's discourtesy, "Perhaps you can tell me who you are first, then I can begin to settle the formalities. You are the one who has breached my property, Madame."

She laughed sickly at Gwendolyn's confrontation. "Am I? Why you silly girl, do you not know where you are? You have entered Wilderbrand Castle."

Gwendolyn crossed her arms and nodded her head. "I have not —" she stopped, doing a double take at the lake behind her. *Oh no, she did enter the property.* The lake separated the two lands, Gisleham Manor on the one side, Wilderbrand Castle on the other.

The woman petted her horse's mane and patted him on his neck. "Insufferable girl, perhaps my fiancé will enlighten you, here he comes now."

Gwendolyn gazed around her and observed a gentleman galloping near. Feeling enveloped all of a sudden, she began walking away from his speedy approach. Descending his stallion of camel beauty, the man strolled to the distressed woman first; they exchanged words, his back towards Gwendolyn.

Gwendolyn overheard the couple shouting and shook her head at the sight of the couple now arguing. She was inconvenienced; after all, she too had every right to be there. She would just have to introduce herself to her new neighbor; enlightenment will soon arrive once he understood she was the new proprietor of Gisleham.

Gwendolyn bent down and pulled a daisy growing wild in the ground; popping back up again she was alarmed at the sight of the gentlemen's magnificent horse trotting over to be by her side. The friendly animal pointed its nose in her face and sniffed its encroachment and she reached out to pet the animal that seemed to curl into her touch. She then peeked over the horse's nose to survey its owner more closely. The man was incomparable in height and towered over his petite fiancée. Sporting charcoal pantaloons, knee-length riding boots, striped grey waistcoat and black coat; he was exceedingly handsome with ebony waves surrounding his swarthy complexion. A shadowy creature to say the least, he turned about with ease, his chest broad and tapering to his lean waist. He accepted the lady's hand on his forearm then leisurely approached Gwendolyn. He appeared self-assured and approximated with gliding steadiness. They're a breath-taking couple, Gwendolyn thought as they came into clearer view, but then…as he drew closer…yet nearer, Gwendolyn's very breath was stolen from her lungs.

"Madame, allow me to—"

Gwendolyn stared at him too, his green eyes rapidly looting her alertness. She tried to fathom how, when and why! Heart thumping in her ears, the booming sound echoed down to her throat. She grasped her neck, covered up her mouth in skepticism. His shocking emergence began to inundate her in deafening waves.

Oh, dear God…could it be?

CHAPTER 3

*H*e watched her body fall to the ground before coming to her aid. Still in shock, he watched a group of horsemen appear before shoving his surprise aside so that he could finally react. One by one, each horse stopped and the rider dismounted causing the man to finally scurry over and bend down to gather Gwendolyn who fainted. Lifting her weight within his arms, he turned to shout at the nearest ear in reach. "Help me get her to the manor!"

"What happened?" Devin asked dumbfounded watching his friend laughably circle around trying to make up his mind which horse to place her upon.

"Here...use *my* horse," Henry advised, equally shaking his head at the indecision.

"Who is she, Katrina?" Amy asked with wide eyes, leaning into her friend.

Katrina concentrated on her fiancé's agitation; she had never seen him so concerned afore. "I do not know."

Continuing to walk with Gwendolyn within his arms, he scanned her body in disbelief. "This cannot be," he said, shaking his head. Looking down at her unconscious, he repeated, "This just cannot be...after all these years...and—and you're alive?"

"Are you taking her to the manor?" Devin asked in an alarming rate. "She could be a thief!"

"Are you questioning my mandate?" The man inquired, turning sharply around and eyeing Devin Hale, his true friend, and solicitor for years.

Devin nodded his head *yes*, and then peered into his associate's piercing green eyes. "No."

The man turned around afresh and proceeded up the horse. "Good, because I am going to need your assistance, now hold her to me."

After aiding his friend with the expired woman, Devin walked over to his sister's side. Katrina pulled up on her horse as well and he motioned for her to stay behind yanking on her sleeve.

The man began his ascent towards Wilderbrand when all of a sudden; Phyllis unexpectedly appeared from the overgrown brush. "Malady—malady, what happened? What happened? Who are you, sir? Where are you taking her?"

The horseman eyed the elder woman scuttling towards him. "And you are?"

"Malady's companion, Phyllis Tallymen, and you are, sir?"

"5th Duke of Norwin, Madame; Earl of Wilderbrand."

"HAVE YOU SEEN HER BEFORE DEVIN?"

"No, I have to say, I have never seen that chit."

"She concerns me, brother."

"Why, Katrina? Your fiancée has been true to you, I have made sure of it."

"I know he has, it is just," Katrina stopped and patted down her dress, removing horsehair from the delicate fabric. "There is an unfamiliar pang in my heart. My fiancée has always been such a puzzle to me." "But surely you have come to know the man dear; you have been his sole companion for the past several months."

"Yes," Katrina paused only to look ahead towards the manor.

"There are times when he makes me feel like I am the only woman in the world." Looking sadly at the ground, she confessed, "Then there are others, when I look at him from across the room, and he has this faraway look in his eye. Like his heart has been damaged and is afraid to love."

"Sister dear, you will be the Duchess of Norwin soon. I will see to it that he marries you," Devin said apprehensively. He knew that's what she wanted to hear. She wanted encouragement, a little boast of confidence and oftentimes a kick in the derriere. His sister was always a little insecure, having grown up with no mother, and a gambling, drunken, neglectful Baron for a father, Devin practically raised her. Devin and his sister grew up in Dover together with Amy and Henry Barton and there were times when he felt such kinship with the Barton twins, it felt natural. He had known for years that Amy was infatuated with him, but after watching the destruction of his parents' marriage first hand, Devin vowed never to marry. While growing up, Katrina even showed interest in Henry, for Henry had been smitten with Katrina for years; his sister was a striking girl, but Katrina kept Henry at arm's length, on reserve until something more promising came along. At nineteen, she should have been married by now, she had so many prospects her first season out. She even had several proposals but rejected every one of them. Devin always felt that she had made the wrong decisions then, but Katrina seemed determined to live a life of luxury, unwavering to locate her knight in shining armor. Katrina always searched for a strong influence from the lack of discipline in her life. He found it in abundance after graduating from the university, but Katrina, his spoiled little sister, latched onto any influential chap that showed considerable interest in her. Enter, Monsieur Antoine Bruneau, a French aristocrat who did not take no for an answer. Devin pleaded with Katrina not to leave with him one evening, but she did it anyway just to spite. The next morning, Devin found her crying in her bedchamber. Later she confessed that Monsieur Bruneau had taken advantage of their privacy and seduced her. Katrina had willingly left with him; she was even seen at the opera with the scoundrel in a scandalous position. He wanted the man arrested, for what, he did not know, but the word "hypocrite" kept bellowing in his ears. Had he not been seen around town doing the very same thing? Ruining young innocents? But this was his one and only sister, his only sibling and the other side of the coin. He would demand a wedding ceremony, an honorable pledge. Devin called for the magistrate, but Monsieur Bruneau had fled to his native country, taking Katrina's innocence with him. The following months were dreadful; Katrina was unhappy, unruly and hard to reason with. She had dodged the shame of an illegitimate child and he finally convinced her that the only way to redeem her inexperience was to pretend that nothing ever happened; to present herself again on the marriage mart under false pretenses. It could work, it had to succeed. Otherwise, Lady Katrina Hale would become repudiated; a spinster, or a married man's mistress and he could not have any of that. Henry came back and his sister was happy for a while, until Katrina locked eyes with the 5th Duke of Norwin and the debonair Earl of Wilderbrand. *Blast it all...*Devin never wanted her to be involved with the likes of him! Bad to worse, the Duke was dangerous, a lethal chap when it came to female awareness. While Devin was known throughout London as a rake hell bachelor, His Grace's allure was considered enigmatic. The Duke of Norwin never offered information about himself willingly so he was always a mystery to others. Devin had seen him in chase attending parties alongside him, the birds all pecking for his aloof consideration. Devin perceived his detachment as conceit, but—after getting to know the gentleman—he learned later it came from caution. Even in the company of other men, the Duke had been coveted and well liked. Devin overlooked the rumors of His Grace's permanent bachelorhood allowing his sister to limit herself to him. She practically begged for the introduction to the most sought after bachelor in all of London, and yes, he was totally against it at first, but the Duke was the one who made the initial contact. It was too late, their eyes met, and it was all over.

Having been engaged to the Duke for the past three months, Devin had continually ignored rumors of their improper commitment, having been seen together throughout London, without a chaperone and very close. It was what she wanted, Devin permitted, and Katrina was finally content. Devin had never been envious of the Duke, rather the contrary; he admired his tenacity keeping a disintegrating merchant trading company, thriving. After graduating from Pembroke, University of Oxford, Devin applied for a solicitor at the Hollinger Commerce Company. Meeting His Grace for the first time had been exhilarating, he had so many high hopes and visions for the future; Devin wanted to be part of it. Working together, side by side, Devin also sparked up a friendship with the Duke he never thought obtainable. The Duke latched onto Devin's candidness and an alliance surged, there was even a special bond between them, a deep sense of camaraderie and they have been inseparable ever since. Being a gifted draftsman, Devin mentioned Lord Henry Barton to the Duke, introducing Henry's artwork to him and the reverie turned tangible. The Duke hired Henry to design all his future vessels, making the Hollinger Commerce Company a well-established merchant trader to rival the British East India Company. In 1784, the India Act settled divided matters between control of governance and trade, clearing borders between the Crown and the maritime companies. While the British East India Company continued to expand its influence to nearby territories through threats and coercive actions, the Hollinger Commerce Company remained in the good graces of the Crown.

"Let us go brother, I do not know why, but I have a terrible feeling about that girl. You know he is not allowed to pay attention to anyone else but me!"

Devin climbed up on his horse, "You are acting like a child again Katrina."

"I just hate to share!"

"Selfish chit," Devin barked back at her.

"I am not selfish," Katrina whined, sticking out her bottom lip.

"And for heaven's sake, stop pouting."

"I do not pout," Katrina griped, whipping her horse with a rider's crop. The black horse let out an ear-splitting whinny, threw his head back and kicked his legs up into the air in defiance.

"Blast it all Katrina, how many times have I told you not to whip that horse that way!" Devin shouted, trying to gallop up next to her surging steed.

"Stop pestering me, brother. I can do what I choose on this estate, it is just a bloody horse!" She yelled back, whipping her horse again. The horse sped up, leaving Devin in a cloud of dust behind her.

CHAPTER 4

"Gwendolyn? Can you hear me? Gwendolyn?"

The Duke had been alone with her for the moment, soaking in her existence. Outlining her chin with his finger, he choked back emotion. *God, she was...startling,* he had forgotten how bewitching she was. He delicately untied the bows to her bonnet and was unguarded by the beauty lying before him. She was saintly in slumber; ringlets in reddish-brown encircled her peach-toned face. Long brunette eyelashes surrounded a haunting stare he always missed. How many nights had he dreamt of holding her within his arms?

The Duke took out some smelling salts from within a jar and held it underneath her nostrils. One quick whoosh across her nose and Gwendolyn began to stir.

By slow degrees, Gwendolyn commenced an endless swim through a current of darkness, her nose stung from a pungent odor and her eyes immediately popped open and focused on the stranger sitting before her. "Where am I?" She asked, sitting up straight and bringing her hands up over her neck. "Who are you? What am I doing in this room?"

The Duke stood up slowly from her side and raked his hands through his black mane, "Do you remember me?"

Gwendolyn surveyed the room, then eyed the stranger again. A wave of confusion passed through her. She instantly recognized her surroundings, but she did not want to know this man. The noble standing before her was a cryptic version of a hallucination brought to life. She gazed deep into his eyes and felt a twinge of reality. "I—It is not possible."

The Duke sat down on the edge of the chair next to her. "What is not possible?"

"Hollinger?

"Yes."

"Lord Jordan Hollinger?"

He shook his head, "No Gwendolyn, it is me, Thomas, but you used to call me *Tommy*."

What! She stood up immediately and began backing away from him. "Bu—but, you're dead. I saw him—the ocean crept over the ship and took Tommy with the surge—" Gwendolyn stopped short and held her hand over her mouth. *It could not be...it just could not be...this man...this disturbing man was Tommy?*

Thomas continued to keep his distance. "I survived Gwendolyn." Within seconds, deep subdued emotions began to stir and Thomas quickly governed his reaction from being so close to his memories. "I cannot believe you are alive. It was understood that Gwendolyn Drummond expired on the ship with the others."

"And I believed Tommy Hollinger died in the ocean."

Thomas nodded his head, "Dear God, what madness is this?"

Gwendolyn swung around and began to pace the floor then eyed his body up and down, disbelieving his existence. "You do not look the same; I thought you were your elder brother."

Thomas pulled up from the chair and glided towards the window. Looking through its pane, he watched his guests slowly emerge the estate lawns. He contemplated the uncertainty of it all.

Right, wrong— wrong, right. He *did* know he resembled his elder brother, hating his reflection each time he passed a mirror, wishing to be an individual, settling for a shared identicalness.

He turned back to Gwendolyn—she was not the same either; grown into some curvy female. He brought his eyes downward up her svelte frame. In her simple blue-black pelisse, she was a little taller, her cheeks were flushed now, her neck, still willowy, her bosoms...*oh heaven help him,* as he slightly turned around...she was flawlessness enhanced. She was absolutely beautiful, beautiful and pleased each one of his senses. Feeling a bit besieged from so many moving attacks, Thomas cleared his throat and continued to distance himself from her. Being in the same room with her, adjacent to the girl he shared his first kiss, brought forth buried sexual desire.

Gwendolyn watched him back away and lean against a desk, crossing his boots in unison with his arms across his chest. Confident and assured, this invader was another person all together, she realized. Handsome in detail, the man was delightfully put together in a sinful sort of way. Her heart began to trip over as soon as she viewed him more clearly. His hair was still an unruly mop of black curls, longer than she had remembered, but the weights of it seem to tame the waves into precision. His nose was still straight, but now had a proud stint to it resting on his tempting mouth. Good Lord, his chiseled jawbone and thick throat were text book besides. It was in his stare, in those light green eyes of his, which caused her to believe it was really her childhood friend. Those heavenly lashed eyes could always take over her sense of certainty. His appearance was just an added bonus to what she used to know of the boy. He was so inviting to look at now; it was challenging for her to even look away. Her close scrutiny of his physique however, caused the raider to offer her a most sensuous grin.

"Do I attain your endorsement?"

Even his smugness surprised her! Gwendolyn was simply amazed by the radical change from the quiet, reserved boy she used to know. She stepped away from him, unexpectedly feeling the urge to wrap her arms around his neck and never letting go. "You," she sighed heavily with the consideration, "have changed, that's all."

"So have you."

"All these years Tommy—"

"It's Thomas now," he corrected her without a beat.

Gwendolyn smiled, "Thomas, yes," and beamed again, "all these years and we never knew?" Persistent giggling on her part suddenly turned into laughter as Gwendolyn clutched her stomach in distress.

"I do not see the humor in this Gwendolyn, if anything, I see a cruel joke."

"Yes," she agreed, erasing her smile, "It has been most unpleasant."

Thomas tilted his head and stared at her again, "Where have you been?" He asked, agitated all of a sudden. "That manor has been vacant for the past ten years. Last I heard the sale of it was suspended in probate."

"In Yorkshire, Kettlewell to be exact, with my Great-Aunt," Gwendolyn softly voiced, thinking about her Great-Aunts demise.

"She is...she has passed on recently."

Thomas' mouth slowly opened, "I am sorry to hear that, I had no idea you had other living relatives...In Yorkshire, you say? I never thought—"

"She was estranged," Gwendolyn cut in, recognizing his vagueness, "My grandmother's sister. My father's aunt, they never spoke...and you? You have been here all along? In the home that you grew up?"

"I was in Bristol for a while and then just recently back." Thomas then felt anxiety fully engulf him, "Did you...did you remarry?"

Gwendolyn stared into his heartrending focus, "No," she pronounced walking backwards away from him again, "But I am engaged to married. And you...are about to remarry as well?"

Thomas' throat closed up, "Yes." He was taken-back; both twenty-six years of age now...and both waited ten years to make that commitment again?

Gwendolyn roamed over to one of the windows and looked out at the beautiful lawn she once ran races on. Focusing on her reflection from within, she noticed the faces that glared back down at her. Quickly turning her head, she eyed the family portraits on the wall; individual paintings of his mother, father, brothers, and then finally one of him. He was young; the boy in an earlier period, *her Tommy*, not the stranger who stood before her looking every bit identical to his senior brother, the portrait at this moment she could not stop staring at. She turned to look at the younger depiction yet again, *oh why had not she seen it before?* He was eye-catching even at his young age! It was only a matter of time he would turn into the charming gentleman he now was.

"Thomas..." Gwendolyn asked seriously now, "...How did we get to this position?"

Thomas directed his senses and cleared his throat. "There was a bounty on my father's life," he confessed quietly, recalling what he knew. "Unbeknownst to the family, the *Junia* stole from a pirate ship and all who bore the name Hollinger was supposed to die."

"Supposed to die?"

"Haven't you ever wondered what happened that night?"

"Yes, of course, I have nightmares to this day," Gwendolyn pronounced without delay.

"Our entire family vanished."

"*Wh—What* happened?"

His menacing gaze only fed her dread. "At first light, one and all were instructed to get dressed, and then forced up deck; everyone, half asleep when the murderers came aboard. They were all tied up and gagged," he voiced eerily, staring into nowhere, "The storm simply a backdrop to a sadistic offense."

Gwendolyn was in shock and hesitantly sat down on the sofa. "And we eluded them, how?"

"By some grace of God, the pirates left us alone. They were not even aware we were in the Great Cabin," Thomas said matter-of-factly, closing his eyes with the haunting realization. "Only our families...one by one, each of them, dropped into the ocean...to their deaths."

"H—how, do you know all this?"

"Captain Porter," he voiced plainly. "On his death bed, he confessed the pirate Red Retropé was responsible."

"Oh dear God...and the threat?"

"No longer valid."

Gwendolyn crossed her arms under her bosom. "Oh my mother, my brother, *my poor family*...and you? What happened to you? How did you manage to survive?"

"I was pressed under the sea," Thomas jarringly recalled, "brushed under the violent current to calm water. I remembered thinking how peaceful it was there, dark, like the night...I'm a good swimmer, you know that," he stopped short and met her stare. "I swam under the tide, then up towards the lighter water. When I hit the surface, a crippling undercurrent threw my body into something solid. I reached and grabbed for it, realizing that I had been thrown into a crate. I climbed aboard and held on for dear life..."

"...I was so distraught," Gwendolyn recalled quietly, "...I ran to the edge of the sheer. I could not see you...could not find you, and the wind pushed me backwards. I began to cry in my lap when I felt someone grab me from behind. Ralph, Captain Porter's first mate, picked me up and brought me to a lifeboat. We managed to outlast the continued waves until a few hours later we happened upon a British ship who took us aboard...*Oh God, why did this happen?*"

Gwendolyn rushed to the doorway and Thomas caught her exit. Gently closing the door in front of her, his significant body hovered over hers in a protective cocoon. "Calm yourself Gwendolyn," he whispered just outside her ear. "Let me take care of this." A whiff of lemon-zest from her hair unexpectedly invaded his senses. Her skirt, brushing up against his thighs, caused his arousal to awaken. Tantalizing deliberations ran through his blood. With both arms on either side of her he could have easily swung her around and properly received her...but he let his arms descend and released his caged embrace.

Making matters worse, Gwendolyn turned around and bore into his eyes. Her wistful expression weakened his assuredness, he wanted to possess her...grab her...taste her...shake her senseless. *Doesn't she realize he would have died for her?* Inch, by every dissatisfying inch, he backed away.

Thomas and Gwendolyn held each other's intent. Gwendolyn wanted nothing more than to run into his arms and cry with relief; the feeling was so tremendous, her heart pounded recklessly with the deliberation. Thomas swiftly encircled his eyes across her lovely face; he wanted to buss his lips across her throat, feel her quiver underneath him in contact, he wanted her so much; his very breath was being sucked from his lungs.

*Mary...*she thought finally. She looked so much like her father and he wasn't even aware! Gwendolyn searched Thomas' eyes for further closeness and when she found it in abundance, she voiced, "Thomas... there is something you should know—"

"We simply cannot wait at port any longer Thomas; we must know who the woman is," Henry exclaimed, startling the twosome out of further intimacy.

One by one, the huntsmen entered. Gwendolyn was so overwhelmed from her entire surroundings, she found herself alone by the window again, watching the amused group unaffected by what just happened.

"I tried to keep them entertained, but all my jokes were already familiar," Devin quipped, meeting eyes with Gwendolyn.

"Please introduce me to this exquisite creature."

Gwendolyn felt a rush of hesitancy; the man was much to forward. *Oh my, he is very good-looking,* she thought, suddenly staring at his exterior. On identical lines as Thomas, the man was just as tall, wearing not black, but blue, of every tint, extenuating his good looks. Uneven shades of blonde hair, azure eyes and a long tapered nose, his mouth formed an avid grin and Gwendolyn blushed instantly.

"I saw her first dear boy," Henry retorted, pushing aside Devin's advance.

He too is fine looking, Gwendolyn thought, examining his façade as well. Uniquely dressed in a coffee tone, the handsome man possessed dark chestnut hair and hazel eyes. *Oh my, each and every man in the room, a prize indeed.*

Thomas noted her lure to both wolves and instantaneously, a sense of possessiveness impassioned him. Henry was basically harmless, being shy and tongue-tied, but Thomas knew Devin's reputation, he was his cohort in pursuit. He further knew that women flock to Devin, and this was one woman he wanted to keep for himself...keep for himself? What the hell was he thinking? "Down boys!" He exclaimed, overriding his emotions back to monopoly. "She is not to be approached men, is that understood?"

Devin crossed his arms in front of him and continued to stare at Gwendolyn. He shook his head and disagreed, "My restraint has yet to be trifled with, but I will try."

Thomas rolled his eyes and gazed at both his friends. Seven winters full of closeness and laughter. He trusted these men... trusted them with his very life. No one here would dare betray him.

Then Katrina fell into view. *Good God, was she standing there all the time? Oh bloody hell...*What was he going to say to her? They were about to be married in two weeks' time! "What I am about to say goes no farther than this room." Thomas halted and eyed Katrina who gathered close. She entwined her gloved hand within the crook of his elbow and squeezed his arm tight. He gazed down at her and felt a rush of guilt.

Gwendolyn sat down and eyed the two of them together. Biting down on her lower lip, she was envious of this girl who had reign to touch him so freely. When she first approached Gwendolyn in the field she stated that Thomas was her betrothed...so this was going to be his new bride? *It is nice to see that he has fallen in love,* she realized. She truly was an attractive woman and the other, who was she? Brunette with hazel eyes, equally as lovely, Gwendolyn felt so panic-stricken.

Coming to her rescue immediately, Phyllis came around the two men and sat down next to Gwendolyn. She grabbed her hand and held it in her lap for reassurance.

"May I introduce Lady Gwendolyn...*Hollinger,*" Thomas let go, feeling the breath being taken from his very chest another time. "My close friends, Lord Henry Barton, his twin sister, Lady Amy Barton, Lord Devin Hale, and his sister, my fiancée, Lady Katrina Hale."

"Hollinger?" Henry acclaimed. "So you are his cousin then? A long lost cousin?"

Thomas began to rub Katrina's hand that was firmly on his forearm. "No Henry, she is not my cousin."

"Not a cousin, then whom?" Devin asked suspicious.

Thomas met Gwendolyn's frightened stare. "Gwendolyn was my... *wife,*" he quietly revealed, feeling Katrina withdraw her hand.

"Wife?!" She exclaimed, suddenly turning unattractive before Gwendolyn's very eyes. "You were married before?"

"We thought the other dead," he voiced, continuing to stare into Gwendolyn's unsure gaze. "Deceased in a tragic accident."

"Thomas, please tell us that you are joking," Devin chortled, pouring himself and his sister a glass of brandy. Katrina yanked the tumbler away from her brother's hand and instantly threw it down her throat.

Thomas turned to look at Katrina, her eyes were full of questions; she was about to explode. "Let me explain," he quietly voiced to her.

"Explain?" She shrieked, waiving her hands up in the air. "You proposed to *me*, Thomas, to me! The banns have all been posted, the preparation...my dress being tailored as we speak!" Katrina stomped her feet twice on the wooden floor and ran out the room, Amy turning as well, followed her.

"I will do it," Devin stated, guzzling down his drink.

"No," Thomas stopped him. "This is my problem, not yours. But I do need your help, dear boy."

Devin grabbed his friend's shoulder. "Anything, you name it."

"I need you to find out when Gwendolyn was declared deceased. Our wedded state may not be under obligation."

Gwendolyn suddenly stood up from the sofa. "My solicitor can tell you that...I met with him this morning," she eyed Thomas then spoke to Devin. "We were there settling my Great-Aunt's estate. My Great Aunt left a will, leaving me inheritance, if there was mention of me to receive property then surely there are documents stating my existence, correct?"

Devin looked at her wide eyes, "She is right Thomas. If there are no documents in existence stating she was declared legally dead, then your marriage—"

Thomas interrupted him and met eyes with Gwendolyn once again. "...Is still legally binding."

"Then we are still married?" Gwendolyn asked, feeling panic rush her neck.

Devin stepped in between the obvious tensions. "There are formalities that can be taken."

"Formalities?" Gwendolyn asked stepping towards Devin.

Devin shook his head at her loveliness, "Uh—*yes, um,* although divorce is infrequent—"

"Divorce!" Thomas suddenly belted out.

"Yes, divorce—it might be the only solution...and a simple alternative."

Gwendolyn stood before Devin now and pleaded with him, "How quick can it be done? I am about to be married as well!"

Devin gave her a roguish grin, "You should have told me before your crimson look my dear." When Gwendolyn narrowed her eyes on him, he stiffened and continued, "A couple of days, five at the most? I do not think it should take longer than that." He then clicked his boots in resolution. "I am off—works to do you know. Nice to make your acquaintance Duchess," he mocked wickedly, turning on his heel and bowing farewell to the unknown woman on the couch.

Phyllis looked weirdly at the debonair young man then grabbed hold of Gwendolyn's trembling hands. "I had an acquaintance once who filed for divorce, she fled to France for isolation," she rationalized, "We live in the country dear, no one will ever know of your partition."

After realizing Phyllis was right, Gwendolyn began to laugh which made Thomas look her way. "Let me know when the papers can be signed, I am going back to Gisleham."

Thomas eyed her walking away. He really should go talk to Katrina. *Remember your fiancée dear boy? The one who ran out of the room crying and carrying on?* But Thomas simply could not get Gwendolyn out of focus. "Where are you staying Gwendolyn? Surely you are not spending the night in that ruin."

Gwendolyn blinked out of her trance observing him following her departure, "No—no, certainly, I am, *we* are staying at The Quail Inn."

"Stay here," he asked cautiously, watching Gwendolyn's face flush with animation. "No, what I meant was, as my guest. You can have your old room."

"The nursery?" She smiled, feeling a touch of repose. "You wish me to sleep in a bassinet?"

Thomas began to smile as well. His heart skipped a beat by her quick humor. "Silly girl, I had Fitzwater and Mrs. Hornebrook restore that room years ago."

"You still have Fitzwater and Mrs. Hornebrook?" Gwendolyn asked astonished. *Oh how she loved playing hide-and-seek with them!*

Thomas let go an adoring grin, "Why certainly, and most of my father's staff. Please say that you'll stay."

CHAPTER 5

"Oh child...the Lord works in mysterious ways," Mrs. Hornebrook declared hugging the life out of Gwendolyn. She was a hefty woman, full of compassion and influence. She used to be under the employ of the 4ᵗʰ Duke of Norwin, but had been joyously working for His Grace for the past eight winters as Head Housekeeper. Having lost her husband twenty winters back, she considered Thomas her only family. Gwendolyn felt overwhelmed with so much emotion from being within Mrs. Hornebrook's arms, her tears turned into a bawl.

"Oh Mrs. Hornebrook—"

"There—there, my darling girl."

"I am so happy to see you," Gwendolyn gushed, releasing her embrace. Mrs. Hornebrook was the closest thing she had to her own mother. She then eyed the short, skinny gentleman to her left. "And Mr. Fitzwater—"

Virgil Fitzwater had been with the Hollinger's for nearly thirty years, servicing the nobles as Head Steward, and had witnessed the births of three Hollinger boys; there was no other place he would rather be, he was already part of the family. "Fitzwater...yes, I feel like a part of me has been reborn, walking through Gisleham, being in this house, seeing...*Tommy*." Gwendolyn stopped and then bowed her head.

"He has changed, hasn't he?" Mrs. Hornebrook asked, watching Gwendolyn's tears disappear.

Gwendolyn stepped away from her and eyed the kitchen quarters. "So many things have changed, Mrs. Hornebrook."

"He is still the same person, deary," Fitzwater chimed in. "He has just improved."

"Improved?" Gwendolyn laughed, feeling a pit in her stomach, a change for the better or for worse? "And now the Duke of Norwin... heavens me, I would have never imagined."

"You knew the title was heritable dear," Mrs. Hornebrook claimed, taking out the teacups for service.

"Yes," Gwendolyn proclaimed, taking a seat. "So was my father's. Just so funny though, thinking of everyone calling Tommy *His Grace.*"

"Yes, and it took him months to finally accept the entitlement," Mrs. Hornebrook acclaimed, handing Fitzwater the service tray. "Did you know that these two children used to cause so much trouble when they were younger?" Mrs. Hornebrook asked Phyllis who was sitting at the farm table.

Fitzwater grabbed the hot teapot and began to serve everyone a cup. "I remember when His Grace and Gwendolyn were ten and got into his father's shaving blades. I walked in on them shaving Mr. Whiskers, the cat's tail. Oh, I have never seen two kids run so fast!"

Mrs. Hornebrook started to hoot, "What about the time when the two of them put frogs in Miss Pinkel's wash basin?"

"The governess?" Gwendolyn asked, amazed that they still remembered.

"Yes...I have never heard a woman scream so loud!" Mrs. Hornebrook chuckled, slapping her thighs with her hands. "She ran down the stairs so fast she tripped on her way down, tumbling through to the lower steps. How it was possible to get up from that plunge and run straight out the door was some miracle."

"It was a sight to behold," Fitzwater declared. "How about the day I found His Grace covered head to toe in honey because the two of them decided to count the bees in a tree hive? Miraculous the boy was not stung."

"Or the time the Duchess found Gwendolyn daring His Grace at a horse race...*oh my,* she nearly fainted at the sight of her daughter wearing breeches!"

The four of them remained laughing when Thomas suddenly appeared. Like the wind blowing out four candles, each one of them shut up and said nothing further.

"You were talking about me, weren't you?" He asked, turning to every one of them and then setting eyes on Gwendolyn.

Gwendolyn's heart stopped momentarily when their eyes locked. *How does he do that? Oh, she has to stop thinking about him so much. You are getting married Gwendolyn...married?* "Not all subjects are about you, you know. You may recommence and do, whatever —Duke's do, Your Grace," she curtsied, eyeing the lines around his mouth beginning to curl. He was going to smile, but he held back.

"Ten winters absent, five minutes back, and she acts like the mistress of the manor," he retorted, leaving them all alone.

Mrs. Hornebrook wondered at the door for a moment and then leaned into Phyllis. "No one speaks to His Grace that way; I am amazed by the way they feel comfortable around each other. Like two halves of the same person." Mrs. Hornebrook stood idle for a second more than twirled around to peek through the door, before whispering to Gwendolyn, "Have you met her yet?"

Gwendolyn knew immediately whom she was speaking about, "Lady Hale?"

"Yes."

"Yes, briefly...she seems quite nice."

Mrs. Hornebrook and Fitzwater both shot looks at one another.

"Seems, is too good a word dear. She purrs like a kitten when around him, but she is an alley cat through-and-through."

Gwendolyn was taken-back, she had never heard Mrs. Hornebrook, talk like that before! She wondered if she was always this over-bearing person who loved to gossip. "Oh?" Gwendolyn asked, batting her eyelashes, the intrigue choking her. "But he must care for her, correct? They are getting married?"

"Yes, my dear, does it distress you to see him with her?"

"Well, I—"

"Oh, I don't know about him sometimes, unsure what possessed him to solicit this engagement; I don't know what he sees in her."

Fitzwater grabbed the sugar bowl and scooped some into his cup with a spoon, "She is quite pleasant on the eyes."

Mrs. Hornebrook swatted Fitzwater on the shoulder, "Dirty old man, don't think I won't tell your mistress about your latest perception—see if I don't."

Oh, dear, God, what did she get herself into? Gwendolyn thought, rolling her eyes away. Mr. Fitzwater has a mistress? Gwendolyn tried to erase the shocked look on her face.

"I say, at least she is more comely than the other's." Fitzwater spurted out feeling the wrath of Mrs. Hornebrook's dagger stare. Mrs. Hornebrook tsked at her daft friend and shook her head.

Others? Gwendolyn then closed her eyes and pretended she did not hear that particular word and what it meant. Knowing her former husband had been frolicking the country looking to replace her, affected her heart in a peculiar sort of sting.

Like Mrs. Hornebrook could read her mind, she subsequently turned to Gwendolyn and lifted up her chin. "I remember once when His Grace used to follow someone around like a magnet," she stated, kissing Gwendolyn on the forehead. "His pull to her was more than an attraction, more like an obsession if you ask me."

Gwendolyn puffed up with sentiment again, her tears bursting at the edges of her eyes. "Never a fixation Mrs. Hornebrook, more like admiration. We were just good friends."

"Married friends."

That darn arrangement! If it weren't for her father's excess gambling and bad judgment in business investments Gwendolyn would have never married at sixteen. She would have been brought out properly at eighteen, introduced to the *ton*, and set the world on fire! She would have never had that burning question lingering inside her mind, even to this very day. *Did Thomas ever love her?* If it weren't for their forced matrimony, would Thomas Hollinger have asked for her hand? "Yes, married, because of the mandatory arrangement between our two fathers," Gwendolyn spat out shaking her head.

"No dear," Mrs. Hornebrook mouthed, disagreeing with her. "I will believe that decree when they prove to me the world is round."

"Her Great-Aunt always stated it was a necessary concordat," Phyllis delivered, reaching out to accept a drop of milk from Fitzwater. "Thank you, kind sir."

"You are welcome, kind woman," Fitzwater teased, winking at her. Phyllis turned crimson again. London was sure full of coy prospects.

"Necessary, indeed..." Mrs. Hornebrook opposed once more.

"In order to save the family," Phyllis continued, "their shipping trade from further debt, the two families had to form a partnership. That the two men waited sixteen years until Gwendolyn was old enough to get married."

"It was all so long ago," Gwendolyn sighed, bowing her head. "Not so long ago, that I can remember when you turned fifteen." "Fifteen?" Gwendolyn inquired, trying to remember.

Mrs. Hornebrook sat down next to Phyllis and patted her hand. "It was her fifteenth birthday. The two families, along with several others were at Wilderbrand to celebrate her birthday. Oh, it was a grand affair; I have never seen so many decorations." She stopped to take a sip of her tea, then moved on, "The Abernathy's brought their son, Barry home from the military institute. Oh, he was a handsome young lad and full of animation when he set eyes on Gwendolyn. A crown of flowers in her long flowing auburn hair, her first grown-up tailored dress, she looked remarkable. All during the party, the Duke's staff and I, used to laugh behind doors thinking how funny it looked, that whenever Barry showed considerate interest in Gwendolyn, His Grace simulated a black panther, ready to pounce."

Gwendolyn stood up and pulled away from the table. "I do not remember that happening Mrs. Hornebrook and I cannot believe you would make up such a story on my behalf." Gwendolyn bent around and headed out the door.

"What did I say, dear?" Mrs. Hornebrook eyed Phyllis, who was standing up as well.

"I will tend to her," she tenderly voiced, "she is a bit emotional from today's events."

THOMAS WENT BACK TO LIBRARY TO POUR HIMSELF A stiff drink. What the hell just happened...what the hell was he doing...what the hell was he thinking? His hands were shaking that's for certain. He looked down at them shuddering when he overheard someone clear their throat. Whirling his head around, he found Henry Barton, his confidant and employee for years. "Oh Henry, still here?"

"Yes, but I am about to depart in a few moments," Henry spurted, walking over to his friend and patting him on his back. "You don't look so good."

Thomas poured himself another drink. "I don't feel so good either."

"She is quite lovely," Henry disclosed, peering out the window, glaring at Katrina.

Thomas doesn't look at his friend, but rather stared at one particular statue solidly gaping back at him. "Yes—*yes*, she is."

Henry continued to stare out the pane. "I was speaking about your fiancée, Thomas; did you forget that you had one?"

Thomas closed his eyes, "No Henry, I have not."

"You know Thomas, Devin confessed to me that Katrina had had her pick of prospective husbands. You weren't the only one who proposed marriage. Katrina was the reigning belle of the season."

He should have been absolutely livid over that remark, should have felt vigilant, should have guarded her from Henry's unremitting interest, but all Thomas felt at that moment was reluctance. "She was at that."

"Can I ask you something Thomas? And you can perjure yourself if you feel you must."

Thomas closed his eyes and tried to get Gwendolyn's face out of his consideration, "Yes, certainly, what is it?"

"What do you feel when you see her?"

Thomas whipped his head around to find Henry heading out the door. "Feel?"

"Yes...*feel*, sense, experience when your eyes meet hers."

"Katrina...or Gwendolyn?"

"The one I believe that's occupying your thoughts at the moment."

Thomas acknowledged his friend and his straightforwardness. "Uncertainty," he uttered evenly. "I once cared for her deeply, Henry. I believed she was gone, therefore, I carried out my life and I am certain she had done the same. We are too different now," he tried to explain away reasons for him thinking of her entirely too much at this point, "with dissimilar opinions. We are both mature and set in our ways. She's probably overcame her appalling habits of slurping her soup, or sneezing into her skirts. The girl I once knew was sixteen Henry, *sixteen*, that woman upstairs is unrecognizable, and yet," he faltered, perplexed by his fate, "She still fascinates me."

"So what is the solution then?"

"Execute the divorce decree and keep my distance, Henry, the farther away, the better."

"WHAT ARE YOU THINKING, GWENDOLYN?" PHYLLIS asked guardedly, observing her pace the room muttering to oneself; she was so concerned for the poor girl.

"It appears that my marriage contract is still binding, Phyllis." "Unbelievable...why your Great-Aunt is probably turning over in her grave as we speak to have you in such a predicament."

"I wish she was here," Gwendolyn cried, burying her face within her hands, spurting into tears. "She would know what to do." Phyllis motioned for Gwendolyn to stop her tread and come and sit down next to her. To her surprise, Gwendolyn rushed to her side immediately and lovingly embraced her. The feeling was so overwhelming; it brought a tear to her eye. "What is there to do child? You have been apart for ten winters dear. He has obviously moved forward, and so have you."

Tears continued to rush down her face. "He is so mature Phyllis and it makes me wonder...I keep thinking of all the *what ifs?* What if we had survived that horrible day? What if we were still together, would we have been devoted? Would we have been content? Would we have had more children? And what of my child now? What if Mary would have known her father? What kind of child would she have been? I would have never met Charles... never would have to break his heart..."

Phyllis grabbed Gwendolyn's head and wrapped her palms around her face, "Break his heart? Why my dear Gwendolyn, why would you think you would have to break your fiancé's heart? Why, when you care for someone, love cannot be pushed aside and buried away."

"But it has Phyllis; love has been pushed aside and buried away. And seeing him again…seeing those incredible hypnotizing green eyes of his makes me want to know the man he has now become."

"Oh dear," Phyllis remarked, letting go of Gwendolyn's face realizing what direction the conversation was heading. "Well," she decided instantly, "I think I know what your Great-Aunt would say."

"What?" Gwendolyn asked, blowing her nose into her skirts.

"At least you have a choice," Phyllis alleged, "the documents won't be ready for a few more days…try and get to know the man, you may find out he has changed entirely too much from the young fellow you used to know. Then your decision will be less of a burden."

"And what if I discover I like how he has improved?"

Phyllis grabbed her hand and held it within hers for a moment, "Then you must weigh your alternatives."

"Why?"

"Because I have learned from Mrs. Hornebrook that his wedding is less than ten days away."

CHAPTER 6

Thomas found Katrina sulking outside by her favorite duck pond; Amy was by her side and looked up immediately at Thomas who stood immobile.

Before approaching her, he wondered what to say. He brought to mind all the other women in his life and how each of them, in their own distinctive way, aided him towards happiness and to get over the first.

When he returned to Britain, solitude beset him and he took comfort in the arms of a barmaid with russet curls. Holding her for hours afterwards, he cried in her arms, beholden to her compassionate character and resemblance. Many nights henceforward he could be found crouched down to Gwendolyn's portrait at Gisleham. Staring at her picture for hours upon hours, until the very sight of her gamine smile pained him to a degree where he was unable to breath.

At twenty and happening upon the season, Thomas was then shocked to realize how many women found him attractive. Practically overnight, he had developed from a lanky lad to a robust, mesmeric male. Confidence then grew with every giggling female he came across, every assessment of an interested woman's eyes. Women of every stature seemed to flock to him and he could not understand why; he did not know how to deal with so much attention and began to withdraw. While most good-looking men relish in their female appeal, their flamboyance sampling every feminine being in sight, Thomas did not. Waking up in the arms of a stranger did not feel comfortable to him and he began searching for compassion.

Never intending on marrying again, he took company of several forlorn widows'. Mrs. Putnam, a widow in her early forties whose husband once a wealthy gent, left her with an estate to run, too much time on her hands and oh so much money to spend. She approached Thomas initially, and showed him how to make love without leaving an unwanted pregnancy. She helped passed the time and Thomas ended their affair when he stumbled upon Mrs. Putnam and her new playmate in bed together. Thomas was saddened to hear that the enthusiastic Mrs. Putnam perished recently in an unfortunate collision when her carriage wheel hit another, thus toppling over with her inside.

Then there was Mrs. Carmichael, a widow in her early thirties. She was a tigress in bed, teaching him how to pleasure a woman at the outset so that their encounter was a more sensual, lasting experience. He liked her very much but she quickly grew possessive and Thomas had no other choice but to terminate their liaison. He had continued his acquaintance with her though, running into her at various social events, flirting with her and vice versa. She was marred woman who weathered well through a broken heart.

Lastly, there was Lady Krausman of German decent, a widow barely nineteen. She was a funny girl, with her clever wittiness that was unsurpassed. He enjoyed her company many times, but she rapidly became desperate. Threatening that if he did not marry her, she would kill herself. Kill herself? Well, he ended their affiliation immediately, and she was still breathing last he heard, living in

Oxbow with her new husband—who looks a lot like Thomas—and their four children.

Enough with the bad relationships; Thomas decided to concentrate on business. Women to him were trivial; his father's legacy evolved into his mistress.

After arriving back in London, His Grace, the Duke of Norwin inherited much more than a title and money. He was in charge of the Hollinger Commerce Company, a maritime lineage passed down from his Great-Great-Grandfather. The *"HCC"* was a sinking undertaking. His father made the right decision by accepting the Earl of Suffolkshire's trade to supply him with ample merchant vessels. Without the marriage arrangement, the *HCC* would be just another bankrupt shipping trade. The export industry to Bengal, India, Madagascar, China, Africa and South America was now his to maneuver. His father was even accommodating passengers for transport to Charleston, Virginia and Boston in North America and Thomas kept that intact as well. Gwendolyn's dowry provided him with endless vessels of every variety: schooners, flagships, brigantines and merchant ships. The first few years weren't without trial though. Pirates in the Eastern Seas to Madagascar commandeered several ships; inundated by infamous pirates the likes of John Rackham, Bartholomew Roberts and Red Retropé.

When construction began; there were orders for ships making the voyage down the Atlantic, around the Cape of Good Hope, across the Indian Ocean and up through the China Sea and back. Tea production was in high demand, enthusiastic customers for the China trades; goods, like tealeaves, silks, cinnamon and firecrackers. The *HCC* began building clipper ships, capable of sailing to China at a rapid pace. Although only a few were being built at the time, Thomas was indeed proud of his short accomplishment. Large and substantial, sleek in profile, with a level freeboard and a narrow, V-shaped hull, her beam was 27 feet, and her keel slanted downward from 11 feet at the bow to 17 feet at the stern. She was considered to be the fastest merchant vessel afloat.

As of late, most of his mercantile cargo was for military usage and aiding the Royal Navy with guns, uniforms, cannons and food. Every quarter, he was fortunate to take on dazzling fortunes from Arabian Kings: gold, silver, elephant tusk ivory, spices, coffers of jewelry and bales upon bales of shiny rare silks. Just recently, he had tried to maneuver away from the slave trade, but that too was good business. But he had concluded that he could get paid evenly for African antelope more sq from human cargo and opted towards the transport of mutton.

Thomas was proud of his triumph; it took him only three years to achieve his goal. And, at twenty-three, Thomas grew into one of the richest men in London and secured respect and admiration from men old enough to be his father. He actually multiplied his father's wealth tenfold and with his suffering behind him, finally looked forward to his future. The subsequent three years have been a whirlwind of invitations, charities and voyages to North America; he was on top of the world when he spotted her from afar.

He wanted to know her immediately not knowing who she was, but watched her materialize across the room. Her gracefulness, so enchanting, felt compelled to meet her. To his amazement, unbeknownst to him, she was his solicitor's younger sister! He unhindered himself and allowed their friendship to grow naturally. So many years wasted on yearning for an alliance that would never resume. He longed to find similar rapport he was obligated to let go and escorted Katrina to several parties throughout the summer. He soon found out that he needed her by his side every moment of the day and plagued Katrina to the physical. Making her his mistress was not complex; she was a welcome participant, her body gratifying his void, her giggle melting his anxiety. Meeting her at clandestine hours, Katrina had been a breath of fresh air, his safe-haven and his confidant for the past several months. Her solace, so welcoming, alleviated the loneliness he seemed to seat within his heart. Her smiles, so lovely, like medicine for his shattered soul; he finally felt released from his misery and asked his mistress to marry him.

"CAN I HAVE A MOMENT ALONE WITH HER AMY? YOU need not go very far."

Amy grabbed hold of Thomas' seriousness. "Certainly."

Thomas waited until Amy was mid-way around the pond until he began to speak. "Ready for the shock of your life?" Thomas quipped, trying to lighten up the severity of the situation.

Katrina gazed up at her fiancé keenly grinning down at her. "You are still married," she said in a portentous tone.

"But not for long," he stated, kneeling down next to her. "Your brilliant brother is working on freeing me as we speak."

Katrina smiled, and then eyed the ducks waddling on the far end of the lake. "Did you love her Thomas?"

Thomas did not want to lie to her; he never had reason to lie. Besides, what kind of marriage would be based on dishonesty? "It was an arranged marriage, we were children; I do not think we knew what love was. We shared a mutual comradeship, and she picked me only because she was my best friend."

That stung. Katrina had never heard Thomas talk that way before about anyone, not even about her own brother, who she considered now to be his present best friend. "Do you love *me* Thomas?"

That was a bold step for Katrina, he thought. He had never expressed devotion to her before, even when he proposed, he could not mouth out the words; his affection towards her shown through tenderness and purchased appreciation, their relationship strictly emergent from repeated liaisons and accord.

She did not let him answer, feeling restriction, feeling a sense of sudden regret. "Because I love you Thomas, with all my heart," she let go along with her hand that grazed his cheek. "And if that means that I must surrender my honor until you are liberated, then I will wait with ungraceful patience."

Thomas grabbed her hand away from his face and kissed the back of her hand, holding it over his heart. He did not want to hurt her but somehow felt he already did.

CHAPTER 7

Gwendolyn had been intently staring at Thomas several hundred feet beyond. He had been chopping wood for hours and Gwendolyn wondered why he had not let any of his servants in his employ do the task for him. She also wondered why he was avoiding her. Eating dinner late, leaving the manor early, gone for nearly the entire day. Two days had passed, and she ached to talk to him.

What a keen frustration for Gwendolyn to once have had his complete attention, to this day be strained to accept intermittent glimpses of him now and then. She remembered when she used to try and dodge him, push him away, yell at him to stop looking at her, or at least give her a second alone! What she wouldn't give to have just a few moments of his curiosity now? What a reversed turn of events! And why did he have to be so entrancing to look at now? It was his body that matured; she recognized in the end, she had never seen a man so sickly sweet with broad, symmetrical shoulders with muscles that would not give. *Gorgeous, yes,* that was the ideal word to describe him at this point; he was mouth-watering to glare upon. Had he always been that way? *No…*She brought to mind the thin, gawky lad he once was, he was bashful to say the least. *And now...dear God, how many other women must have fallen in love with him at first sight?* Oh God, she was hurting inside at present. She wanted, no throbbed to have his sole concentration again.

"Heavens me, what could be so fascinating?" Katrina asked, arriving alongside Gwendolyn raising an eyebrow in aversion over Gwendolyn's brown silk morning dress.

Gwendolyn had not counted on Lord and Lady Hale to arrive at that very moment. She watched another opportunity go by, as it seemed very unlikely for her to get Thomas alone with the manor energized with preparation for the evening's festivities. Learning from Mrs. Hornebrook that a planned dinner party was set for that night, Gwendolyn was reluctant to spend the evening there.

"I want to go into town," Gwendolyn spurted out suspiciously, continuing to look out in the distance.

Katrina laughed and followed Gwendolyn's concentration. "He is quite tempting, is he not?"

Gwendolyn turned to look at her. She was wearing a white satin bonnet with ostrich feathers and gold braid. With a pink embroidered spencer jacket, puffed shoulders encased her cotton percale dress with muslin flounces. She appeared absolutely faultless, but Gwendolyn felt there was another side to this alley cat and she was apprehensive to experience her claws. "I would not know, I once knew the boy—that over there...is a man."

Katrina smiled seductively, licking her lips. "Yes, and quite an attractive man at that." She traced around Gwendolyn and surveyed her attitude, "You should have seen him in battle my dear —he was absolutely breath-taking in action."

"In action?"

Katrina clicked her tongue, "On the prowl? Lurking around? After every form that happened to wear a skirt?"

Gwendolyn's blood began to boil. *God, she hated this girl!* "How did you two meet?"

Katrina gazed out at Thomas now and watched him intently as well. "I was invited to several parties he had hosted, but never got familiar enough to be introduced. Seems Thomas over there likes his fun, spirits...and games. Oh his social events were all the rage of the season. There was not a female within a hundred kilometers uninvited to one of his affairs." She laughed and then looked over at Gwendolyn who was not amused. "Oh, but I guess there was."

Gwendolyn swallowed her contempt and began to walk forward, Katrina followed slowly behind. "And when did you two meet?" She repeated.

"Thomas owns a shipping trade; you knew that, did you not? Well, my brother Devin applied for an opening in one of his employ. They became instantaneous friends and invited my brother everywhere. Devin escorted me to one such social highlight and aided my encroachment."

"I see," Gwendolyn stated, holding up her dress and marching on.

Katrina sustained her stride. "Do you Gwendolyn? Because according to Thomas, you were once the best of friends, and after we are married, I do wish to keep my husband in high spirits and hope to remain acquaintances."

Gwendolyn stopped and bore into Katrina's spiteful blue eyes. *Friends with her?* She would rather befriend a cockroach. "If you do not mind, Katrina, I would like to speak to Thomas alone."

"But I do mind, Gwendolyn," Katrina voiced with disdain. "You are headed towards *my fiancé...*" she stopped and eyed Thomas again. "And since neither one of us is accompanied by our companions, it is uncustomary to approach a man alone; especially one who is as vigorous as the Duke of Norwin."

Gwendolyn did not realize how close she was to him. Now only a few feet away, Thomas had stopped chopping wood and stood and stared at the two women's unannounced materialization. His shirt, by some means, escaped his upper body. He stood panting and grasping for breath and carefully laid his ax down by his leg.

His broad chest was covered with disorderly black curls and he glistened from the strenuous activity, welcoming the sun that bronzed his skin. His pantaloons appeared much too relaxed to withhold his muscular thighs and yet, they appeared painted on.

Thomas grinned from ear to ear and powdered his hands once again, rewrapping the ax. "To what do I owe this pleasure?"

Katrina bit down on her lower lip and practically ate the man alive. "Devin and I are here for our Thursday feast with several of the *ton* dear, did the ritual escape your mind?"

Thomas did not look at her and swung the ax around. His taut strapping arms flew up over his head and came down with a whack aside the lumber, splitting it accurately in two. "No, I did not forget Katrina," he strained to say through splitting, "and why are you here Gwendolyn?"

Gwendolyn regained her composure. Sweat began to drip down the center of her back from his disreputable flaunt. Her fingers itched to touch him and she clasped her hands behind her rear to disguise her craving to do so. "Don't you have someone to do that Thomas?"

Thomas did not bother to look at her and continued on with the undertaking. "Yes, but I prefer to do this myself. I like to take out my frustrations on stagnant blameless trees."

Gwendolyn began to hoot from his morbid humor and apparent private joke. Thomas gazed over at her and grinned himself. The warmth from his smile and the allusion in his eyes caused her mouth to go dry. "Since you are rather fond of my absence I would like to go into town; can you arrange a driver for my carriage?"

He knew exactly what she was hinting at. The last couple of days were excruciating to say the least. He was so excited to have her here it had been pain-staking torture not to converse with her. Nevertheless, Thomas stayed his course, "You cannot leave Gwendolyn."

Gwendolyn gazed around her and pinpointed Katrina; she had

suddenly walked over to Thomas' backside and perched herself on a massive tree stump. "Why ever not?"

Thomas split a log in two before saying, "I cannot have you traipsing around town spilling your existence when I am about to get married, you see."

Seeing his point all too clearly, she retorted, "So you intend to keep me hostage?"

Thomas chortled, "You are free to roam the acreage Gwendolyn and no one intends to keep you imprisoned to your room. We still have ample horses to ride around on; there are even several delightful ponds you have never seen before surrounding the grassland. I think you would enjoy the restoration of Wilderbrand."

"Sounds like a splendid idea, I haven't ridden in over a month. I will just go find a cozy little spot by a quaint little pond and write a letter to *my* fiancé. Tell him how much I miss him and apprise him of recent measures." Gwendolyn huffed and began to walk away. She circled around and inquired, "Do I have your permission to use your horse?"

Thomas smirked again, "Certainly." He was rather enjoying her company, and she was withdrawing her verbal jostling? "But do not feed her sugar, she won't eat her regular diet if you spoil her...I quite like the way she is now."

"And what way is that?"

"Submissive."

Gwendolyn's heart began to pound again. He said it so huskily, she felt like throwing herself into his arms and kissing that bare chest of his. She eyed Katrina who kept seated, "Coming Katrina?"

Spreading out her skirt alongside the cut-off trunk Katrina continued to sit and turned away.

"If I recall, that tree used to ooze sap...and well, ants and beetles love sap, don't they Thomas?" Gwendolyn turned around and smiled and began her trot up the hill.

Katrina immediately jumped off the tree trunk and began patting her backside.

Thomas grinned and watched Gwendolyn tramp away. Unconsciously, his foot moved forward, he was going to accompany her. He instantly recalled always following her and stopped dead in his tracks. *No. Stop. Do not pursue her.* Gwendolyn was always the one in control, relinquishing his capability to her, ruling their friendship; he was forever trailing in her wake. What would it be like to have her shadow him for a change? She was now his hostage, as she put it very nicely.

He stood frozen, heart pounding fierce, without a doubt, it would be a valuable challenge, absolute compensation if he could win her full attention. He brought to mind their wedding night when he first realized how he could gain the upper hand, to be assertive...well, that won't be so difficult now; he had been that way for years. He could just continue being his same assured self... *no, that won't work either; he was always mush around her.* No, it had to work, it will succeed...but for what purpose? Good Lord, what was happening to him? Confusion, disorder, he was not used to so much instability since he was a lad! Daunting, intimidating, nerve-racking...he knew this would happen... he knew he was in big trouble when he laid her down on that blasted couch. He was once her personal dunderhead, but no more!

He continued to look at her...by God; she was a vision, even in retreat. Her sensual neck was exposed with her bonnet missing; she even glided across the lawn appearing inviolable in her swan-like grace. Outlandish thoughts ran through his regulations, unusual temptations, unlike any other he had ever known. He thought about tackling her from behind, pulling her down to the ground and bussing her neck with all the passion he was feeling since first seeing her. What would she do? Relent, or kick him? The very thought swirled deliciously from side to side.

Idiot, he was still a fool for her. He shook his head a few more times trying to get that foolhardy imagery out of his mind.

Realizing that Katrina was watching him like a hawk, he rolled his eyes around and curved to see her glowering at him.

Katrina stood in front of him with her arms crossed, "Charming girl, your childhood bride. The sooner you get rid of her, the better."

Thomas eyed his fiancée's measured advance, "To what consequence?" He asked gruffly.

"Go get ready for the party Thomas," Katrina purred, drawing near in her cat-like sashay. With an index finger she indolently poked him in the chest, slicing it down towards his midriff, resting on the front of his pantaloons by design. She brought her eyes up his lanky, well developed body and met his entranced gaze. "And may I suggest a cold bath?"

CHAPTER 8

To her respect, Wilderbrand Castle had not changed much. Constructed in the Fourteenth Century, the manor had once been a fortress housing nobles safely with its rather sizable moat surrounding the "H" shaped constructed block castle. Thomas' Great-Great Grandfather, the 1st Duke of Norwin had the lagoon packed full with dirt, and the turf, over the years had grown into a deep dark emerald green from all its mossy nutrients. The land was still extensive, nearly forty-thousand acres with a working farm, stables stocked full of horses for breeding and competition, as well as, not one, not two or three, but four separate residences for all the household staff. The Hollinger's were known for that, keeping their servants content and close at hand.

The ride around the property proved positive to be a relaxing and enjoyable experience. At Thomas' guarantee, Gwendolyn found undiscovered ponds around the castle, uniquely designed pools covered with geese, ducks and swans lazily swimming. Falling in love with the ambience straight away, she had assembled herself on a blanket next to a beautiful pond surrounded by wild flowers and assorted grasses.

"Cherish," the glorious buff Arabian with dark mane and tail she remembered first seeing when she saw Thomas again, was quite affectionate...and *female*. Thomas mentioned once or twice that his horse was a girl, had he not? With all that bare skin of his distracting her senseless she wondered how she was able to articulate two words much less listen to the rascal. *Cherish* was very friendly, in fact, she constantly wanted to be petted; sniffing the blanket, nibbling Gwendolyn's writing paper, her skirt...her hair. The horse would not stay put, so Gwendolyn had to repeatedly walk it out to the meadow and force her to eat the tall green grass, but Cherish kept trotting over to Gwendolyn relaxing by the pond nonetheless. Gwendolyn rolled her eyes and scolded herself for not following previous instructions; serves her right for not listening to Thomas in the first place, Gwendolyn had fed her sugar.

She wrote Charles an extensive letter, explaining to him about current events and her length of stay. Gwendolyn had already explained to her fiancé about Mary's father, but did not go into detail. Only offering that her husband was lost at sea, leaving her a widow at such a young age. It was a treasured, special memory she had not wished to share. No one needed to know her pain, her misery, or why she chose to stay unmarried for ten winters.

Odd, how the things you took for granted were so sorely missed once they disappear. Like his smile from one of your jokes, or the comfort of his arms around your shoulders when you skinned your knee. The way they were so inseparable, even when apart; always thinking the same thing, finishing each other's thoughts. She oftentimes cried herself to sleep at night, missing him so. She could not wait for Mary to be born. The miracle inside her womb was her refuge; singing lullaby's, reading children's stories, talking to her unborn child when she felt lonely. But then one night in June, Lady Mary Elizabeth Drummond Hollinger came into this world. She did not even mind the ache of birth; she could not wait to hold his child in her arms. And when her Great-Aunt handed her the baby, Gwendolyn cradled the infant and cried into her little body for hours upon hours. Kissing her tiny head surrounded in black wavy curls. It was like Thomas was still with her, a chance to live again, to communicate to her through his descendant.

Oh, she could have remarried. Could have married Viscount Tapps of Moxley and had more children. Her Great-Aunt took her back to London when she was eighteen, she even went on a picnic with the comely Viscount, and he seemed interesting enough. Having known him since Gwendolyn was ten, her Great-Aunt thought they would have alike empathy, but Gwendolyn was not responsive; she chose not to know him.

At nineteen, Gwendolyn was then introduced to a widower, fifteen years her senior. Baron Switzer had two small daughters, both around the same age as Mary. The girls all got along so well, playing, laughing, but Gwendolyn did not like the way the Baron showed his affection towards his children. Under intense suspicion, Gwendolyn knew the youngsters might be surrogate companions to the man until he found himself a suitable wife; he was constantly cuddling the girls significantly. Gwendolyn did not want to subject Mary to any future harm if her intuition was correct.

Then, at twenty, her Great-Aunt wrote to a friend in Bedfordshire. Her acquaintance had a son who could not seem to find a bride. Untitled, but wealthy, Patrick Smead was a timid chap who doted on his mother relentlessly; running to her side as soon as the woman tapped her teacup. After watching him scurry around the large, overbearing woman several times during her visit to their estate, Gwendolyn simply stood up and walked out the door never to return again.

Men did not equate…no one compared.

For many winters, Gwendolyn and her daughter were a team.

Gwendolyn was oftentimes in awe of her child, her spirit and curiosity. She loved to hug her, and her daughter loved to be held. It was only until Mary showed interest in the local livestock that she had met Charles.

It was not love at first glance or anything similar to that, but when his gaze met hers, Gwendolyn was intrigued. There was also something about him that made her want to know him. He was not obviously handsome, but was decent enough for her, with a charming façade, facial hair and warm, brown eyes. They were friends first and it was easy to like Charles, he was not a pushy male like the other men in town, he was gentle and kind, and whenever a new calf was born, he would always ask if Mary could come by the dairy to visit. Charles had been the most polite man she had come across in the village and around her age, all the eligible bachelors much too old or way too young to consider. Gwendolyn desperately wanted more children and she was sure by Charles' gentleness with Mary, he wished for them too. Charles was a likable gent, courteous and un-presumptuous showing considerable interest in helping Gwendolyn raise her daughter throughout the years.

Charles was also a hardworking man, owning a dairy farm was tedious work. A thousand-acre farm expanding over the rolling fields of Kettlewell, Charles was also an essential man. He was a big fish in a small pond and Gwendolyn liked him that way.

Gwendolyn remembered weeping the night her Great-Aunt passed away; she was outside her cottage when Charles sprung up behind her. His compassion was tender, genuine and she flew instantly in his arms. His maleness and warmth was a sense of comfort and he kissed her on her forehead. That soothing kiss, led to one on her lips; wrapping her arms around his neck and shoulders, allowing him to taste her. It only lasted a couple of moments, but within that time, she knew for certain that she would be spending the rest of her life with him.

It was beneficial to have a good rapport with your future

husband and Gwendolyn and Charles could talk for hours. Holding hands continuously, Mary on the one side, Charles on the other; taking walks through the grassland picking up flowers and stones. She could always make him laugh, and he could always melt her heart with his consideration. Gwendolyn liked the feeling of his big arms around her, he made her feel protected, and that's just what she needed in this time in her life, to be taken care of, to feel serene and treasured.

She was so lonely and longed for physical contact, that one night she allowed him use of her body. It only happened once, it was fast and awkward, but afterwards she felt tranquil…precious. He held her in his full-size arms and she felt his love. For the first time in her life she had complete devotion from a man. And Charles had loved her, told her often, but to this day, she had never reiterated her feelings towards him! Oh she knows she should, she also knows it was truly unfair but she had always had trouble expressing her true emotions. Her heart would begin to pound, her throat would close up and she just could not mouth out the words.

Her wedding was supposed to be in the next couple of months; a country wedding in a little church in Kettlewell, with no more than ten people in attendance. She had hoped that her Great-Aunt would be able to see her get married again, but sadly enough; she became too sick to hang on. The past several years Gwendolyn had taken care of her the same way her Great-Aunt took care of Gwendolyn, with kindness, affection, and patience.

And to get married for a second time after so many years of being alone? This time, she wanted to be married, to be someone's wife, quite different from her marriage to Thomas. She was too young to understand how to make him happy. Married atop a ship, Gwendolyn had never been more apprehensive about a union. Only coming to the perception that she would be joined to a reserved boy, who happened to be her best friend, both complying with their father's indissoluble debt.

No doubt entered her mind whatsoever when with Charles. He

would make a fine husband and a good provider, and she could move on, living a sensible life in Yorkshire on a farm. The reservation she had now was unimaginable; to mull over the fact that she doesn't want to return back home? She wanted to continue being under his roof, near him, by his side, trying to get closer to Thomas than ever before? What was wrong with her? Here, she had this wonderful man waiting homewards for her and she did not want to depart to be with him? She would rather be Thomas' prisoner then be liberated with Charles?

What was it about Thomas now? Was it the fact that he bore a resemblance to the celebrated Jordan Hollinger? She remembered when she and Thomas would be sitting on a bench in front of the estate, out of view of the carriages that drove up, and low and behold, out popped some hysterical father, ranting and raving, claiming that Jordan compromised their daughter. Jordan would never come out the door obviously, only the Duke of Norwin, sending the poor gent away. Jordan had been in the house all evening, surrounded by dozens of witnesses, how could he have touched anyone?

Jordan had a certain charisma...a magic that surrounded him; you wanted to get to know him, be in the same room...touch him. Why, just looking at the man caused a girl's heart to flutter. Sexual magnetism, yes, that's what it was and Thomas possessed that as well. Without a doubt, having other women finding Thomas irresistible was wildly enticing; owning his self-assurance. Why would she be drawn to such conviction? She never cared for certainty before, but having Thomas hold his weight within his peers was also very intriguing. He never used to be like that! Thomas was shy, introverted, it was only when she provoked and prodded him that he lashed out. And now, no longer understated, no more intimidated by her presence, she found herself lured, more so than she ever was before. What caused him to turn around? Was it another woman? Or did it go deeper than that? Was he hardened by life and the events that occurred? Losing his family all at once, like her, maybe, creating an outer shell of armor that no one was able to penetrate, an unbreakable shield of wisdom, control and confidence caused by insurmountable turmoil?

She would try though, to get through to him, if he would permit her to do so. Not only was he her first husband, Mary's father, and best friend...he was funny, kind, compassionate, admirable, strong, brave, interesting all rolled up into one impressive build. Someone she used to worry about tremendously, if not extraordinarily. Repeatedly dreaming of her wedding night when Thomas suddenly transformed into that fascinating male...

"You're mine now, and as your husband, you have to do what I say..."

I recalled gasping at his rapid strictness. I had never heard his voice so severe. His tone set off a counter attack but was immediately doused by the odd transformation of his face. His expression altered... which was so bizarre, I was already well acquainted with every feature on his mug but I was suddenly so attracted to this stern air. In fact, his whole demeanor changed, his attitude... that look of his, it made me want to know the texture of his lips, allow him to come across the surface of mine. No longer my equal, no more my comrade, Tommy transformed into someone very interesting.

"Now, I'm going to kiss you."

"You are?" I asked in disbelief. Amazing how forgetful a peck on the lips could be, like the one he gave to me when we were pronounced man and wife. But now, as my heart pounded in my ears like drums, I gazed into his interest and promptly found myself looking forward to our first real kiss.

He hesitated, and then ran his thumb across my mouth. I stared at him for a moment wondering what the heck he was thinking. I could not wait for him to kiss me...and then he did.

His lips were nice, soft, and gently pressed against mine. Tender, then deep, then tender again, shooting weird darts directly into my stomach, awakening feelings felt deep within. I didn't even know those sensations existed, but there they were, and my body wanted more. The ambiance felt amazing; did it feel the same for him? I kept thinking why we hadn't tried this before. We had been alone countless of times, not chaperoned, we were best friends bursting at the seams with curiosity. We could have easily stole scores of kisses and I scolded myself then and there why I never insisted we at least try.

Kissing him felt incredible though, unleashing my inhibitions to finally touch his naked body. I reached for his neck, wrapping my arms around his back and shoulders and the physical contact was all it took. There was no going back; I liked how his skin felt underneath my fingertips…I liked it too much. His male skin was rigid, and I was surprised to find so many muscles I hadn't noticed before. He kept kissing me however, each connection different from the first, increasingly eager and when his tongue suddenly pushed through my lips, a gratifying moan escaped both our throats. I met his ardent exploration in a delicious, languid impatience like we had been kissing for years. It felt so natural…it felt like heaven. Too much heat passed between us now as the tastes of him unlocked my desire to touch, sample and be aware of every gift he had to offer. I felt him tugging at my nightgown, and with the aid of my own hands, I was instantly released from my gown and undergarments, and, Oh God, I did not want the vibrations to end! His hands roamed far and wide, alongside my neck, down my arms, to my lower back, around my buttocks until they reached up and cupped my breast. It only startled me, his heat on my skin; I even anticipated his fondle which made me flinch. He instantly withdrew his hand, but I quickly grabbed it back and led it back down to my breast.

He looked into my eyes and I got lost again in the deep green of them. "Oh God," he continued, brushing his lips hotly across my lips in tiny little kisses, "…You are so beautiful Gwendolyn, so sweet, my sweet, sweet girl."

Those words…his enunciation… the exhilaration from his expressions produced such a thick fog of passion, my reservations suddenly vanished and something wonderful fell into its place. I watched with round eyes as he kneads the small mound then bent down and leisurely suckled. With his searing mouth, the wet gratification surprised and delighted me, I wanted to *offer him something else, but what else could I give him? I watched in awe as Tommy swiftly shifted to the other, licking and filling his mouth, looking every bit as wonderful as it felt. I did not know how to make him feel as good, so I grabbed his head and ran my fingers through his thick black mane. I had never felt his hair before, coarse on the ends from the sea wind, silky-soft by his scalp…and, oh God, the smell of him? Unexpectedly sensing some new essence; my nostrils wide and greedy, sopping up the heavenly scent of soap and masculinity. He quickly brought me to a blistering temperature, an inferno of sensations that needed to be extinguished. My body burned; oh God, it felt like fire, so much heat flared amid my junction when Tommy suddenly covered my body with his, adding pressure where I ached for it the most. I was so ready for him, for it, for whatever he was about to do and felt the bulk of his weight bear down on me with something hard and foreign entering in one lively swoop. I did not know what to expect, but I felt instant pain. My slight yelp buried beneath his lips confirmed my discomfort.*

"I'm sorry," he whispered now, "So sorry."

He should apologize; I remembered thinking—that definitely hurt, and then we laid very still…our chests moving up and down soaking in some kind of anticipation. And that's when I realized what was really happening. Tommy was… inside of me? I felt it move and adjusted to the fullness and all I kept thinking was how mind-blowing it felt…how utterly fantastic to be able to receive the mystery of him in the place where I kept secret.

I pushed against the breadth and tried to meet his rhythm experiencing tingling convulsions spread through from my stomach up my spine and down my back. When I arched up to welcome the wondrous sensation, Tommy impelled one last time then collapsed into my chest nearly out of breath.

He remained on top of me heaving, and I did not mind in the least. His body was wet with perspiration, but I did not seem to mind that either. He was suddenly closer than ever, and my heart cried out to get virtually aligned. My mother was right, our wedding night was memorable, and for the first time in my life, I was elated to be a girl, happy to be his and glad to be married. He smelled wonderful that night, and my future didn't seem so bleak. He was mine forever, and, without a doubt; I found a fresh diversion to share with a cherished friend.

"Did it continue to hurt?" He whispered against my lips, continuing to kiss me.

"No," I blushed, caressing the sides of his cheeks. I wondered if he would want to try it once more.

He gave me another devastating smile, "Want to do it again?"

I laughed, and then closed my eyes. "I was just thinking the same thing."

I remembered thinking how much I loved him and how much I wanted to tell him so. I brushed back hair that mottled his face and, oh God, I loved him with all my heart! Loved how his body felt naked, inside...kissing, on top of me. But then I instantly recalled him not wanting to marry me and right away tears began to swarm my eyes...

GWENDOLYN SIGHED HEAVILY AFTER RECALLING THAT wonderful memorable night, and sadness as well as tears quickly approached. Recollecting her wedding night brought forth agonizing deliberations. Was she really in love with Charles? She was incredibly fond of him...always looked forward to conversing with him, but good God, why wasn't she in love with him? She should be in love with him; she agreed to be his wife! Charles had never brought forth that kind of passion. Not once had he looked upon her with the same sort of eagerness. Was she simply marrying him for companionship? Would their marriage be one-tenth of what her first short-lived union was? Would Charles ever be able to spark fervor in her with one simple glance? A grin...Or just him standing there? No, and Gwendolyn felt troubled realizing the awful truth, and in the same breath, she felt like a fool knowing she once loved Tommy Hollinger so deeply and he never returned her love. It took her years to get over him...and now he was alive? Looking every bit as dashing, even more so, beyond handsome, stealing all her thoughts, she was utterly confused. This titter-totter of emotions had engulfed her so fast; it was driving her crazy. She doesn't know which way to turn, or move, one moment she wanted to run and hide, the next she wanted to curl up into his arms and stay there forever. His mesmerizing spell was choking her to death, at any given moment, poke her in the arm and she would positively scream!

And what was this ridiculous notion of thinking Thomas would eventually pop up unannounced behind her? She kept turning her head in anticipation of his sudden emergence. What stupidity to think he would really want to continue to spend time with her! Resume their past childhood friendship? He was not the same boy, he was a man and everything had changed. What could they possibly have in common now? Memories? Swimming? Frogs? Mary? *Oh, God, Mary...*he was still in the dark about his daughter and Gwendolyn felt bad swallowing the surprise.

There...she did it again; turning her head around in hopes of seeing him coming near. But to no purpose, no one was around, it was just she and the darn horse...she, alone with her wandering perplexed stupid optimism. Which was worse? Having him actually standing there unannounced, or her continually wishing she were where he was?

But Gwendolyn had to remember that they both accepted a pledge, an oath of marriage. She knew Thomas was extremely principled and would never break his commitment. Huh, and that's a laugh, would he even want to? Would she ever be able to break hers? She hated to know she would be hurting a friend, but, oh God, she would walk away from Charles in a heartbeat if she ever found out that Thomas felt the same. But Gwendolyn knew in her heart that he may not. He never loved her before, so why do so now? He was probably head over heels in love with Katrina nonetheless. Oh, how she envied Katrina at this point! What did she hold to actually earn a voluntarily proposal from an amazing man like the Duke of Norwin?

CHAPTER 9

A carriage arrived at the manor early in the morning. Every day, Thomas would get up at dawn and head out the door and remain absent till evening. Gwendolyn studied his routine daily and decided to sabotage him on his way outdoors.

Gwendolyn stood centered in the foyer waiting for Thomas to come downstairs. The sun had just peeked over the hillside and a chill had been in the air. Appropriately dressed in her seaside coat, gloves and bonnet, Gwendolyn waited patiently when she heard the sound of a door being shut and quick footsteps stride alongside the stairwell to descend the long staircase.

"Gwendolyn!" Thomas asked surprised to see her, "What are you doing up so early?"

"I could ask the same of you. Where do you go?" She asked, judging his buff pantaloons tucked into brown riding boots, his beige Carrick, loose with large sleeves overlapping both hands. *God, he looked absolutely tempting…* she had never seen clothes look so categorically accurate on an athletic physique.

Thomas grinned and put his hat atop his head, "Gwendolyn, I am the owner of transoceanic cargo. My vessels are some of the finest in all of England. Someone has to make sure everything is in working order," he remarked, opening up the door to find Devin about to knock.

"Good morning, friend, how was breakfast?"

"Fine, Devin, ready to go?"

Gwendolyn stood upright and proceeded on with them. "Thomas, can I come along? I won't be in the way, I promise. There is something I would like to speak to you about."

Thomas then bowed to her and led the way. He helped her into the carriage, and to Gwendolyn's amazement, Katrina was already inside.

"What a pleasant surprise," Gwendolyn voiced, feeling a bit surrounded.

"I ride along with him every morning," Katrina voiced, eyeing Gwendolyn and then gazing out the window.

Thomas noted his fiancée's anger. "By the by Gwendolyn, what is it that you wish to speak to me about?"

Gwendolyn gulped and shut her mouth tight. There was no way in hell she was going to tell him about his daughter with an audience. "I would like to visit a tailor I heard so much about."

Thomas looked at her curiously, "A tailor?" He quipped, crossing his arms about his chest. "Does this tailor have a name?"

"Madame LeFleur...I hear she is the best seamstress in all of London."

Katrina arched a brow and snickered, "Why, she is. I need to visit her myself, why don't I accompany you with an introduction?"

"That is not necessary," Gwendolyn voiced, eyeing Thomas seated next to her, his hands between his thighs, casual and unaffected by the altercation that was about to awaken.

Gwendolyn then gazed over at Devin; he too was busy admiring his fingernails, biting and clipping them with his teeth.

"I insist, Gwendolyn, Thomas has an account there, don't you dear?"

Gwendolyn quickly eyed Thomas and caught his deliberate distraction.

"Madame LeFleur? Why yes, I do have an account there."

"Then it is settled. We will drop my brother off at the shipyard, while Thomas escorts us both to Madame LeFleur's."

When they arrived at the shipyard, Gwendolyn got out of the carriage a bit overwhelmed. Not only was being enclosed with Katrina uncomfortable, the shipyard took her by surprise; it was a massive, giant productive seafaring industry.

"I haven't been here since I was a child," Gwendolyn recalled, walking around the construction.

"Still pretty amazing, isn't it?" Thomas stated proudly, suddenly feeling Katrina's gloved hand wrap around his forearm.

Gwendolyn turned away from the assembly and focused on Katrina's hand binding Thomas' arm. A rage of protectiveness entered her heart as her eyes met his. "And what exactly is being built here?"

Thomas cleared his throat, "I generally build commercial vessels built for merchants, three-mast, square-rigged carriers. But, as of late, built for merchants, three-mast, square-rigged carriers. But, as of late, footer. A well-trained crew could load her heavily with armed cannons, easily taking out any pirate ship. My team has constructed one hundred, thus far."

"And all this, used to be my father's?"

Thomas began following Gwendolyn unconsciously; she began walking around farther into the construction which concerned him. "Gwendolyn, watch yourself, you never know when a plank might come loose and conk you on your head."

Gwendolyn laughed, but did not bother to look his way. "I know where to walk, thank you," she said, holding her skirts and continuing to walk the grounds.

"You know Gwendolyn, I was thinking," he carefully verbalized with Katrina still at his heel, "that since your station has made my life most comfortable, I would be willing to pay you clearing with the divorce. How does twenty-thousand pounds sound?"

Katrina pulled back on his arm and choked on the implausibility that he would offer her that much money. Thomas turned around and scowled at her.

Gwendolyn now looked his way as he turned around to meet her cynical eyes. He seemed serious…too sincere for some reason. "Twenty-thousand pounds? Are you really all that prosperous?"

Thomas stood mesmerized by her uncertainty. Why would she even think that he was not? Or would not be? "I forgot to mention, a year. The figure is based on an amount that would be offered annually."

Gwendolyn's heart escalated. *Annually? Was he insane? Did a plank conk him on his head?* "I will have to decline Thomas," she revealed modestly, "I do not need anything from you—we have all that we need."

Thomas stared at Gwendolyn like she had three eyes in the center of her forehead. Almost immediately, he was inundated with questions from his manager and had to leave Gwendolyn momentarily. Katrina did not dare leave him alone and accompanied him back to the office on the wharf where he generally did business.

Gwendolyn stood idle and surveyed the vastness of the great shipyard. Timber was scattered amongst the ground like modest sticks. Woods of every variation: rock maple, white oak, cedar and pine. *Twenty-thousand pounds indeed*…Gwendolyn next ambled over to one man centered amid the chaos giving orders. "Excuse me, sir? May I have a word?"

The man's eyes lit up and quickly walked over to her. "Yes, mum, watch yer step, what is it that ya need?"

"May I ask you a question?"

The man kept staring at her; women have been to the shipyard before, but none as radiant as she. "Yes, mum."

"Have you worked here long?"

"Yes, mum, all m'life."

Gwendolyn's eyes grew round, "Really? Then you must have been under the employ of the Earl of Suffolkshire."

He lowered his gaze, "Yes, mum."

Gwendolyn noted his dismal response. "Why the look of dejection?"

"The Earl was a terrible business mon, gambling away his profits, never paying wages; had to barter the hand of his daughter to save his production." Then he paused and his eyes grew broad. "Was he was yer father?" He asked without a hint of diplomacy.

"Why yes, how did you guess?"

"I remember ya coming to the shipyard once," he remarked truthfully. "Running after yer brother, ye tripped into mud."

Gwendolyn then blushed and looked oddly over at the large ships being built. "So many years ago, mister—"

"Cornwall, mum. Edmund Cornwall, at yer service. The Duke of Norwin has been the best employer in all of London, mum; do not mind mentioning that to ya. He has kept a roof over me head and food in me stomach for the past seven years. God bless him, yer husband."

Gwendolyn did not bother correcting the man. He seemed genuine and kind. She smiled and lifted up her skirt, "Mr. Cornwall, would you be so kind to explain to me what these men are doing? I would like to know more about my father's venture."

"Certainly, mum, please follow me."

Gwendolyn followed Mr. Cornwall around and met teams of craftsman like carpenters, dubbers, joiners, caulkers and fasteners all working together to convert the designers' vision into reality.

Henry Barton, Thomas' supervising engineer, showed Gwendolyn his models. He explained to her the vision of creation, step by step. With a mallet and a gouge, he first shapes his model before taking it to the mold loft. Once there, the model's curves enlarged to full size are traced on the floor with chalk. Flexible battens, temporarily pinned to the floor are used as guides for tracing and ensuring smooth arcs. The chalk lines are used for wooden templates for the ships ribs. Outside, timbers are sculpted into structural rudiments and curved, usually steamed in ovens until they were flexible enough to bend into a hull formation. Thousands upon thousands of wooden fasteners called 'treenails' are split by hand for utilization.

Thomas and Katrina then joined Gwendolyn, Henry and Edmund. Thomas eyed Gwendolyn first, but she quickly looked away. He was wondering what she was doing amongst the timber, wandering around with the two men. His heart pounded strangely when he noticed Gwendolyn giving Henry extra awareness.

"Everything is so interesting Thomas," Gwendolyn raved, bringing extra attention to herself from all the men in the group. "What are they doing over there?" She expressed still curious.

Thomas eyed the derricks in view. "Come with me, I will show you."

"If you do not need my assistance any further, Lady Hollinger, I should be heading back," Henry announced, speaking to her, but then setting eyes on Katrina. Katrina lowered her eyes in her usual inhospitable way.

"Yes, of course, certainly, do not let me keep you Lord Barton. Your visions are quite exceptional, it was most informative," Gwendolyn pointed out, smiling at him graciously.

"Thank you," he accepted, tipping his hat and bowing goodbye to the rest of the group.

Thomas eyed Gwendolyn watching him saunter away and raised his eyebrow. "Come Gwendolyn, I will explain to you what process is being completed here."

Gwendolyn was then escorted to another vast area where a horse driven derrick was lowering a massive white-oak timber, making the ship's keel—the backbone of the hull. Thomas explained to her that the men guided the timber so that the butt, which has been engraved on a stepped diagonal, will form a snug locale on the keel blocks. The intersection, called a hook-scarf joint, will then be clenched with yard long iron spikes, known as drift bolts.

On a raised area built on either side of the keel, the ribs are assembled from sections that been cut to match the shapes of the mold-loft templates. One by one, the massive horseshoe-shaped ribs are elevated upright and fitted onto the keel. Once they are up, the keelson—another composite of joined timbers—was bolted along the hull's centerline, combining the framework tightly against the keel.

On scaffolding that surrounded the hull, a dubber uses an adz to flatten sections of the frame so that the planking would sit securely in place. Operating with a big auger, a borer drills holes through each plank and into the frames at the rear. A mallet man follows him, securing the planks by pounding hardwood treenails into each drill hole. Later, another yard hand will saw each treenail off flush when complete.

Thomas escorted Gwendolyn to another location where the deck beams were being installed. "Yard hands support the knee. Knees are cut from a single piece of wood and are used to reinforce the joints where the deck beams meet the frames. Truly a team effort for all involved, three yard hands are used to support the knee, while a fourth worker pounds the lumber to wedge the knee firmly into place. A fifth man is needed to drive drift bolts through another knee to fit that into place, until each beam will have a hanging knee set under it and a lodging knee on each side."

"Fascinating Thomas," Gwendolyn pronounced in awe, hearing a distinctive boinking sound coming from another dismembered ship. "What is being done over there?"

Thomas walked along the footpath with Gwendolyn, Katrina and Mr. Cornwall. "Well, a team of caulkers are sealing the deck. We use oakum and tar-soaked hemp between the planks. That caulker over there is holding a long-handled hawsing iron which the mallet man is striking and driving the oakum into the cracks, creating a tight water seal."

"You seem to know so much, Thomas, I am so impressed," Gwendolyn ranted, causing Katrina to squint her eyes.

Thomas swallowed his fun and eyed a vessel that was about to be launched. "Gwendolyn, come with me, I want to show you something," he said excited, walking away from Katrina and meeting Gwendolyn's stride towards the wharf.

Gwendolyn was then amazed to come face to face with a massive completed ship about to enter the ocean. She watched with wonderment as a pair of yard hands pound away the blocks of wood that supported the keel. As each block was knocked away, the weight of the hull was thrown onto piles of beams built up along the hull's underbelly. The beams appeared to be greased as the heaviness of the ship begins to slip, allowing the craft to move down the incline and into the water.

With a booming sound of plummeting keel blocks, the ship enters the water stern first, causing a tremendous splash.

"She will be towed later to my rigger's wharf and fitted out with her permanent masts, yards and sails," Thomas expressed happily, energized from Gwendolyn's apparent satisfaction.

Gwendolyn gazed up at him smiling down at her. "You have done a tremendous job here Thomas; you have made your father proud."

"Thank you Gwendolyn," Thomas beamed, suddenly being called over by another foreman. Thomas nodded his head for acknowledgment and turned to Mr. Cornwall. "Escort the ladies back to the office Cornwall; I will be there in a few."

"Yes, sir," Mr. Cornwall established, watching Thomas head off to speak to the supervisor.

Katrina lifted up her skirts and schlepped back towards the wharf where Thomas would be. "So much nonsense probing and carrying on about the shipping business."

Gwendolyn grabbed her by her shoulder and spun her around. Mr. Cornwall raised his eyebrow at the perceptible hostility between the two women.

"How dare you insult the very foundation of your future? You should be proud of the accomplishment Thomas has managed to maintain. You could not possibly imagine the joy it is for me to witness my father's legacy being fully controlled and administered properly. For something Thomas never wanted to be a part of in the first place, I am pleased to see he has shown nothing but ability to preserve and sustain supremacy in the maritime industry."

Katrina raised her nose and proceeded onward, leaving Gwendolyn and Mr. Cornwall hastily behind.

Later, Cornwall entered the private office where Thomas and Devin had been arguing. He waited off to the left of them till the end of their spat before handing Thomas a handful of papers.

"What is this?" Thomas asked, grazing through the reports.

"Ye wanted to see the progression of the *Sea Witch,* Your Grace."

The ship *Sea Witch* was a competitor's masterpiece, and Thomas watched her progression continuously. "Yes—yes, quite right, I did." Thomas repeated, skimming through the figures on the document. "Thank you Cornwall."

"Well, if you are done disagreeing with me Thomas, I am off to work on some certain paperwork for a certain gentlemen friend of mine," Devin jested, lifting his brows.

Thomas rolled his eyes and gazed beyond his exit. Katrina was standing outside now, with Gwendolyn unhurriedly arriving up next to her.

He sat there a moment and watched Gwendolyn from a distance. Katrina ignored her presence in her standard pretentious behavior, while Gwendolyn fidgeted nervously playing with her handbag under her coat. They were waiting for him to take them to the tailor, in suspense just outside the vast windows.

He did not want to compare the two women, but felt he needed to. They were like night and day, sunlight and evening; hair of gold, tresses of auburn, blue eyes, brown, both the same height, with a slender shape, but oh so different in behavior. Equally graceful and unique, yes, poised and exceptional; both owning the same qualities he found irresistible in a companion. And who demonstrated that engaging persona to him foremost? Some girl he used to know...what was her name again? Oh yes, Lady Drummond of Suffolkshire.

Edmund eyed his employer boring at the two women and replied, "Thought yer wife was deceased Your Grace. Entirely surprised to see her today. If yer still married, who is Lady Hale? Can I be ya for a day? Parading around Bristol with yer wife and mistress in tow."

Thomas grinned, and then looked up at Cornwall. "Ha! Good one Cornwall. Never you mind, you ole buggar. Now, go back outside and revive the troops. We have to finish that clipper soon, cannot have those Yank's beating us at everything."

CHAPTER 10

*M*onique LeFleur, a French deserter, began sewing when she was a young maiden. Having worked with the famous tailor, *Leroy*, the dressmaker for her highness, Empress Josephine and her Court, Madame LeFleur was renowned throughout London for her unique vision and designs. Once a beautiful red head in her heyday, her hair had been aged with streaks of grey and the lines of maturity showed brightly on her artificial rouged cheeks.

"Madame LeFleur, so nice to see you again," Katrina voiced, striding into the Parisian parlor putting on heirs. "Is my gown ready?"

"Oui Mademoiselle," she voiced, "are you ready for a fitting?"

"That is why I am here."

Gwendolyn waited for Katrina to introduce her, but Katrina only snubbed her presence, and through squinted eyes Gwendolyn watched Katrina stroll into another section of the parlor.

Madame LeFleur clapped her hands a couple of times and several ladies in waiting came to her side. She shouted at them in French and each one of them darted towards a different area of the shop. She turned towards Gwendolyn and raked in her appearance; focusing on her unique hair…it was a deep reddish-brown, similar to hers when she was younger. The young woman was absolutely divine with soulful doe shaped eyes and pink lips. Did she come with Lady Hale? No, Lady Hale would not be caught dead parading around town with a woman more striking than she. Then who was this lovely woman? "Allow me to introduce myself, I am Madame LeFleur. What may I help you with Mademoiselle…?"

Gwendolyn began taking off her gloves and bonnet, "Drummond," she covered herself, "it is nice to meet your acquaintance. Undergarments?"

Madame LeFleur gave Gwendolyn a syrupy smile. *"Tous vêtements ici,* everything here. Muslin braces; morning fichu; crinoline dresses; corsets; chemisette with frills even leather shoes."

"Splendid."

"Would you like me to set up an account?"

"Oh—no, I will settle everything today, thank you."

"Very well, I have several dresses already completed that you would quite like."

Gwendolyn caught Thomas strangely pacing in front of the store windows in the corner of her eye. She slowly went to the casement and watched him pace back and forth, forth and back, contemplating whatever; funny to see him scratching his head, mumbling to himself, and waiving his hands up in the air. "You are too kind Madame, but I am looking for a ball gown…something different."

Madame LeFleur looked intently at Gwendolyn staring outside the window. She turned to look at whom she was gaping at and noticed the Duke of Norwin on the other side. "Ah—to catch the eye of a certain gentlemen, perhaps?" She probed.

Gwendolyn laughed and then looked away, "Yes…"

. . .

OUTSIDE, STRIDING UP AND DOWN THE FOOTPATH, Thomas weighed his uncertainty. Strange, outlandish thoughts ran through his noble principle. *Gwendolyn wanted nothing from him? Why, that's absurd.* He even offered her more than he contemplated giving her. Unbelievable that she rejected the offer, with no hint of emotion. *Damn her! Why was she always so hard to figure out?* All that he had now was once hers and she doesn't even long for part of it? She wants nothing, needs zilch...and what was this *"we"* business?

MADAME LEFLEUR BOWED HER CHIN AND SAID BRASHLY, "I have the perfect dress." She clapped her hands again and quickly directed a maid in French and the maid disappeared behind a curtain. To Gwendolyn's surprise, Thomas came through the door, and greeted Madame LeFleur with pleasantries.

"*Bonjour,* Your Grace, it is so nice to see you again. *Votre belle fiancée* is in the back, attempting the most sensational dress...the one you had made for her."

Gwendolyn continued to pretend she did not notice him standing there. Thomas imagined she was not there either and addressed Madame LeFleur.

Madame LeFleur raised her eyebrow in suspicion as the duo purposely tried to sidestep one another.

"*Oui, bon, mais cela est pourquoi je ne suis pas ici,*" he voiced, moving away from Gwendolyn's hearing distance.

Gwendolyn whipped her head around and eyed Thomas without hesitation. *That's not why he is here? Then why is he here?* And when did he finish learning French? His intelligence took her by surprise.

A maid who presented a delightful lustring grey dress with white ruffles encasing its neckline and bodice suddenly distracted Gwendolyn. Gwendolyn nodded to the maid that she wanted to try it on and the maid escorted her to a dressing room.

"*Alors s'il vous plait,* Your Grace, why are you here?" Madame LeFleur asked with enticement.

"I will settle Lady...Miss...*her,*" he voiced under his normal tone pointing at Gwendolyn's egress, "account Madame, make sure she obtains everything she needs."

Madame LeFleur looked at him with restriction, "*Oui,* Your Grace, it seems Mademoiselle is in need of a ball gown...something unique, she asks."

Thomas noted the woman's directness. "Unique?"

"Oui," Madame LeFleur repeated, studying his curious posture and apprehensive movement.

"Madame LeFleur, remember that gown that I wished for my fiancée last month, the one that she refused to wear?"

She knew immediately what he was speaking of, "Oui, the emerald one? Classic, Venetian splendor, a magnificent gown, *cette robe?*"

"Yes, the dark green, that one."

"Oui, it is still here."

"I wish to purchase it for the woman, make sure she does not leave without it."

Madame LeFleur was taken back and tsked at him, "Your Grace, why you are worse than most Frenchmen I know. *Homme honteux,* shame on you—procuring a dress for your mistress, while your betrothed is in the other room dressing."

Thomas noted the indifference in her accusatory tone, "Madame LeFleur," he said assuredly, "there is but one person I allow to address me in such an impudent manner and she is in the other room. As for my acquaintance with that woman, she is not my mistress nor will she ever be...she is my *family,* and I will take care of her," he remarked, puffing up with further disdain. "Now, if you wish for me to withdraw my account from your establishment, please state so accordingly, *comprenez-vous?*"

Madame LeFleur nodded her head and curtsied low. "Oui, Monsieur."

"I expect to see the emerald dress in her purchase, good day Madame," Thomas pronounced, placing his hat back on his head just before he left.

Gwendolyn came out moments later, brushing down the elegant grey lustring dress. She was admiring herself in the mirrors when a blur of cream satin took her focus. She did it on purpose; Gwendolyn realized as she turned around and eyed Katrina wearing her wedding dress. Breath taking was all Gwendolyn thought. *Absolutely, awe inspiring…and oh so devious.*

On Romantic lines, the dress had a standing pleated ruff, with a train of lace extending several feet. With bands of ribbons decorating her waistline, shirt and sleeves, the front neckline was draped in muslin with hundreds of eye-catching pearls dotting the bodice.

Gwendolyn immediately glanced away and felt Katrina's presence at her neck. "Thomas had the satin imported from India. The lace was imported from Holland, and my headpiece was made in Spain. Thomas made sure that I was the most beautiful bride," she quietly voiced in her hair, "and ordered all new gowns for me on our honeymoon voyage to the West Indies."

Spiteful, spiteful girl, Gwendolyn thought, swallowing the urge to rip off that dress. "Thomas has good taste in costumes."

"He never loved you, he told me so."

A direct bite; her toxin, sedating her throbbing heart. Gwendolyn bit down on her lower lip, "It does not matter—I never cared for him either."

"He is mine and will always been mine, and no one, not even a former—" Katrina held in her maliciousness until Madame LeFleur was out of hearing distance, "Dalliance of his can take him away. Because that's all you really were to him. Thomas requires more from a woman than just reciprocal friendship, he needs a warm body to embrace him in the dark…touch and hold him in return. He is very lustful, *my Tommy*, and appreciates a woman's body and how it feels next to his."

"Enough—"

"Last evening when he took me to bed, he overwhelmed me with his passion, *by God,* the man is gifted—I could hardly keep up. Thomas requires warmth, not words."

Gwendolyn lifted up her jaw, and with every possible piece of dignity she had remaining, she voiced, "If you are fond of your tongue, Katrina, I would watch what I say."

"Are you threatening me? Why you meager girl, you no longer hold importance to him."

Gwendolyn withheld her misery. "To look at you on the outside Katrina, you are a vision of perfection, but to know you on the inside, you are nothing but a heartless parasite and one day you'll get your comeuppance." Gwendolyn ran around Katrina's venomous form and bumped right smack into Madame LeFleur.

"Mademoiselle, why are you crying?" She asked, holding Gwendolyn by the shoulders and soaking in her sadness.

"You have such beautiful dresses here Madame LeFleur," Gwendolyn lied, wiping her tears away, "I am crying with joy because I cannot wait to take them back home with me."

"You are leaving soon?"

"Yes, the sooner, the better," Gwendolyn uttered, bowing her head.

"Then I will have your purchases packed for you at once."

CHAPTER 11

Gwendolyn head up to the far east tower of Gisleham Manor where she was always able to see Wilderbrand from its window sill. Sitting on the casement ledge, Gwendolyn rolled up in a ball and started to weep. *He's alive and he's still drifting away...*

Her restraint from seeing him daily took over in a stubborn way. She didn't know how to deal with the fact that her authentic consortium was to be kept concealed, while his second marriage to Katrina was to be rejoiced. Having never been jealous of another woman before, she resented Katrina for being able to prepare for their upcoming wedding, which meant Katrina was able to see Thomas. *Oh!* Gwendolyn hated feeling like this...this persistent tug at her heart. What she wouldn't give to have just a little piece of his attention! So many years of longing for their close friendship, she wanted to continue on with it, not move it aside. It was like he was purposely avoiding her and each and every time she heard he was away; her heart broke just a little bit more because of it. She hated leaving Thomas without an explanation yesterday, having taken a separate carriage in return to Wilderbrand. She did not see him at supper that night and he was off again this morning.

"Malady, I have never seen you cry so much," Phyllis quietly voiced, arriving up next to Gwendolyn. She looked out of the window and saw the tower of Wilderbrand beyond in the distance. "A fortunate girl like you shouldn't have to weep for substance when she has the universe a plenty."

Gwendolyn began to laugh and wiped away her tears, "Are you speaking about Charles?"

"And a fine man he is Gwendolyn," Phyllis agreed patting Gwendolyn's hand. "Why, we've been here no more than five days, and His Grace has shown nothing but common courtesy to you."

"He is avoiding me," Gwendolyn sneezed into her skirts. "There is something different about Thomas now," she reasoned, turning to look at the tower again. "It seems I cannot detain him longer than five minutes to detect it."

"Why don't you talk a walk in the sunshine maybe that will make you feel better? Being in this house only makes you grieve."

Gwendolyn touched her friend's face with admiration, "You are absolutely right Phyllis and I will go take a walk in the sun."

Odd how just a few days ago she was at the same lake, melancholy for the attachment she had with a boy, when at present, she had been awarded a glorious gift to continue the connection with the man.

Stopping at the water's edge, Gwendolyn suddenly was taken over with memories of her and Thomas as children. Diving into the water from the oak tree's ridge, daring each other to see who could swim the lake the fastest, burying treasure by the shore's grassy rim. *Buried treasure?* She recalled excitedly.

Gwendolyn instantly looked down and tried to remember the last time she was there. Her and Thomas were playing shipwrecked buccaneers and decided to bury her mother's jewelry chest. *Oh yes, the jewelry chest!* Feeling energized all of a sudden, Gwendolyn roamed the surface, trying to recall where the box had lied. Kicking off her slippers, she ran aimlessly all over the grass speculating its location. After several mind-boggling minutes of trying to find the container's mystery position, Gwendolyn finally gave up and threw her hands up in the air, surrendering to the abolished mission.

"I believe it is over there."

Gwendolyn turned around and felt her heart drop, the vista of the man subtracting a mouthful of air. A frilly white loose shirt, buckskin pantaloons tucked into leather riding boots never looked so well on a male before. Feeling the saliva deserting her mouth, Gwendolyn blushed and turned away. "Oh?" She barely got out, licking her bottom lip. "For some reason, I thought we buried the chest closer to the water."

Thomas shuffled through the wheat grass and headed straight for her. Passing her to some extent, he surveyed the ground and the stability of the dirt. "As I recall, the lake was extensive then. The water level has gone down tremendously. The oak tree used to be by the water's rim, remember?" He said, pointing to the massive milestone. "We used to dive from that branch there into the deep end. We could not do that now, we'd hit solid ground."

With his dynamic shape unquestionably enticing, Gwendolyn sighed heavily and marched away from him. Thomas immediately followed her, and Gwendolyn smiled inwardly. He *was* a magnet, she thought happily, nervously wringing her palms onto her skirt. "Then, if I recall correctly, then it should be right here," she playfully voiced, pointing her toe to the ground.

Thomas idly looked down at her bare foot. "I beg to differ," he protested in jest, walking passed her. "I believe it should be...right *here,*" he claimed, digging his heel into the ground.

Gwendolyn smiled then looked down at his boot. "well...we'll just have to see about that," she voiced, buckling to her knees, plowing the earth.

"Gwendolyn, you'll get dirty."

"So?"

"Aren't you coming to the party?"

Gwendolyn looked up at him and brushed away some hair that fell in her face, "You wish me at your engagement party?" She sniggled, "So I am finally allowed liberty?"

"I've been thinking."

"Does it hurt?"

Thomas smiled inwardly and looked away from her, "I will introduce you as my cousin. Henry nearly thought so, why not everyone else? In any event I would like to see you enjoy the rest of your stay, I cannot appear to be inhospitable."

"Phewy to your honor," she retorted, "tis your ego that I have always tried to challenge."

Thomas leaned down to help Gwendolyn with her search. She had dug a deep hole and he was beginning to wonder if he was incorrect. "That's an understatement if I ever heard one," he agreed.

Gwendolyn snickered and remembered his recollection. "I was always trying to dare you at something or another was I not?"

"Testing me is a better word for it," he added, cropping up dirt with both hands.

"I was able to dive farther than you," she said with a sense of triumph.

"Little did you know back then…I let you."

Gwendolyn's mouth flew open wide. "Why you big lout."

Thomas cupped his fingers into the dirt one last time and scooped up the soil around the small chest. "Ah-ha!" He exclaimed, puffed up pleased with himself. "I knew it was here!"

Gwendolyn sat down now and tucked her legs to the side. "Bigheaded oaf," she kept teasing, picking up the chest and unlocking the latch. Gasping in awe that everything was still there, Gwendolyn's jaw fell to the ground.

"Close your mouth Gwendolyn, you remind me of some of the goldfish in my ponds."

Gwendolyn smiled inwardly again and admired all her mother's old jewelry: Rings, pendants, necklaces, combs, ear bobs and a tiara... priceless. "I bet," she uttered, admiring a necklace, bringing it up into the sun, "I could throw a rock farther than you across the lake."

Thomas looked down at her lips, "And what do I get if I win?"

Gwendolyn lowered the necklace and watched his eyes meet hers. "You may have your choice of jewels in the chest I just unburied."

Thomas chortled, "You unburied? Ha!" Thomas stood up with Gwendolyn and arched his brow. "I accept the wager," he said, picking up a rock. Walking towards the water's edge, he flicked it towards the lake, skipping it across the water nearly to the middle.

Gwendolyn watched the rock submerge and then picked up her own stone. Showing his shocked gaze that it was indeed larger than his he just threw, Gwendolyn flipped it perfectly and eyed it as it frolicked several times above the basin to a point farther than his.

"Very good," he seemed satisfied by the performance. "I see you have been practicing."

"My daughter loves the water as well," she spurted unconsciously, "we challenge each other to a competition—which could throw the farthest."

"Your daughter?" He asked thunderstruck.

Gwendolyn brought her hands up over her mouth. She did not mean to tell him so abruptly and nonchalant! Thomas suddenly stood grave, unsure and shocked. Oh so traumatized! "Oh God Thomas, I am so sorry, I tried to tell you, tried to get you alone, but you have been so busy, never at the manor, always away, always with Katrina."

Thomas tried to mouth out the words, *"Wh—what,* are you saying Gwendolyn?"

Gwendolyn reached out for him, but held back her contact.

"You have a daughter Thomas," she cried, releasing tears of joy. "Her name is Mary; I named her after my mother."

Thomas ran his fingers through his hair, pinning it back with clasped hands. "I...have a child?"

"Yes," Gwendolyn cried, wiping away tears from her cheeks.

"How? I mean, oh God, I know *how*," he shook his head, suddenly feeling foolish to a degree, "But when?"

"Ten years ago," Gwendolyn voiced with despondency. "When we returned to Yorkshire, I was so sick; my Great-Aunt thought I might have gotten yellow fever. Vomiting and sleeping all day, I was bedridden for three months. When the doctor was finally able to examine me thoroughly, he gave me the news." Gwendolyn suddenly stopped and recalled her vivid joyful tidings. "Three months enceinte...Pale and thin, I was never happier."

"Never happier?" He repeated, gripped to her every word.

"Ecstatic Thomas!" Gwendolyn exclaimed, suddenly glaring into the sky. "Oh so jubilant..."

Thomas was enthralled by her admission. "Why?"

Gwendolyn brought her head down from the heavens to meet his eyes, "Because, Thomas...having her meant I would never be alone."

Thomas felt the urge to wrap his arms around her body and pull her into him. *Oh...dear...God,* the circumstances intensified. He had a child...a daughter with Gwendolyn...a descendant to solidify their short union? He suddenly felt an unpleasant yearning, an unfulfilled ache to know his seedling. "What...what is she like?"

"Oh God Thomas, you should see her, she looks so much like you," she suddenly laughed with liberation.

"Like me?" He asked astonished.

"Pitch-black hair, green eyes, skin so tan, it turns chestnut in the summertime. She is precocious, fun-loving...curious. She hungers for affection and has a quick temper. Oh, let me tell you Thomas, I oftentimes have to scold her for being so direct."

"How is that?" He invited, intrigued.

"One time she disobeyed me and ended up getting hurt. Oh she was all right in the end, but the disobedience served purposeful. She was so agreeable after the incident; she turned into a different child.

She is like that, Mary, her personality topsy-turvy…but with all her unpredictability, I consider her my sanctuary."

"And why is that?" Thomas asked, further absorbed.

Gwendolyn stared at him and searched his face for the apparent clarification. "Isn't it obvious?"

Thomas thought he knew the resolve but wanted to hear it confessed. "Enlighten me."

Because she was my gift from you, Gwendolyn thought, but said instead, "She was a continuation of our wonderful friendship and cherished memories…a token to hold through life."

Thomas could not withstand his mania any longer and grabbed Gwendolyn into him. "I do apologize that you've had to raise her alone," he whispered openly, caressing the back of her head.

Gwendolyn felt instant comfort from within his enclosure. His body warm, like a tepid bath; soothing her frosty skin on this frenzied day. *And, oh God,* the smell of him, her nostrils rejoicing from fresh laundered linen, musk from some unknown scent of his and magnetic masculinity. "You do not know how many years I have wanted to hear you say that," she voiced, closing her eyes. Slowly, she allowed her hands to roam up his muscular back… never in her life had she felt anything so exhilarating.

Thomas' unpredicted contact with her body caused an unanticipated spur he had not counted on in midday. He wanted to do more than just hold her. He wanted to pull down her bodice and examine new heights, drag her to the dirt and buss his lips across unforgettable bare limbs. He commanded his stance and let go of her quickly, setting her back several feet away.

Gwendolyn opened her eyes and nearly lost equilibrium. Dizzy from dreaming of a life within his arms, she quickly blinked back to reality.

"I must get back," Thomas voiced gutturally. "I forgot I had a meeting in Essex. We'll talk later Gwendolyn," he expressed hastily; "I wish to know more about Mary."

CHAPTER 12

*I*t truly was a magnificent engagement celebration. *Months of preparation must have been involved,* Gwendolyn thought, passing the elegant table settings in the banquet room; mirrored tabletops, expensive linens, the finest imported china, gold-rimmed crystal with buckets of champagne everywhere. Extravagant pink Hydrangea centerpieces, sterling silver galore, *stupid ninny,* what was she thinking?

Gwendolyn was hesitant to attend, but after what happened that morning only lured her further in; she wanted to earn Thomas' confidence again, secure that spark she managed to ignite and if that meant she had to swallow her pride and overlook the etiquette of their conflicting arrangement, then so be it.

Reaching the ballroom at last, Gwendolyn stood wavering, soaking in the stage before her. The men dressed mostly in courtly black, while the women wore attire of every coloration like a spattered rainbow across the parterre.

Unique in an octagon design, the ballroom was decorated with painted panels of warm brown and luxurious red velvet. More masculine in motif, busts of Roman heads of state protected every corner, while several bays of plush benches for intimate conversation divided the walls. Several opened French doors welcomed the guests to an outside veranda with towering columns covered in overgenerous draping foliage. Burning fire lamps were scattered about to help soothe the chilly air from the breezy nighttime wind.

Then the music...*ah,* the violins, the cello's, the orchestra was heavenly, no doubt the finest musicians money could persuade away from contracted opera houses. Wealth was obviously demonstrated this evening, success Gwendolyn used to be a part of but on no account measured until this moment. It was never important to her in the past; she was content living in the country, but now living at Wilderbrand meant existing with Thomas and Gwendolyn wanted to be a part of it.

In the corner of her eye, she noted several bachelors springing to her entrance, each one of them patting the other on the shoulder. She knew she looked presentable; she planned on wearing the silver lustring she purchased the other day, only to open up her trunk of new dresses and found one that took her breath away. In all her haste, she had not remembered procuring it. It was an emerald hued silk gown commemorative of the Fifteenth Century; a fitted off the shoulder evening dress with a white brocaded underskirt, it incorporated flowing chemise slashed finestrella sleeves with hints of gold integrated throughout with ribbon that crisscrossed at the back to tie at the posterior. Wearing a radiant diamond studded necklace with dropping pear shaped emeralds she found in her mother's jewelry box, her hair was. finished up in an elegant coiffure with jeweled combs she also discovered which matched perfectly with the dazzling embroidered gemstones that dotted her attire.

Amy, who was standing alone, spotted Gwendolyn's spectacular entry. "Why, Lady Hollinger, you look absolutely stunning. That emerald gown, with all the gold and exquisite handiwork, I have never seen its counterpart! Oh, and the necklace, such a fine display of opulence."

Gwendolyn focused on the gap between Amy's teeth as she smiled. Growing up, she would have considered Amy a good friend but she learned through Mrs. Hornebrook that Amy was Katrina's close confidant since childhood, and was considered a foe, or at least a collaborator. "Thank you Amy, you look beautiful as well, but you do not have to call me that name, call me Gwendolyn," she let go realizing that Amy had brightened up with her consent. "Tonight I am simply the *cousin.*"

Amy let go a wink, "Yes...the cousin, Henry had me swear to the secret details. A mystery I shall take with me when I depart."

"Leaving so soon?"

"Not the party, but rather London; my last affair I must say," Amy gushed despondently. "I will be leaving tomorrow to join my ailing aunt in Manchester."

"Oh, I am sorry to hear that."

"As am I," Amy voiced, looking away, her brown eyes searching the ground. "I was hoping to be married by now, seeing it is my third season."

"Third?" Gwendolyn asked, astonished. "But you are such a lovely girl, any hopefuls?"

"I am afraid the only gentleman who has approached me was fatefully compared to the only one who mattered."

With saying that, Gwendolyn followed Amy's heartrending stare. Lord Hale was in a corner speaking with a young lady who had been fanning herself from his obvious rogue attention. "Have you set your cap for Lord Hale?"

Amy turned red, flustered and grabbed at Gwendolyn's arm, "Oh please, you mustn't say anything. Why if Katrina knew, she would tease me till the end of days."

Gwendolyn giggled and held her hand over Amy's, "Your secret's safe with me Amy, I mean you no harm."

"Thank you Gwendolyn."

"How long have you," Gwendolyn stopped and eyed Lord Hale again, "Been infatuated with him?"

Amy began fanning herself, "Since I can remember, actually," she cut short, trying not to look his way, "When I came out in my first season, Lord Hale chaperoned Katrina and Henry escorted me; all of us on familiar terms. We were a happy foursome and at times I thought the four of us would marry, until the Duke appeared."

Gwendolyn's mouth suddenly became very dry. A confidence, she thought. Another secret was about to be revealed. "Thomas"

"Yes," Amy quietly exposed, "he was the most sought after bachelor in London and he showed interest in Katrina. She dropped her acquaintance with my brother and clapped eyes on the Duke. His Grace has the greater title than my brother, obviously, and well, Henry was so heartbroken, and I do not think he will ever get over her."

Gwendolyn gulped and turned away. Thomas stole Katrina away from Henry? *Unbelievable*...looking around at all the dancing couples, she spotted Thomas with Katrina in the distance. He had not noticed her concentration of his locale, but Amy did.

"Does it hurt you to see him with another woman?"

Gwendolyn sharply turned around, that was very fearless of her to ask. She searched her eyes for compassion and found it in abundance. "Hurt me?"

"Yes, does it distress you to see him with her?" Amy asked again, squinting her eyes at Katrina's boast of accolade. "Because if I were in your position and my marriage to an unequalled man was securely mine, I would not allow anyone to breach it."

"May I have this dance, Lady Hollinger?" Henry asked, bowing down to her.

Gwendolyn blinked out of her incertitude and noted Henry's composed manner. "Why certainly, Lord Barton."

He winked at his sister who smiled up at him. Offering his elbow to Gwendolyn, she grabbed his arm and was proudly escorted to the line of couples already in precession.

Henry was not nearly as tall as Thomas or Devin, but he was striking just the same. There was also something else about him, engaging, that Gwendolyn could not help but stare. His poise and quiet manner gave him an air of intelligence mixed with anonymity. He was all businesslike the other day, but she did detect a sense of suffering. Unlike the other gentlemen here this evening, Henry was not a showy fellow. No, Henry Barton carried a burden so deep; it surfaced on his face when you were lucky enough to get close to him. He seemed uncomfortable by her inspection though, and purposely gazed away at nearby couples completing their waltz.

When Gwendolyn caught him finally looking her way, she expressed, "Are you enjoying yourself this evening Lord Barton?"

Henry grabbed hold of her soft shoulder as he spun her form around. "I am ecstatic if you must know."

Gwendolyn thought that was a nice choice of words for one so obviously disturbed. "I can see that," she quipped, "You are practically dancing on the ceiling."

A smile escaped his lips, "That obvious?"

"Yes, do perk up Lord Barton."

Henry smirked, giving Gwendolyn her answer and then voiced, "I am surprised to see you here."

"Oh no—not you too," Gwendolyn snorted, being twirled around more so than she was supposed to. She was surprised to see the apprehension shift.

Henry caught Gwendolyn's backside and pulled her in intimately so that he could whisper in her ear. "Be careful," he quietly voiced while drawing away.

Gwendolyn stared into his hazel eyes once again. His shyness disappeared and self-assurance emerged. He was not flirting with her, oh no, this was something else entirely. His 'be careful' had been anchored with some hidden meaning: Careful of whom…or of what? Gwendolyn expected she knew the resolve, why she was here in the first place and why she was one determined fool. To get close to Thomas, to still see if she could grab his attention away. That sole concentration of his, even from his own engagement party and fortune hungry fiancée. Was Henry here for the same selfish reasons? She would stake her life on it. *Oh yes, they were two peas in the same cramped pod,* Gwendolyn affirmed; under the same cruel hell. It must be very challenging to watch the person you love, fall in love with someone else and then marry them right in front of your very nose.

"Why are you worried?"

Henry shrugged his shoulders, "May I be frank?"

"If you feel you must."

Henry grinned at her openness, "I have the distinct feeling we are both on the same mission."

Gwendolyn guffawed and threw her head back. *Bulls-eye!* "How true."

Henry gazed deep into her eyes. "I do not wish to see you hurt as well."

Henry Barton shrieked loyalty, Gwendolyn thought, and then snickered, "A lost cause? You think we are glutton for punishment?"

Henry laughed aloud, more so than he should for other couples around them began eyeing the two of them together. "Oh, it has been predestined," he expressed, bowing to her at the recession of the waltz. "You are quite humorous; I can see why he likes you."

"Ah, a compliment, thank you Lord Barton."

"You are something else."

Gwendolyn rolled her eyes, "And criticism as well, how fortunate for me."

"Oh, please accept my apologies, my tongue sometimes," Henry swallowed, regretting he opened his big fat mouth. "You are quite different."

Gwendolyn laughed aloud bringing more attention to her. "What, pray tell, did everyone think I would be like?"

"Like Katrina, I suppose."

"And we are that distinct?"

"Very much so, in fact," Henry breathed, pulling her body into his again and whispering into her ear, "You are so dissimilar, I am starting to believe that Thomas will make the right decision."

Gwendolyn languidly leaned away; his breath on her neck was making her tingle. Whispering back, she voiced, "And this makes you happy, why?"

Henry looked intently into her eyes, "Because I might gain from his failure to appreciate what he has."

GWENDOLYN SAID SHE WAS NOT GOING TO ATTEND, SO Thomas did not bother to search for her presence. But most of his guests were pointing now, some of them even making outrageous observations. *At what... or at whom?* A couple out on the dance floor, he realized. Curiosity got the best of him and his eyes caught hold of the lustrous jade dress spinning around in the vastness; it was Henry and Gwendolyn...and then Gwendolyn alone, as he brought to focus the zenith to his ultimate doom. Gwendolyn bestowed vivacity, her copper hair set in bangles about her face, the dress exquisitely adapted to her form. Just as he imagined in doing so, he stood motionless in awe of the illusion before him; a panorama of a long ago hallucination rapidly appeased.

CHAPTER 13

Walking outside in the moonlight, Gwendolyn suddenly stopped on a hill just above the ballroom and soaked in the captivating violins that echoed up the embankment. Nearby crickets added to the romantic music as she transfixed on the waltzing couples. *His engagement party*, she thought dejectedly. Gwendolyn didn't know what to feel at this point, Amy only contributing to the assumption she held towards Katrina, that Thomas' so-called fiancée was nothing more than a social climber. What about Thomas? She could not allow him to throw himself into another impulsive wreck. She had to warn him. Had to tell him somehow, but why? Why does she feel the need to rescue him? They were no longer close—he had another confidante, and why does everyone keep asking if it troubled her to see him with another woman? She was so drawn to him and was so afraid of what to feel…but *yes*, yes! It did bother her. She longed to be by his side, moped around because she could not.

Her gaze halted at the sight of Thomas now dancing with Katrina; him, in his fancy togs, her, in a picturesque ball gown of light pink spinning in motion. Thomas looked so handsome gazing down at her with affection, clearly appreciating what he had. A familiar pang pierced through her heart at that moment. A shooting pain every time she thought about them together. Were they compatible? Does she make him laugh? She wondered what ensued within their first conversation, what they speak about now, and what he felt when he kissed her. They do kiss...he's had to have kissed her, probably even...*oh God*, Gwendolyn thought while closing her eyes feeling that proverbial ache inside her heart, and they probably do it often...A passionate man like Thomas would not want to wait for his wedding night and would not pause to seduce his fiancée. Katrina said as much, that she and him...that, they...*oh God!* She had to stop imagining them both together!

A crunch of leaves at the rear startled Gwendolyn. Straining to see in the darkness she fathomed Lord Hale heading towards the tree she rested upon.

"There you are Lady Hollinger, why are you hiding out here in the dark?"

"With so much to comprehend Lord Hale, I felt the need for some fresh air. Why are you here?"

"Because you are," he voiced huskily.

Gwendolyn's pulse began to race. That was quite scandalous. The moon was also quite dangerous that evening as Gwendolyn could not help but stare into his azure eyes dancing in the moonlight. Gad, he was handsome! Dirty blonde hair combed flawlessly around his collar, a sporty physique as well as fashionable, the type of man you just couldn't help but stare at for his sheer symmetry. Devin Hale was to be avoided at all costs. Katrina said that Lord Hale and Thomas had been close friends for years now; she could only imagine the kinds of mischief the best friends let loose on London. Diverse from Thomas in every way, Devin was sunbeams across the horizon, compared to Thomas' alluring obscurity and Gwendolyn felt a little odd feeling so envious of their close friendship. "You like to shock me."

He laughed and gazed over at the windows beyond. "No, just my nature, I guess. I like to see how far I can push a person."

Gwendolyn snorted, "And such candor."

"May I have the pleasure of a dance, Lady Hollinger?"

"A postponement, Lord Hale?"

"Call me Devin."

"Only if you call me Gwendolyn."

Devin let go a roguish grin, "Unquestionably."

"Would you mind accompany me on a stroll?"

Devin extended out his arm as Gwendolyn gently seized it. She felt comfortable with him for some reason and felt her body more relaxed.

"I could not help but notice you are without your companion," he teased, trying to meet her stride. "No one has informed you of my disreputable reputation?"

Gwendolyn smiled inwardly, "You are trying to distress me again, Devin. Unlucky for me, Phyllis likes to drink her spirits alone and sleeps 'til sunrise."

"How promising for me," Devin smiled devilishly.

"Devin, you simply must cease and desist."

"Why?"

"Well…because for one thing, I am engaged."

"I find that challenging," he retorted, brushing his hand over hers on his forearm.

Gwendolyn rolled her eyes and proceeded down the hill. *Another man who loved challenges…*oh, she would have to keep her eyes open with this one. "I am curious, what do you find intriguing about me?"

Devin let go a daring grin, "You are not a young innocent, and yet I find you virtuous. You contain a certain gracefulness, and I find that to be fascinating."

Gwendolyn blushed, and then thought about Amy. "What kind of woman attracts Lord Devin Hale?"

"And you are also forthright," he teased, shaking his finger at her. "I find that welcoming."

"You are avoiding an inquisition Lord Hale."

He gazed out in front of him and replied, "Besides the attributes I just described, she has to be brunette. There is nothing like a female with dark, mysterious allure...She has to be about your height, around your built, with your charming qualities."

Gwendolyn cleared her throat...his straightforward charisma was out of the ordinary, she even felt her blood beginning to boil. She had to change the subject, and fast. "The ball is lovely, does Thomas have them often?"

"Frequently, a few years back. He always tried to keep his mind busy. Long days at port, continuously away on business...did I embarrass you?"

Gwendolyn smiled, "Huh—I think I will keep you guessing. How long have you known him?"

"Thomas? Exactly seven years. When he arrived in London, I aided him with his company."

Gwendolyn tightly held onto Devin's elbow as she continued to walk through the grassy field towards the manor. "And your sister? I assume you approve of their impending nuptials?"

Devin halted and grabbed Gwendolyn by the shoulders. He circled his eyes around her face before saying, "My sister loves Thomas with all her heart. Any other woman who would have to wait until her intended divorced his first wife would have scampered away. But not my Katrina, she is smart, she is determined, and she is also grateful for what she has."

His statement only added to Gwendolyn's persistent confusion. "I genuinely hope so."

Devin's hands still remained on her shoulders and his thumbs carefully grazed her soft skin that was exposed. He was going to kiss her, she thought frantically, feeling herself drowning in pools of aquamarine. *Must... scurry...away!* Gwendolyn broke free from his confine only to be grabbed back by her waist and brought straight into his chest, feeling the length of him, his heat, his ardor rapidly seizing all her principles.

Devin had never felt desire so strong before and yet, kissing her seemed terribly wrong, but his physical mind set was hard to ignore and he leaned forward to tempt her with his lips but Gwendolyn refused to greet his desire but rather stood there immobile waiting for him to do something or at least act contrite. "You know I want to kiss you."

Gwendolyn noted how quickly her body reacted to his magnetism. "Yes."

He circled his eyes about her face again and said, "You know I have never been envious of him."

"Him?" She asked knowing exactly who he meant.

"I've admired him," he admitted, "but never *envied*...until now."

Gwendolyn swallowed hard, and watched with spherical eyes as he attempted to lean in to kiss her again but held back.

Instead of releasing her however, he expressed softly, "God, you are beautiful."

Gwendolyn accepted the flattering remark and smiled, "I like you Devin," she expressed delicately, placing her palm in the center of his chest. "I like you enough to keep you in the highest regard after this moment."

Devin stiffened up from her touch. "Yes," he agreed, stepping back away from her. "Yes, indeed," he said taking in a deep breath before letting go a huge sigh.

"We can," Gwendolyn said, stepping towards him and placing her hand back on his forearm. "Be friends?"

Devin perked up, "As special friends?"

Gwendolyn rolled her eyes; he just would not give up! "As silly friends," she added, trying to detour the sexual tension.

"As humorous friends?"

"Yes!" She exclaimed, glad that he finally got the point.

"Yes," Devin agreed, patting her hand then guiding them forward. "Joking friends," he continued to play.

"Ridiculous friends," Gwendolyn said next, practically skipping through the grass.

He allowed her to skip away before saying, "By the by," he coughed again feeling foolish to a degree, "Thomas was bombarded with questions about you a few moments ago and mentioned to all the guests that you were his cousin, so you may come out of hiding my dear and dance with me."

"A persistent and determined friend," she tsked at him.

"That was my intention, I do assure you," Devin quipped, back to his same brazen self.

Gwendolyn giggled and did a double-take when they arrived at a familiar setting; a sizable conservatory full of vegetation from all over the world. Orange, lemon and apple trees, king palms, bamboo, tropical ferns, orchids, tulips and roses all in full bloom.

"Have you seen the greenhouse?" Devin asked, watching Gwendolyn light up like a firefly.

Her mouth flew open wide, "Oh, I used to love to come here when I was a child!" She exclaimed, letting go of his arm and running towards the dwelling around like a toddler.

Inside, Devin laughed aloud at the sight of Gwendolyn roaming from foliage to flower. She looked like a little girl discovering plant life for the very first time. Picking leaves, smelling flowers, touching and caressing, he relayed, "I must say Gwendolyn; you do make a charming addition to all this glamour."

Gwendolyn blushed and smiled appropriately at him. "Why Devin Hale, you are absolutely dreadful."

"I do try."

Gwendolyn shook her head, "You are a wicked man."

"And an absent one I might add."

Gwendolyn's smiled dropped at the sight of Thomas filling the entrance. He was not amused and stared straight at his friend.

"Lose something Thomas?"

Thomas shook his head at his friend's mockery as he made his way in. "There are several ladies in the ballroom dying to dance with you. It seems you have spread yourself around this evening dear friend and need to fulfill your many pledges, just holding you to your dance card your wickedness."

Devin bowed in defeat, "Quite right dear friend, but before I leave, Gwendolyn has also pledged a waltz with me, will I see you later inside?"

Gwendolyn blushed and realized he was baiting her, "I wouldn't miss it," she played along watching him exit.

CHAPTER 14

Thomas watched Devin amble away before setting eyes on Gwendolyn. Lowering his gaze, he surveyed her attire downside up.

Gwendolyn's heart tripped over several times from Thomas' close scrutiny of her appearance. Why does he keep affecting her body that way? Hands down, he was the most handsome man she had ever seen. Black was definitely his color, his cutaway perfectly designed for his magnificent mold, he made Devin and Henry look absolutely common.

"Forget something?"

Gwendolyn noted his frivolity, his hands across his chest and the questionable look in his eyes gave him away. "Yes, and it seems you are just the person to refresh my memory."

"What about your fiancé? Or should I ask, *is there* a fiancé?

Gwendolyn twisted her lips. "How dare you question my sincerity, Thomas? Charles is not imaginary by any means!"

"Charles?"

"Yes, Charles…His family owns a rather large dairy farm in Kettlewell," she stated proudly lifting her chin up in the air.

Thomas walked over to a nearby Philodendron growing out of control. He reached out and touched the plant. "I wish to meet this farmer of yours."

"Why?"

"I want to know what his intentions are," he stated quickly, continuing to ravage the fern.

"I told you what his intendment was you silly nincompoop," Gwendolyn reacted irrationally. "He *wants* to marry me!"

Thomas quickly met her unreason. As if Gwendolyn just poured a bucket of hot water over his head, deep-rooted history began to bubble. She was the only one who could uplift embedded passions and Thomas was swiftly disconcerted. "What makes you believe I didn't want to marry you?"

Gwendolyn's fury erupted as well. "You *never* wanted to marry me Thomas—"

"How do you know that for certain?"

Gwendolyn was dumb-founded. How did she know that for certain? Well, her memories back-peddled fast...their fathers disagreeable pact... *err,* Thomas arguing with his father...*err,* Thomas looking nervous as hell in front of the monsignor...their consummation...doesn't he object as well? "You hated the idea of our joining, and, as I recall, you yelled at your father and told him how you despised him for forcing you into the arrangement."

"Key word here is forcing, go on." Thomas ran his fingers through his hair in frustration. He let loose strands that were neatly combed behind his ears.

Gwendolyn focused on the hair that seemed to dangle on the sides of his face. The swinging lock seemed to hypnotize her as she forced herself to glare away. "You...*you,* practically stomped your feet in protest Thomas, please do not try and deny that now."

"Why you misguided wench," he quipped, surrounding her. "What you saw, or should I say, think you observed was me ranting to my father balking in the way he enforced us to take your hand."

Gwendolyn's mouth flew open to attack. "Why you arrogant

swain! You cannot stand there and tell me honestly that you had any desire to marry me!"

Thomas laughed sickly at her remark, "Desire? Yes...let's do talk about desire *my dear wife."*

Gwendolyn could not believe he finally acknowledged her rightful state. Oh, if Katrina were only there! Then she could have heard her fiancé admit that Gwendolyn was the true Duchess of Norwin and not she. Gwendolyn watched Thomas pace in front of her with his hands on his hips; he hastily kicked up dirt and yanked off that stem he was admiring before.

Thomas took another good look at the girl who always managed to turn his world upside down. He wanted to divulge all that he was feeling, but held back. As a timid, indecisive, shy young lad, he desperately desired Gwendolyn. Following her around, watching her intently as she innocently arched her back in front of him. Naively undressing in front of him before their summer swims, imagining himself pressing his lips against hers, on the crux of her neck, setting his mouth on her breasts and taking her for hours. He would go home each night to soak himself in a cold bath—he desired her so much! Does he confess that little tidbit? Would it even matter...would it change anything? He had been dreaming of her relentlessly since her advent, imagining his tongue dancing with hers, across her much healthier bosom and damned-if-he knew-why, was haunted nightly by the illusion of her naked body across his empty bed! Does he allow her to know that? *NO!* He thought tentatively—he must move forward, carry on with his stupid plan. "Are you happy Gwendolyn?" He asked instead.

Gwendolyn was prepared for her retaliation but was blown away by his sudden change in direction. "Happy?"

"With him? Does your farmer make you happy?"

Gwendolyn's stomach churned. She thought hard and said, "Yes... yes, he does. Does your debutante make you happy?"

Thomas stared at her for a long moment before saying, "Yes."

It was no use. They had truly grown apart; no longer the

children with the same interests, the similar views and bound future and Gwendolyn winced from the further cuts he managed to carve and began to walk away. She nearly tripped over a potted Bird of Paradise that—out of the blue—grew in her path as she continued to walk backwards. Thomas sprung forward and held her tightly confined. Only then did Gwendolyn realize that her back was against a statue, solid and cornered.

"What is it going to take to have you back in my arms?" Thomas murmured into her ear only to languidly pull away.

Gwendolyn was staggered looking up at him. She couldn't breathe; she couldn't even think—and felt instantly drunk from his sudden burst of particulars. Did he really say what she thought she just heard? "Don't tease me Thomas."

"I am not one to pretend, Gwendolyn, and as your husband I still hold liberties to procure advance of my wife."

*Yes...oh yes...*she wanted that too! Advance on him. Assault him was more like it. Wanting to yank off his cravat and kiss his throat, chest, down to his...*Oh God!* His embrace was enfolding, her bosoms melted into his chest, her nipples hardened from his unguarded charge. "What exactly do you want?" She asked in breathless anticipation.

"To kiss you," he stated with a hint of indecency, "just once... one last time."

Gwendolyn felt her face being cradled as Thomas leaned in to kiss her; lips so silky soft...gentle, temperate, parallel to a kiss felt long ago. Misleading that kiss, his talent turning famished, as his slow, careful taste of her grew ravenous in greed. Thomas besieged her backside with his arms, reached up to her neck to keep her position under his control. Opening up her mouth with his tongue, the compulsion fed and exploded every ardent sensation she subdued and she met his coercion with much of her own. Meeting his silky dance, thrust for plunge, taking, giving, receiving and flinging her wanton body towards his. Through her dress she could feel the heat seeping through his waistcoat and shirt. His body against hers was rewarding and yet, the length of him fully pressed into hers was not fulfilling enough.

Arms nearly crushing her, lips behind her ear, down alongside her neck, his hands roved to the front of her bodice, fondling her breast, kneading, wheedling her flesh to his eager mouth. Drawing her hips to his loins, he enclosed the space between them, expertly placing his leg amid hers, spreading her bearings until she practically rode him in rapture. It happened too quickly, much too fast, he was hot, hot, and hot; it was not enough, merely a tease. His body could not take it anymore; his appetite for her was unyielding. He was not prepared for so much passion to erupt—he knew from past experience that he couldn't fake what her body made his feel. His hands roamed freely underneath the many layers of her dress, alongside the smooth texture of her thighs, in between her legs, sensually rubbing himself on a pressure point until he heard her moan in his mouth...

That's when Gwendolyn flinched realizing their interaction went way too far. "Oh God, stop...please...just stop."

Thomas was out of breath; he pulled away from her momentarily only to kiss her lightly on the lips. "Must I?"

Gwendolyn received his one last kiss then became totally embarrassed; realizing the possibility...the, indiscretion...what were they thinking? She tried to fix her gown to its original state. "Look at me, look at what you have done!"

Thomas blinked out of his trance. "Me?" He retorted; realizing she had withdrawn his shirt restricted to his trousers, his cravat, unraveled, spilled in front of his waistcoat and the front button of his shirt undone. "My clothes did not liberate themselves, you naughty girl."

Gwendolyn noted his tousled attire, "Oh! Insufferable!" She was more ashamed of her actions, what the heck came over her? "What, pray tell, do you think was about to happen?"

"I sense the course was mutual."

Gwendolyn concentrated on Thomas twirling his cravat in front of him in a tease. She fixated on his sinfully pleasing mouth and turned away, blushed, unruffled herself. Why did she feel so lustful when around him? Her actions were untamed; she had never felt anything like that. He was also too clever these days, "What course?"

"We were about to make love."

"We were?" *Oh dear, they were…*it was what her body craved, was it not? Amazing what direction the body will take you once you give it a nibble.

Thomas bent over and tried to see her face more clearly. She had turned around and began to stroll away, tucking and brushing herself down along the way. He tracked her, only to grab her by the arm and whirl her around, "Is that a blush? Are you blushing, Gwendolyn?"

"No," she rejoined, regaining her poise.

Thomas smirked and was engorged with gratification, "Well, I must say, whatever the consequence, it was nice to finally see you receptive."

"Huh!" She respired, realizing he was right, "That outburst was not civilized, Thomas."

"When is passion ever polite?"

"Passion?"

"Gwendolyn, we have always encompassed it, you and I. Why does this shock you?"

Gwendolyn closed her mouth and looked intently at him. He had this satisfied cast upon his front. *God, he looked wonderful,* kissable, yes, she wanted to kiss him again and again. Was that what she was feeling all along? Passion? Oh God, she hated passion, and she despised him even more for having detected it first. "There is no you and I…it was…nostalgia, that's all." Gwendolyn tried to expunge the fanatical sensation she was encompassing. Encompassing? Yes, rather hard to ignore all sides of her bursting with desire for him.

Thomas smirked, "Do accept my apology Gwendolyn, but my

reflection turned into an investigation...it must have been the dress."

Blasted man, she thought, hesitating when she realized he was the one who purchased the gown. "You did not."

"I most definitely did."

She tsked at him, "So inappropriate."

"But suitably appropriate to your shape...just like I imagined."

He said it so huskily, that Gwendolyn nearly grabbed his head to her bosom for a second time. "No more gifts, Thomas."

He started to hoot and brought his eyes down and then back up again to meet her bravado. "Gwendolyn, consider yourself fortunate that you have found a partner who likes to share his fortune."

Gwendolyn let go an insensitive smile, "A partner, Thomas? I do not see our partners in this span."

Why does she keep reminding him that she was still not his? Thomas was, nevertheless, encouraged, his green eyes sinister and persuasive. "Consider it a souvenir then, for a most pleasurable interaction."

Gwendolyn marveled in the way he spoke, his voice deep and swaying. "Do you give gifts to all the women you have interacted with?"

"Only to those I expect to be intimate."

"We were not about to be intimate."

"We'll see how long you deny yourself the pleasure. Not many stand where you are now and not want to satisfy their gain."

His erotic grin nearly discharged her moral fiber; she laughed moronically, only to close her mouth. "So there has been many?"

"Many what?"

"Women."

Thomas sensed that she was probing. "I am no rake Gwendolyn, but I do hold a certain finesse with the softer sex."

"Your kiss hasn't improved that much," she managed to say, watching with spherical eyes, his second attempt to test her.

Thomas leaned in skillfully, not touching her anywhere else but his intended target. Gwendolyn stared at his approaching brashness, hesitated, and then naturally parted her lips to receive him.

Thomas stopped just inches from her kiss, circled his eyes about her face and grinned into her surrender. "You see...you still want me."

"I do not." Gwendolyn promptly replied. *Liar. Oh yes...*she did, she really, really did. She doesn't want to be quarreling with him; she wanted to collide with him. And, *oh dear God,* as she continued to be tempted by his suggestive glare, she wanted to carnally lie down. One kiss was not enough...she wanted him naked now and buried deep. She was so in love with him, she recognized instantly...*Still in love with him...*in love with a man who savored her on his engagement supper to another woman!? Damn him! Why did being reunited have to be so bloody complicated? Gwendolyn quickly overruled her runaway emotions. "The devil take you Thomas Hollinger," she declared on her way out the conservatory only to stop at the entrance to turn around. He was still so confident, and she loathed that puffed-up chest of his. "How dishonorable you have become, *Tommy.* The sooner I leave here, the better...you're just a distraction...you and your...*clothes.*"

CHAPTER 15

Thomas arrived back at the gathering in a purely primitive manner. The fury his infant bride influenced was not of this earth. He had never felt that kind of insatiate need with any other woman...not even within his private moments with Katrina. *God, he was...obsessed.* Her words, her eyes, her hair, her body and that kiss—the burning desire she inflamed in him! God, he knew this would happen! Give that woman just a little bit of his interest and she would be smothering him with her gratifying attention. This little game he had been playing had not gone according to plan. *Bloody everlasting hell...the devil take sexual attraction!* Idiot, fool! He was always trying to catch her true position, forever trying to trip up her true sincerity. Why was she always so hard to pin down? And now, he had to sever being standoffish, the diversion suddenly gone fishing. The further time he spent with her, the more he wanted to spend. Want, desire was substandard to what he was feeling now. Not since the yearning of getting back to Britain had he sought after something so badly. He was a man at her mercy, anything that she demanded, he would hand her.

Thomas stood possessed and imprisoned by Gwendolyn's nonchalant allure. She was waltzing with Devin now, smiling, carefree and enjoying his expertise. *The devil take him as well!* Why does he feel so envious of Devin's arms? He's never envied Devin, not one little bit! In fact, as he eyed several other bachelors eyeing his forgotten treasure, the vision of her dancing with any other man practically ate him inside out. *Oh, bloody hell...*he wanted to punch anyone who laid eyes upon her...*Good God, what was happening to him?*

"Take me to your room?"

He felt her presence, but was concentrated on the reflection before him. Katrina had flounced up behind him and enfolded her arm within his.

"What, why?"

Katrina watched her brother dancing with Gwendolyn and thought how finished they looked with one another. She then eyed the many guests glued to her presence and awarded the gossipmongers a taste of her good fortune by leaning into Thomas intimately. Through clinched teeth, she lowered her voice, "Because my dear Thomas, that incensed look on your face show's charm to others, but I know what prurient desire lies behind those dark eyes of yours."

Thomas turned to look at her, she was indeed, a beautiful woman besides; her blonde curls set about her milky white complexion, her exquisite laced ball gown made of pink satin, a bodice cut lower than was fashionable enticing added male attention than was proper. This was his supposed engagement celebration, what was wrong with him? He should have been exultant, and yet, he had never been more miserable!

He knew how it would appear if he were to be seen walking away from her, but he did it anyway and noted the reaction of some of his close by guests. Katrina stood alone now, with Thomas withdrawing from her affection.

Just then, the queen rumormonger herself, Lady Trousley,

cornered Thomas. A rather portly woman who liked to squeeze herself into the latest fashion whose assets oftentimes spilled out because of their tension. "Trouble in paradise, Your Grace?"

Thomas regained composure, "None, Lady Trousley."

"Your dear cousin is quite the belle of the ball, why haven't you introduced her to us before?"

Thomas caught sight of the jade dress twirling around in the corner of his eye, "She has been in Yorkshire, Lady Trousley, only here for the wedding."

"Yorkshire," Lady Trousley repeated with ridicule, "how posh," she wheezed, and then sailed on, "Even so, her face seems quite familiar."

"Yorkshire," he repeated hoping she'd go away.

"Her family from London?"

"No," he said, rolling his eyes.

"Suffolkshire?"

Chatty cow, Thomas thought, shaking his head at her obvious nosiness. He had better shut her down and fast. "If her presence seems familiar, love, it is because I was unsuccessful in keeping our relationship unnoticeable." He then bestowed one of his deadly grins and gave her a playful wink. "Very hush-hush Lady Trousley and I do hope I can count on you to be discreet about such matters."

Lady Trousley began fanning herself from Thomas' rascally behavior. Her intuition had been correct and after having tea with Madame LeFleur that afternoon, her assumption about his acquaintance with his so-called cousin had been right on marks. Gwendolyn Hollinger was no more than the Duke's mistress? First to marry his communal mistress, now to parade one around? Shame on him for displaying her more or less common and inviting her to his own engagement party! Allowing her to present herself as a relative? Absurd! Indecent, if you ask her—why the man had no morals; and equally wicked—did she not just bump into another one of the Duke's mistresses at the dessert cart?

"Scandalous," she let go, fanning herself to a degree of blowing herself over.

Thomas excused himself and headed towards the conservatory once more. Tried to recollect what just happened. Scandalous, shocking, wicked? Something inside of him popped, ruptured and oozed. He was being attacked from all sides because of it; this war of emotions inside his heart. Marrying Katrina felt incredibly wrong all of a sudden. Wrong, improper and inappropriate...An unhealthy, horrible decision! He still cared for Gwendolyn, he realized conceding. The problem now was how to break a bloody pledge. He had never broken a promise his entire life! But he would fracture one now without hesitation if Gwendolyn divulged mutual attachment. Rip it, stomp it, kick it away if she would reveal her true feelings. He had not been intimate with Katrina since setting eyes on Gwendolyn. It was that auburn enchantress who held his sole desire now and he felt nothing less but suffocation.

Finding his legs halting atop a hill, just above the ballroom, Thomas soaked in the captivating violins that echoed up the embankment. Nearby crickets added to the romantic music as he transfixed on the waltzing couples. *My engagement party,* he thought dejectedly, watching the wondrous dance. He then focused on Gwendolyn dancing with Devin. Where would they be if they had survived that horrible day? If they were still together, would they have been devoted? Would they have been content? A blissful family...with Mary now...and more on the way. *Oh God,* he thought, while buckling to his knees. *I am still in love with her,* he realized...in love with his best friend...in love with his wife.

Devin escorted Gwendolyn to a corner in between their dances. She had not danced in such a long time and she had forgotten how much she enjoyed it. Devin was a wonderful partner and she felt at ease with him the more time they spent together. Special friends, indeed; it was odd to feel so composed with a man so quickly, but that's just how it was, instantaneous...yet weird. Devin excused himself for a moment to fetch them something to drink when Gwendolyn felt the analysis of several eyes. Numerous guests stood around her whispering and commenting amongst themselves, no doubt mentioning to one another that she was Thomas' cousin. *Cousin? Huh! If they only knew the truth.*

There was one individual, a woman in particular, who was standing just a few feet away that seemed to give Gwendolyn one intense inspection. In her forties, she presumed, but still quite striking decorated in a black and red evening gown with ostrich feathers jotting out from within her elegant headpiece. She was standing with a younger gentlemen, no doubt her son...or maybe her escort, as Gwendolyn quickly noted the man's vulgar closeness as he whispered sweet nothing's into the woman's ear.

She kept staring at Gwendolyn, which made her feel uncomfortable. Just then, Devin returned with two glasses of bubbly champagne. Gwendolyn stood in front of Devin, her back towards the woman and quietly voiced, "Devin, who's that woman?"

Devin leaned in, bent his head down to Gwendolyn's obvious confidentiality and asked, "Which one?"

"The lady who keeps shooting daggers at me."

Devin eyed Mrs. Carmichael barely a few feet away. He acknowledged her presence by bowing his head slightly, scanning her attire from toe to tip, and then saying adieu with an agreeable smirk. He had enjoyed her company once or twice a few years back, but knew Thomas had a rather lengthy engagement with the avid Mrs. Carmichael. "The widow, Mrs. Carmichael, no doubt she came here to get a good look at my sister."

"Your sister? Whatever for?"

Devin closed his mouth, he said too much. "Katrina caught Thomas. She is probably green with envy."

Gwendolyn turned around again and continued to sip her champagne. Out on the dance floor, happy couples waltzed away. She spotted Katrina standing alone across the ballroom and noticed her despondency. Her shoulders slumped, her hand covered her mouth and she gave the impression that she was on the verge of tears. "Speaking of your sister."

Devin whipped his head around and pinpointed Katrina. He observed her stance and brotherly alarm skyrocketed. He immediately walked forward, and then remembered he was with Gwendolyn. "You'll excuse me?"

"Yes, of course, go."

Gwendolyn eyed Devin stride over to his sister and embraced her shoulders. They exchanged words, and then Devin held out his compassionate arm and escorted his sister onto the dance floor. Gwendolyn decided to use this time to search her thoughts when she stumbled upon a barrage of black and red ostrich feathers.

"Look at her...look at how fortunate she is," the woman shrilly expressed. "Mrs. Carmichael by the way and you are Thomas' cousin?" After Thomas unexpectedly broke off their affair, Catherine Carmichael went into seclusion. Depressed for months, the only way she could climb out of her gloom was to bed another man. And that's just what she did, testing several in fact, but no one else compared and she missed Thomas' friendship more than anything.

Gwendolyn took a long sip of her champagne, "Yes," she barely voiced, "Lady Hollinger."

Catherine humpfed, a well-used disguise. A few years back, Thomas introduced his mistress succeeding her as his supposed cousin as well. "Nice to make your acquaintance, I was beginning to wonder about the mystery surrounding Thomas, his family perishing at sea so many years ago. Simply tragic...nice to see he found a relative to claim."

Gwendolyn was taken-back. How did this woman know his past? And she addressed Thomas so informally...by her tone, *intimately...good God, no.* "Lady Hale will no doubt make a beautiful bride, wouldn't you agree?" Gwendolyn asked trying to provoke further legitimacy.

"In addition to being a well pleasured woman."

Gwendolyn raised her eyebrows. She had been correct. Mrs. Carmichael had been one of Thomas' mistresses? And why was she looking at her so impishly...what was she trying to imply? "Were you and he?"

Mrs. Carmichael lowered her eyes and raked in Gwendolyn's loveliness in emerald green, "But I thought everyone knew of our liaison dear. Thomas had been my escort for many years...he never mentioned it? The scoundrel. I am not surprised to see so many of us here tonight. He has kept polite alliances with all of us, you know. Gave every one of us a token of his parting goodwill—his eternal gratitude. Friendship is very important to the man, so do not allow him to break your heart! And if you are waiting on him to show his devotion, you are in for a world of disappointment. You are better off accepting what he has to give and thank God he gave you fleeting interest. He is a cad through and through, why else would he be flaunting any of us around? The man has no conscience. He has never allowed himself to feel, or to love, my guess he is probably not even in love with Lady Hale."

Gwendolyn was stupefied. Mrs. Carmichael thought she was his mistress? What a laugh, but why did his past sting so brutally? How many mistresses did he have? Or *had* for that matter? Gwendolyn's head began to spin around and around, pinpointing every woman Mrs. Carmichael seemed to spot out. The red-head in the blue gown, the brunette in yellow. Gwendolyn could not take it anymore and decided to concentrate on the woman before her. Why would Thomas court Mrs. Carmichael? She was mature, yes, but uniquely diverse from Katrina's obvious fresh beauty. Eyes of hazel, pert nose...auburn hair... like her mothers, nearly the same shade as hers. Another strange stab afflicted her disposition. "Excuse me Mrs. Carmichael, but I feel a headache coming on."

"Yes, of course, certainly."

Gwendolyn hesitated, looked at her oddly, and then quickly left the woman's side.

CHAPTER 16

Gwendolyn was alone now, inside the Roman Room, admiring all the frescoes painted on the walls. Angels, cherubs and Poseidon, the Greek God of the sea, all-playing wistfully in an ocean full of ships.

Beginning to pace the scope, Gwendolyn began to bite her fingernails. Thomas kissed her, and kissed her well. Kissed Katrina. Kissed Mrs. Carmichael. Kissed many women. The red-head in the blue gown, the brunette in yellow. Herself, a few, a dozen, hundreds, *oh bother! Damn that sexual magnetism! The devil take it all!* She wondered what Mrs. Carmichael got as her departing gift?

Whipping her head around, Gwendolyn was startled by the sight of a man slowly approaching. With her mind being so preoccupied, she did not realize he had slipped in unannounced. He looked familiar... and he was. Viscount Adam Tapps of Moxley, a former beau. "Viscount Tapps, so nice to see you again," she smiled, extending out her hand. "I am alone here."

The Viscount was still as handsome as ever. He bowed, kissing her glove directly. A little taller than herself, he had long, dark brown hair bordering his piercing brown stare. Yes, he was staring, a rather concentrated glare. "I will only be a moment...How are you, Lady Hollinger?"

Gwendolyn inhaled; she had forgotten how intriguing he was. Why was she not interested in him before? *Oh, that's right.* "I am doing well Viscount Tapps, how are you?"

He encircled her, admiring her dress with his gape, "You look remarkable. Still searching for a husband, I do hope. I am quite available to take on the task."

Gwendolyn blushed and stepped away from him, so much trifling going on this evening; first Devin, then Thomas, now him. "Hard to believe you never married."

He grinned, and then turned away from her. "Not so hard I suppose, I am quite finicky."

Gwendolyn giggled, and Adam gazed down at her lips as she did. She closed them instantly. "Silly to hear you compare yourself to a feline."

He guffawed himself, realizing what it sounded like. He instantly remembered her humor and was smitten. "No comparison, simply an observation...I have a specific preference for a chosen mate."

Gwendolyn's mouth opened slightly, his seduction was quite unique. She stood staring at him too now, until the door closing whipped both their heads around.

"Am I intruding?"

Viscount Tapps eyed Thomas walking towards them. His severe deliberation indicating that he was not the least bit pleased. "Your Grace—I...I was just getting better acquainted with your cousin here."

"She is not my cousin, and you bloody well know it—Adam." Thomas and Adam go way back. They used to be school chums, until Adam Tapps cheated on a test and blamed Thomas for giving him the answers. Since that day, he had never trusted him and there were even countless times after that incident that would substantiate future mistrust. He knew that Gwendolyn was not his cousin; Adam grew up in the same social circles as the Hollinger's and Drummond's, but now resided in Hampshire. The only reason he was invited this evening was because of Devin; he was one of Devin's benefactors.

Oh, Gwendolyn could not believe it, Thomas had changed right before her very eyes, rapidly transforming into some predatory animal, his glower was constricted—nearly brown with opposition, his chest puffed up, his fists were even clenched at the base of his legs. *He did resemble a black panther;* she thought...a fierce possessive being. "He was just leaving, weren't you Viscount?"

"For the record, Thomas...I have known she was alive even before you did, I just chose not to disclose that information for purely selfish reasons," Adam grinned, winking at Gwendolyn, "I wanted to relish in your shock as I introduced her to you as *my wife.*" Adam remained steady for a few more seconds then turned on his heel when he noticed Thomas' face turning purple. He left without further ado. He knew Thomas was a better swordsman, the better aim and did not want to be forced into something he could never wake up from.

"What does he mean *by wife*—what was he talking about?"

"He was a former beau of mine—"

"He was what?"

Gwendolyn noted his stunned looked. Even though she knew it was not the time or place to divulge such delicacies, she felt she needed to explain. Thomas made her feel like she had been caught with a lover, but why? Oh God, it was no use, this war of emotions going on inside her heart. "Did you really think I would stay a widow forever, Thomas?"

"You mean you and him?"

Gwendolyn paused at the sight of him shaking his head and heading out the door. "There were even several beaus after him, all fighting for my hand." His incredulous flight kept steaming away. Had she injured him that much with her statement? "Do not walk away from me!"

Thomas painstakingly remained at his exit a few feet away; he was so upset with her. "This is easier to do than to look at you right now, Gwendolyn."

Gwendolyn narrowed her eyes, "Why you conceited hypocrite! You cannot stand there *jealous* when I have met your Mrs. Carmichael and have probably even conversed with *God-knows-who-else-you* have-bedded in addition to be constantly thrown together with *your* fiancée!"

Thomas stood still; a foreboding expression embraced his face. So she met Mrs. Carmichael, good, then maybe envy will turn Gwendolyn around. But why was she so concentrated on the other women in his life? Or Katrina for that matter? He met her accusation as a revelation. "Why, are you covetous of them?"

Gwendolyn guffawed and shook her head, "You do not understand this do you? We both waited ten long years to remarry. You obviously care for Katrina, otherwise you would have not asked for her hand. I obviously care for Charles; otherwise I would have not accepted his proposal."

Just once, he wished she would make up her mind. Disappointed once again, he remarked, "You slay me, Gwendolyn, you really do. Go— *stay,* kiss me—*run away*...you make me dizzy! You are just an excellent tease."

Gwendolyn stared at the door slamming for a moment and became enraged herself. She wanted to scream! She wanted to throw things, but there was nothing in the room to shatter. Huffing and puffing, she wandered to another part of the space and tried to focus on the frescoes of angels on the plastered dome ceiling above her. They were staring down at her with those haunting black eyes of theirs and she wanted to throw something at them too for being so bloody cheery.

Wringing her hands at the sides of her dress, she began to

shake them—they were tingling. Why did she feel the need to rattle him so? He called her a *tease*…was she always one? Which part should she have omitted? Should she have kept that part a secret about the Viscount? Should she have not mentioned that he was a former beau…or the part where several men tried for her hand? She thought he was dead; she had to go on with her life. He thought she was dead too, he had to do the same. She knew that a gorgeous man like Thomas would not lack for female attention, and, *oh God,* the thought of him lying down with another woman made her ill. Was that why he was angry too? Did it make him feel sick as well with the thought of another man touching her?

Startled by the door opening back up again, Gwendolyn eyed an older gentlemen walking towards her. *Oh no, not again.* She just wanted to be alone. He came in closer…yet nearer. He looked familiar, but she could not quite pinpoint the name. It was on the tip of her tongue. *Oh, what was his name?* "I am alone here, sir."

"Yes, I know," he ominously let go.

Gwendolyn's breath quickened realizing his intention.

"Do you know who I am?"

Gwendolyn gulped and surveyed the man more closely. His age, mid-fifties, she guessed, his hair striped with grey through a blondish brown. His eyes, blue, his face…*yes, she does know who he was.* "Baron Huxton?"

"Yes, Lady Hollinger. I do apologize for frightening you; it is just… that when I saw you across the room, and then dancing in the ball room just now, I could not believe my eyes. You look so much like…*her.*"

Gwendolyn blinked back her anxiety and realized he was talking about her mother. She knew she resembled her, but no one here tonight was supposed to know that…to recognize her, she knew now that the secret might be out. "Who Baron Huxton?" Gwendolyn asked gently.

"The Duchess of Suffolkshire, you are at least, related?"

145

"Yes," Gwendolyn confessed, pleading with him, "But you mustn't tell anyone. Please Baron Huxton I beg of you."

"Then you are related?"

"Yes, she was my mother."

The Baron bowed his head and paced away. "Yes," he said softhearted. "Mary had a little girl...I met her once, Gwendolyn, correct?" He expressed, wiping his brow with a handkerchief. "The Drummond's were in association with the Hollinger's, were they not?"

"Yes," she expressed with anxiety now.

"There was a contract."

Gwendolyn closed her eyes, "Yes."

He looked down at the ground, "Yes, I do see the delicacy in this matter."

"Yes, Baron Huxton, so I do implore you to stern confidence."

"Yes, Lady Hollinger," he replied, encircling her and then bowing to her nobility, "Your Grace, I will do it for Mary." He then leaned up against a pillar in back of him. "Did your mother...did your mother ever mention me?"

Gwendolyn's heart dropped a little lower at this point. *Mention him?* She tried to search her memory. Baron Huxton was her mother's married man? "Oh Baron, yes... she did talk about you once," Gwendolyn conveyed, covering up her mouth with her gloved hand within seeing the Baron's heart-breaking collapse. The man looked miserable all of a sudden, on the verge of tears. He bent over as if in pain.

"Your Grace, when I saw you dancing in the ballroom my heart burst wide open," he confessed, leaning back on the pillar. "I have always loved your mother. I wanted to marry her, but my father contracted me to another," he revealed, suddenly doubling over in pain. "My wife died just recently," he gushed, holding his abdomen, "And I have never shed a tear."

"Never shed a tear for your own wife?" Gwendolyn repeated in disbelief.

"No," he continued to weep, "not one. The only grief I have ever felt was the day I heard of Mary's passing—I loved her so."

He bent over and cried in his hands and Gwendolyn reached out for the man, placing her hand on his shoulder. His soul shattered into a million pieces. She never wanted to be in that position...and vowed to never be. "Baron Huxton, you'll be glad to know that my mother did indeed love you in return."

The Baron's surprised elated look brought tears to Gwendolyn's own eyes. "She—she did?"

Gwendolyn nodded her head in confirmation. Baron Huxton was so elated; he grabbed Gwendolyn into his arms and held her there.

"What am I interrupting *now?*"

Gwendolyn and the Baron immediately broke apart. Within seeing the host in the doorway, Baron Huxton repositioned his stance and coughed away his grief.

"Nothing happened Thomas; this one does not concern you."

"Everything concerns me Gwendolyn when a lack of decorum is not met under my roof," Thomas stated, his eyes full of annoyance and rage staring straight at Baron Huxton. Thomas doesn't like the Baron either; he used to push his spoiled daughter, Joan into his sphere.

Gwendolyn noted the intense expression on his face and immediately walked over to Thomas and placed her palm in the center of his chest. In a calm, gentle voice, she uttered, "We were talking about my mother," Gwendolyn expressed gazing at the Baron now. "I was just telling the Baron where the memorial was... in Yorkshire, remember Baron Huxton? In the graveyard, at St. Paul Church?"

Baron Huxton's eyes lit up and nodded his head in appreciation. "Yes," he agreed, "yes, we were discussing just that," he verbalized, stiffening back up and walking around the two.

Thomas looked down at Gwendolyn still infuriated. He wanted to devour her, brutal passion still riding him hard.

Gwendolyn closed her mouth once more and stepped away from him, creating a much-needed distance between their obsessions. His sudden burst of protectiveness was a bit overwhelming and Gwendolyn did not know how much more she could take without giving into her need to be intimate with him. She was on the verge of doing something she would definitely regret...something, oh so reckless.

CHAPTER 17

"*L*ady Hollinger, what was your cousin like when he was a child?"

They were sitting down to formal dinner, another couple, besides Lord and Lady Hale were invited to the small affair. Gwendolyn looked up from her strawberry tart to address Lady Evelyn Moore. She was a striking young brunette with dreamy blue eyes whose family married her off to a titled husband for wealth. Her husband, Lord Curtis Moore, the Earl of Trenton, being seventy winters her elder.

Gwendolyn smiled down at her dessert, so many memories dashed inside her head; she doesn't quite know which one to focus on. *How lucky,* she thought, to have shared a past with someone whom everyone wanted to be familiar with. She thought about all the fun they used to have, like the time she and Thomas both had loose teeth and decided to yank each other's out with strings, or the frightened memoirs reminiscent of when they went sailing in her father's cruiser and the wind blew them offshore, fifty kilometers away from port. Thomas had to use his skills he learned from his brother about utilizing the wind speed to his lead and navigated them back to safety. She remembered how grateful she was and crushed the life out of Tommy when they got to shore. Funny, how you suppress the contented recollections and only memorize the unpleasant ones. Then, her fifteenth birthday, she does recall that now...

I was sitting at the table with a group of girls my age. We were all giggling and pointing at the boys across the room. We were eating my birthday cake, when one of the girls, Joan, a girl who spent most of her time in the country with her mother, spurted out, "How do I get Jordan Hollinger to pay any attention to me?"

"Oh Joan," one girl complained, "the only girls he pays any attention to are the ones that are rumored to give into his seduction."

"And how, pray tell, do you know any of this?" Joan asked with one brown eyebrow high in the air.

"Heard it whispered last month," The girl nonchalantly assumed, "unknown if there is any weight behind the gossip, but look at him, how any girl cannot succumb to his disposition!" She giggled profusely, causing all the other girls, including myself to take another look at Jordan's outward show.

Surrounded by ladies of every social class, Jordan kept the females interested with his dry wit and external charm. He was too vain, I concluded immediately, until he caught me staring at him as well and his temporary curiosity caused me to roll my eyes to catch Joan staring into another direction.

"Who's that boy over there?"

"Who?" Another girl asked.

"That one, over there, the boy with the dark hair, who is he?"

I finally turned my head to see whom she was speaking about, I could not tell. The only boys I could see en route of her pointing finger with dark hair were Adam and Tommy.

"Oh, Joan, you know who that is? Why, that's Jordan Hollinger's younger brother!" I heard the girl squeal. "He is so handsome; he is similar to his older sibling."

Joan's eyes lit up in wonder, "Really? So, he's our age then? With no unsuitable reputation?"

"Yes," that squeaky girl shrilled, "he is also very sweet, you would like him, he has the most gorgeous blue eyes."

I stared at the both of them. What the heck was going on? Did the sugar from the frosting on the cake go to their heads? Have they lost their minds from eating bad fruit? "Green," I said, which made them both turn my way. "Tommy's eyes are green."

Joan asked amazed, "So you know the Hollinger's?"

"Haven't you heard? They're family friends," Squeaky spurted out matter-of-factly.

"And you have been sitting there silent as a church mouse and haven't gushed your acquaintance?" She quipped, slapping my hand that was in my lap, "Shame on you." She then quickly turned her head to consider Tommy once again, only this instance, took her time at it. "Do you think you can introduce me?" She asked me now with puppy dog eyes. I watched her face turn from mine and followed her eyes to see if I could figure out what she found so fascinating. Tommy and Adam were side by side, both of them the same height with their arms animated out in front of them in conversation, they looked normal to me, and so non-fascinating. I turned back to Joan and her face was still absorbed.

"Oh Joan, do you think you have set your cap for him?" I heard Squeaky inquire.

I viewed Joan slowly nod her head yes, and just like that, I couldn't believe it. A threat invaded my special comradeship. I didn't want her setting her cap for him. I didn't want anyone setting anything on him. Tommy belonged to me. I got up from my seat and marched over to where the boys' stood. Not caring that I left the girls dumbfounded with my abrupt rudeness, but on a mission, a conquering urge to protect what was mine. Arriving quickly at my intended target, I yanked at the back of his collar and motioned for Tommy to come and follow me to a nearby corner.

"See that girl over there, no, don't look her way, I think she likes you," I said, trying to figure out why my heart swelled up beyond comprehension.

"The blonde girl?" Tommy asked, gazing over at her. He appeared to give

Joan too much inspection, as I watched his eyes turn from inquisitive to interest. *"What is her name? She is kind of cute."*

"Cute?" I remarked, gazing over at her myself. I tried to figure out what he found so fascinating. Long blonde hair, dark brown eyes, she was even wearing the same style of dress I wore. *"She is Baron Huxton's daughter, Joan. Why, do you like her?"* I asked, feeling the beats in my heart beginning to escalate.

"I don't know...do you think I should go talk to her?"

I stared at Tommy still looking in her direction. Could not believe that he would leave me to go and speak to a stranger. My heart hurt now. It got large, swollen, and kept beating in an unpleasant, stubborn way. Just then, I wanted to injure him just as much as he was wounding me. *"Go ahead, I am going to go and talk to Barry Abernathy anyway."*

Tommy closed the space between us and stared me down. Squinting his eyes in annoyance, he voiced, *"Barry Abernathy? Why, he's Andrew's age. What would a chap like Barry show interest in a child like you?"*

With my hands on my hips, I twisted my lips, *"He's already shown interest in me you nitwit—he's practically glued to my heel,"* I retorted, walking away from him. *"Watch."* In the corner of my eye, I could see him; Barry Abernathy, so tall, with wide shoulders, two years older than I. I could not understand why he was so fascinated, having never been introduced to him before. The farther I walked away, the farther Barry would follow me. I turned to see if Tommy was following me as well, and he wasn't? I stopped cold and watched him pace over to Joan and Squeaky to introduce himself. A bizarre darting pang pierced through my heart...he was not allowed to honor her wishes! Upon my huff, I noticed in my peripheral view that Barry was still within arm's length. I decided to see how far he would chase me and scampered over to the horse stables. I knew I was without a chaperone, but I didn't care. That throbbing ache inside my chest would not go away.

"See now," I heard him say, *"slow down, I cannot talk to you if you do not slow down."*

I turned around; I didn't realize I was running! *"What?"* I asked, my arms draped across my chest in a standoff. My heart started to beat *ungovernably now, realizing that we were alone, inside the stable with no one else but horseflesh.*

"Happy birthday, Gwendolyn," Barry quietly voiced, stepping into me, rapidly stealing all my air.

"Th-thank you," I said, wondering what the glint in his eyes, meant. I stepped backwards, turned around and walked in farther into the stables. "Have you seen the horse my father gave me? The Arabian?" I asked sheepishly, hearing his footsteps behind me. They were like echoing, thunderous sounds inside my thumping ears. I halted at the hatchway, and in a flash, the gelding trotted over to me for a petting. "Isn't she beautiful?" I asked, stroking the horse's mane and then gazing over at Barry.

He was staring right at me; looking at me in an irregular way. "Yes," I heard him say in a low tone, "yes, she is."

I noticed him reaching for me and I wanted to run, but my legs would not move. I was spellbound, he was going to kiss me, but I still could not move! Suddenly, his hands were on my waist...dear God, he was touching me, and he did not even ask. Swiftly, Barry enclosed the space between us and I felt his warm hand on the edge of my breast, his other hand grabbed at my neck and before he finished his attempt at tasting me, Tommy came out of nowhere and toppled Barry horizontal.

Tommy and Barry were on the ground now, in the dirt, kicking hay, pulling, punching, hitting, and strangling one another. I screamed at Tommy, trying to get him to stop, but he wasn't listening to me. I bent down and yanked at his coat and tried to drag him away. Tommy was enraged; I had never seen him like that before. He cursed at Barry who was still down in the dirt, and before I knew it, Tommy ran away and I rushed after him...

GWENDOLYN SAT TRANSFIXED ON HER MEMORY OF THAT day. Too many deliberations bounced around in her head. She was older now, wiser, and did not grasp what was happening back then, but, *oh God,* she comprehended it now. She had seen that look before...the first time on that day, secondly, on her wedding night, and thirdly, the other night at the ball. So much emotion, heat and craze in those fair green eyes. Thomas' face was full of passion; it was enthralling, it was mesmerizing... it was...kind of like...now? Gwendolyn impulsively drank down her goblet of wine and decided to focus on a story less disturbing.

"Oh, do tell us that one," Evelyn voiced, energetic with glee, "The one that you just remembered and turned crimson."

Gwendolyn swallowed and gazed down at her plate, careful not to look at Thomas, no, do not look his way. He was probably wondering what the heck she had recalled. Nodding her head, she uttered, "Um... well, there was one particular story I'd like to share."

"Do tell us Lady Hollinger, your dear cousin is such a mystery," Evelyn decided, gazing at Katrina with envious eyes.

At the head of table, Thomas leaned back casually in his chair and set eyes on Gwendolyn. Gwendolyn sat up tense in her seat and declared, "Thomas was shy—"

"Shy!" Evelyn began to titter.

Her husband pinched her leg underneath the table. "My dear, please refrain from any further spirits," Lord Moore asserted.

"Close your eyes and go to sleep," Evelyn nagged at him. "Now, Lady Hollinger, do go on, I do apologize for my outburst."

Gwendolyn smiled and gazed at Thomas who had remained intently looking at her, he was so wickedly handsome she could not bear it. *Oh God, what would it look like if she flung herself across the table to kiss him?* She studied his pretext before saying, "He broke his arm once."

"I forgot about that," Thomas added, grabbing his chalice of wine and taking a sip.

Gwendolyn turned from him and began to speak to Lady Moore; "We were by the lake, in the summertime. It was very hot that day, and we decided to take a swim. Andrew..." she stopped suddenly, swallowing from feeling overwhelmed with the memory that Andrew was now deceased. "Andrew, Thomas' brother, built a raft, and we decided to steal it."

"Steal it!" Evelyn squealed again, making her sleeping husband jump from the noise. She patted her husband's hands underneath the table and Lord Moore carried on with his snoring.

Gwendolyn's smile grew with each regained memory of that fateful day. "I did not want to of course, but the future Duke wanted to see if it could sail."

"Sail?" Evelyn interrupted again, "But I thought you said it was a raft."

"Evelyn, if you do not mind, we would all like to listen to this interesting story without any interruptions," Katrina announced, making everyone feel a bit uneasy. "You may precede, Gwendolyn."

Gwendolyn's claws began to jut out beneath the table. Blasted girl, she thought, Gwendolyn wanted to scream off the top of her lungs that she was the Duchess of the manor and should not be directed so informally! But Gwendolyn sustained her smile and concluded, "We thought it could sail, because we were very young...six years, I do recall now." She turned her head and saw Thomas gazing at Katrina. They shared a fleeting look and Gwendolyn grew envious. "Tommy—I mean, *Thomas*, grabbed the back, and I pulled the front until the raft floated on the water. We drifted around happily, pretending we were soldiers on his majesty's ship, when I decided to stand up to hoist sails and tipped over our vessel!" She laughed, hearing everyone chuckle along with her. She clogged again and eyed Thomas. This time, he leaned back into his chair and stared at her with an indebted gaze. Her mirth weakened, when she realized he knew exactly what came next. "We swam to shore, dragging ourselves out of the water, head to toe, wringing wet, when I decided to disrobe." Gwendolyn halted and eyed the guests; they were all very quiet and intrigued, hanging onto her every shameful word. "I was wet you see, and damp, sticky, my leggings full of water, I felt like a bathed cat. I urged Thomas to do the same, and when we were finished...we were nude." Gwendolyn circled her eyes around and everyone had their mouths open. Katrina, whose eyes were narrow and full of fury, promised revenge in the very near future. Old Lord Moore was fully awake now and engrossed in her every wicked detail.

Thomas just sat there, grinning from ear to ear. "Finish the story Gwendolyn," he pressed her.

"Heading back towards the estate, our governess spotted the two of us, running around exposed as Roman statutes, and chased us roughly trying to catch a limb or two. Slippery as we were, she was unable to; constantly bending over, missing us like oily little piglets between her fingers. Thomas continued to run away from her when he did not see the tree in front of him and ran right into it."

"His Grace...broke his arm...on a tree?" Evelyn bellowed off the top of her lungs.

"Yes!" Gwendolyn snorted with her. Everyone began to roll with amusement, even Thomas, who grabbed his goblet again and chucked the remaining wine down his throat.

"Excuse me, Your Grace, but we have an unexpected visitor."

Thomas acknowledged his butler who peeped in through the door. "Who is it Fitzwater?"

"A mister Charles McMillen, sir."

Gwendolyn gasped and stood up from her seat, "He's here?"

"Yes, malady, should I receive him?"

Thomas stood up from his chair and threw down his napkin, "McMillen, Gwendolyn?"

Gwendolyn straightened up her back and met his annoyance, "Your point being?"

The table was hushed at once; having just been introduced to the most enjoyable story heard in decades, to straight away feel the tension between the two childhood culprits.

"Your fiancé does not happen to be Scottish now, is he?"

Gwendolyn crossed her arms in defiance, "Your point being— Your Grace?"

Thomas kicked back his chair and headed towards the far end

of the dining room area. He suddenly froze realizing his upper back was saturated from a propelled strawberry.

"Where are you going?" Gwendolyn demanded about to throw another piece of fruit at him.

Thomas swallowed his annoyance then slowly wiped the gooiness away from his person, "To see what is cluttering my hallway."

"What are you going to do?" Gwendolyn inquired, watching Thomas halt then turn on his heel.

Thomas cocked his head to one side, "...I am going to invite him to play tidily-winks!"

Every guest glued himself or herself to his hasty exit while Gwendolyn rushed around the table to meet his stride. A gamine smile appeared on her lips, instant gratification spun out of control knowing he was now envious of her current beau. "Why are you so angry?"

He did not bother to look at her. "Who's angry?"

"You are."

"Am not!"

But now Gwendolyn was mad. *What was he going to do?* She yanked at his coat and pulled him off balance. "I do not see why you should be so upset Thomas, you are not the one who's going to marry him."

"Who's upset?" He let out with twisted anger.

"You are!" She snarled back at him.

"Am not!"

"Am too!"

Thomas regulated his emotions and straightened out his waistcoat. He turned to his friends all staring at the both of them arguing and replied, "I apologize for the explosion."

"At least he's not *French*, Thomas," Devin quipped with a snicker, directly eyeing Lady Moore.

CHAPTER 18

*P*ushing Thomas aside, Gwendolyn managed to beat his footing and ran towards Charles first, whirling herself around to clamp the man's extensively wide arms.

Thomas stood agape—the man was huge! A giant, burly, robust gorilla was what he was: Wool cap atop cropped reddish-brown hair, dim eyes with a mustache and beard a bit overgrown and in need of a trim, farmer's suspenders holding up worn trousers over bulky mud boots. He petted Gwendolyn's small hand within his enfold and stared at the black panther before him.

"Ye must be the stately Duke," Charles mocked with his distinct Scottish brogue.

"I am," Thomas stated, watching his guests all pour into view.

Katrina arrived on the scene behind him and stood by his side. "I am Charles McMillen, here tae collect me fiancée," he roared unruly, gazing down at Gwendolyn.

A rush of possessiveness passed through Thomas. He was not about to let some brute take over his control. "She is not going anywhere."

"Och now, yes she is," he rumbled in a deep, growling voice.

Thomas noted his friends who had all gathered around. "Nothing to see here, may I suggest tea on the veranda outside? There is a lovely moon, the air is warm and light, I do assure you it will be quite comfortable," he hushed down and spoke to Katrina in her ear. "Be a dear and direct them outside, I will meet you in a moment."

"Only a moment Thomas, and not a moment longer," Katrina demanded quietly, waiving her arms in misdirection. "Shall we go to the garden?

Thomas stood erect and sized his opponent once more. The two men met eye-to-eye, on the verge of attack. Gwendolyn noted the tension brewing and yanked at Charles' large arms. She was not about to witness a primeval skirmish between a gorilla and black panther.

"Come Charles; let us go to the library."

Charles kept his eyes on Thomas the second they arrived behind closed doors. Unaffected, and within his realm, Thomas lurked around his desk and took a seat in his leather armchair.

Gwendolyn sat beside Charles, who, by this time, relaxed and held her hand. Thomas took out a cigar from within a small chest on his desk, lit it and then pointed the smoke at Gwendolyn's fiancé. "Care for one? Or is smoking too courtly for you?"

Gwendolyn's mouth flew open wide. "Thomas! Behave yourself; you are trying to provoke him."

Thomas noted the man's scarlet ears, and yes, *indeed*, he was trying to provoke him.

"Shush me sweet, the mon is merely trying tae rattle me," Charles uttered wisely, "He knows he willna triumph, in fact, it does me good tae know he's already ben beat."

Thomas fastened his teeth on the cigar and bit down. The wrath that fused within him was out of place and inexplicable and doesn't quite know how to handle it. Here sat Gwendolyn's betrothed; an odd sort of beau if you had time to think about it. What was it that attracted him to her? Big and beefy, is that the kind of man she loves? With all that wavy red hair and dark eyes to boot, not a bad looking creature in a bizarre sort of way. Switch eye color and paint a beard on Thomas and they could be twins... what? Thomas had to blink twice in order to get that little illustration out of his head. No one was good enough to replace him in the husband department and this stocky monster was certainly not worthy of Gwendolyn. "Beaten? At what sport?"

Charles started to laugh, but clearly he was not amused. "The pursuit of interest, I wood say."

"I do hold a slight advantage."

Charles' face turned beet red now. "But from Gwendolyn's letter, ya'll be grantin' her a divorce and she will be free of ya."

Free of him...hmmm, he thought shrewdly, liberated is no good, Gwendolyn was *his* friend, *his* companion and *his* wife—and besides, *he saw her first!* Thomas swallowed his exhale until smoke came out of his nose and nearly his ears. He resembled a dragon, his eyes verdant, fixated with hatred and conflict. "And what if I do not grant her a divorce?"

Charles stood up and inflated with protectiveness, "Ya'll be giving her a divorce, or ya'll be dealing wit' me."

"Dealing with you?" Thomas laughed wickedly. "And what could a simple farm boy challenge a clever competitor like myself with? Arm wrestling?"

"Och now, notae bad idea," Charles acknowledged, nodding his head.

Thomas brought his eyes down to the gorilla's arms. Big, hefty, muscular...he swallowed his dignity. To beat him would take a miracle. "When and where?"

"How 'bout right now?" Charles challenged him.

Gwendolyn stood up and brushed down her skirts. "That is it," she demanded, positioning her body between them. She held one palm to each of their nearing chests. "I have heard enough, no one is challenging anything to anyone, do I make myself clear?"

Thomas smirked and met eye-to-eye with Charles once more;

the two men staring each other down, sizing one another up. Gwendolyn was pushed aside by both of them and Charles began rolling up his sleeves.

Thomas yanked off his dinner coat and then ripped off his cravat. Rolling up his sleeves too, he stalked around Charles, guesstimating his contender's strength.

Gwendolyn ran over to Thomas and quickly pleaded with him, "Do not do this, you are going to lose…he has never lost a match before. You do not know what you have gotten yourself into, please Thomas, and concede."

Thomas tore his eyes away from his challenger for a moment and looked into hers. "Worried about me now, eh?"

Gwendolyn huffed and stomped her foot, "How incorrigible you are! No, you egotistical fool! I was merely giving you forewarning!"

Too big for his breeches, Charles squatted down next to a nearby chess table, and skated his forearm across the counter clearing it from all game pieces. Thomas serenely knelt on the other side of him and placed his elbow firmly on the granite surface.

"If I win," Charles wagered, placing down his ante, "Me fiancée leaves wit' me this very eve."

Thomas arched one black brow, assertively addressing him, "And if I win, your fiancée continues to stay."

Charles let down his enormous elbow onto the stonework with a thud, "Agreed."

Gwendolyn covered her eyes from any further stupidity and began to pace the room. "This is ridiculous!" She exclaimed, waiving her hands in the air. "Do either of you want to know how I feel?"

"NO!" They both said in unison.

Concentrated eyes glued on one another, their hands gripped instantaneously; Thomas on the left side, Charles on the right, all the strength, power and vigor showing instantly in their strained grimaces.

Gwendolyn began to gasp at the sight of Charles easily bearing down on Thomas. She wanted to entwine her arms around his and support his losing brace. Oh how could Thomas be this brainless? What on earth could this solve? Men! She will never be able to figure them out. Gwendolyn clutched her stomach from the distressed vision before her and shook her head. Closing her eyes with the realization that she was going home with Charles, Gwendolyn turned towards the door about to exit. She heard a bang of knuckles behind her and placed her palms on the outlet.

"I'll be stayin' at The Quail Inn 'til the papers are signed," she heard Charles say behind her.

Whipping her head around Gwendolyn was surprised to see Thomas rolling down his sleeves. An intense, wild, victorious contortion embraced her gape. *Dear God, he won.* He actually beat Charles McMillen, a five-time arm-wrestling champ, with ribbons and medals to prove his strength. She swallowed hard and followed the loser to the entrance foyer.

"Only a couple more days Charles, then I'm coming home," Gwendolyn mouthed to him, feeling his defeat.

"Are ya Gwendolyn?" He asked quietly, wrapping his large hand around her chin. He leaned in and gave her a small peck on her lips.

"Yes, Charles," Gwendolyn voiced watching his face pull away from hers.

Charles stared at Thomas in the backdrop. "Then I'll be seeing ya," he voiced, placing his wool cap back on his head, exiting out the door.

CHAPTER 19

*W*alking along a ship's deck, Gwendolyn felt the rush of rain and wind across her face...she wiped off wetness, but suddenly felt dry...a thick cloud of fog embraced the hull...she continued to walk forward, her feet damp and moist from not wearing any slippers...she was cold, she was drenched and eyed a tall figure in the distance. *Tommy*, she realized...and before she can reach out to touch him, he jumped over the ledge in one alarming hurdle...she cried out to him, but he does not hear her? She ran towards the sheer but sees his body floating face down in the water...crying, and on the verge of insanity, she felt compelled to join him...

GWENDOLYN SAT UP FROM BED DRIPPING IN SWEAT. Gasping for air, she realized it was her recurring nightmare. She hobbled out of bed and rushed towards the vanity. The basin was bare. The water was gone.

Grabbing her lamp, she lit a fire stick and enflamed the wick inside. Once outside her door, she looked up and down the silent hallway. Everyone was asleep, she realized, and descended the long corridor. The manor was pleasantly still and eased Gwendolyn's apprehension. She passed several closed doors on her way towards the staircase then stopped at the sight of illumination from underneath a closed door. *His room,* she recognized and wondered why he was still awake.

Slowly opening the door, she wheezed at the sight of Thomas sitting in a lounge chair, guzzling an open bottle and staring into a blazing fire. He was bare-footed in breeches, an unfettered white shirt exposing his neck and chest. His hair was in disarray, untamed and cascaded above his shoulders. He doesn't hear her approach and Gwendolyn silently sat down on an armchair aside him.

Heart thumping inside her ears, she assembled opposite him gazing into a sullen fire. He still had not responded to her advance and she felt odd watching him stare dejectedly into the blaze.

"I do not like your intended," he suddenly whispered into the conflagration.

Gwendolyn let go a smirk, "I do not like yours either."

Thomas grabbed his bottle and held it to his chest. "Unexpected, how two people who never warmed to the idea of wedlock, suddenly find themselves both desirous of marriage?"

Gwendolyn fought back her tears and brought her legs up into the chair and crossed them under her long wide chemise. "You are lucky he allowed me to stay...he does not trust you."

He yanked the bottle away from his chest and took a swig of the comforting alcohol, "With good reason."

"Yes," she confirmed, "you must keep your hands to yourself."

He cursed into the flare and continued to stare at the blaze. "No worries Gwendolyn, after tonight, consider me the perfect gentleman."

Gwendolyn laid her chin on her knees, "When have you ever been above reproach, Thomas?"

Thomas brought the bottle up to his lips and cocked his head, grinning slightly, he let go a "Touché."

Gwendolyn watched him drowning his sorrows and his depressed look. "Thomas," she asked gently, "Devin has expressed that he has only known you for seven years. What happened to the rest of the three?"

Thomas now looked over at her. Gwendolyn's hair had tumbled down the sides of her shoulders like an auburn waterfall. She appeared striking in spite of her commonplace nightgown. She handed over a smile that truly puzzled him. "I was detained."

Gwendolyn sat silent, watching Thomas suddenly shiver. "Detained, from what?"

"I did not tell you everything Gwendolyn," he expressed, turning away from her and gazing back into the flames.

"Another riddle?" Gwendolyn asked sweetly.

"An understanding," Thomas let go sluggishly, the alcohol damming his reason. "My crate was adrift for nearly four days," he confessed shrilly. "Some Portuguese fisherman found me afloat. Bringing me aboard, they fed me molded bread and rotting fruit, thinking that would save me." He stopped coldly and took another swig, wiping his jowl of liquid that missed his lips. "They stranded me on a foreign land, with no one to aid me, no one to acknowledge the fact that I could not speak a word of Portuguese and left me to fend for myself. I was weak and tired, and hungry... oh so starving. I started stealing food, anything and everything that I could make a run for; fruit, vegetables...sometimes even sausages. Occasionally, I was able to eat what I stole, most of the time...I was flogged. After two pain-staking years, I finally found an English ship that set anchor. I tried to explain to them who I was, but no one believed me. My father's shipping commerce had become inoperative since his death and all *HCC* ships were being ordered out of action. I then befriended the British captain who offered work for food. I even entered arm-wrestling contests to help me achieve my goal. It took me another year Gwendolyn," his voiced cracked as he lowered his head, "Twelve long months, lifting those bags of wheat the size of horses, to achieve passage back to England."

Gwendolyn sprung up from her seated position and lurched towards him, wrapping her arms around his neck, pulling him into her warmth. He was trembling, frightened and she tried to console him by massaging her fingers through his hair and rubbing his back. "Oh Thomas…"

Thomas dropped the bottle on the floor and blanketed his arms around her backside, resting his head on her midriff. Crossing his doom, he closed his eyes and felt a rush of zeal from being so close to her sympathy. He allowed his hands to roam her spine, down the small of her back, to her derriere.

Heart pounding in her throat, Gwendolyn felt her desire beginning to escalate. Oh God—his hands felt so good…her body awakening from his blind groping. "I should go," she quietly voiced.

Leaning his head slightly away from her, he said, "Yes…yes, you should. Go back to your room Gwendolyn; it is not appropriate for you to be in mine."

"Why you despicable man."

"Yes, that's it…hate me, go ahead and hate me."

Gwendolyn was tongue-tied, emotions bursting at the seams. "Hate you? I just wanted to comfort you…it is what a friend would do for another friend."

"You and I can no longer be friends," he stated in a cold harsh tone.

Gwendolyn stood away from him and his indifference, "We were once the best of friends."

"In another lifetime," Thomas uttered gently suffering from his repeal.

"True friends are hard to find Thomas," she beseeched. "I would hate to have to go through life knowing that your friendship was no longer obtainable."

Thomas threw his posterior back into the chair. *Good God, she was ...beautiful, how was he ever going to get her to leave?* "Could you do it Gwendolyn? Could you?" He asked with all honesty. "Meet me on the streets of London, you with your husband, me with my wife. Look at me strictly as a friend and converse with me by the same well-wishes?"

Gwendolyn searched his subject for some remorse, but she could not find it. His words were painful to hear, afflicting her reasoning in the worst sort of sting. "It would take some time, but yes, I think—"

"Because I could not," he interrupted her.

"Why not?"

"Because every time I look at you," he paused to search her objective. "Every time I see you, Gwendolyn...with mutual esteem or just you standing there, I want to pull up your skirts and ravish you for hours."

Gwendolyn's mouth closed up and her pulse pleaded leniency. She scanned the fire beside her and then looked over at Thomas. She could tell by his posture that he was still inflexible, but his eyes showed proof of hesitancy. She could have him now; have him once...one last time. "Every time?" She whispered carefully.

Thomas' mouth suddenly went dry. He felt a throb uncoil in his abdomen. What was she doing? He watched in disbelief as Gwendolyn unclothed herself and stood before him, naked and unprotected from his vigilant charge. "Trickery demeans you."

Devious to a degree, Gwendolyn purposely stood in front of the flames to outline her physique with the fire's orange glow. "No deception Thomas, merely a test." She was still his wife, he was still her husband, and their longing seemed suited and within acceptable limits.

Thomas grinned and rested his glare on her ruby-red nipples darting towards the sky. "Then I fail unmercifully."

Feeling her breath quickening, she watched him disrobe while still established in his chair; he pulled his shirt up over his head, unbuttoned his breeches tugging them off his feet. Stationed only a few feet away from her, his penis sprung free, his undress, merely an enticement, inspired her recklessly, his physical body powerfully apt in ideal proportions. "You are a beautiful man Thomas Hollinger."

Enthralled from her sheer existence, Thomas grabbed her waist and ran his hands up her bare stomach climbing towards her breasts. Hovering over her peaks, so soft and plump, were those luscious cherry stems. "Men aren't beautiful Gwendolyn, they're simply built for potency—now sit on me," he persuaded roughly, bringing his eyes up to her gaze.

"Well, my friend," Gwendolyn murmured, raking his shoulders, his manhood and lower body, "Your traits are taken too lightly." Gwendolyn then stepped into him and sat on his lions.

Almost immediately, Thomas pounced on her hair, pulling it down until her throat was exposed to allow his mouth to buss her neck and ear with over-zealous exploitation. "Never miscalculate me minx," he groaned in her lobe, "I shall make you pay for your taunting discord."

His fervor passed through her too quickly, meeting his obsession with her own burning journey...through his hair... around his neck... down his sinewy backside. Happy to be in his arms...joyful to be by his side...blissful that he was alive again, Gwendolyn grabbed hold of his face and kissed his lips with hungered anxiety. Thomas pulled her body in closer and opened her mouth with his tongue. Slow, tempered searching turned fanatical and immersed.

Breaking away from the vortex, he breathed, "Hold me tight, love... good, now lean away."

Gwendolyn did what was she was told, draping her arms encircling his neck, declining...*and oh God*...his hot mouth on her breasts gratified her in ways too wonderful for words. The silkiness of his tongue on her skin, the gentle tenderness, both foundling and appetite of his starved need, caused her to cry out for mercy.

With one hand gripping her rear, the other searched the smooth triangle of hair between her legs. Opening up her threshold with his finger, he found a greeting of moist acceptance for the other finger that entered. "Oh God," he exhaled, "So tight, so sweet…my sweet, sweet girl."

Feeling absolutely scorched from his cajoling words, Gwendolyn met his wide-open mouth with vehemence and felt Thomas insert another finger directing her rhythm. Instinctively, her hips began to move into the sensation, trying to capture its pleasure, liquefying her intention to pure honey.

"Keep moving," he urged, "Don't stop."

Gwendolyn followed his instructions and felt a rush of limitless satisfaction between her thighs. My wonderful teacher, she thought while riding him intensely. Thomas' tireless hot mouth continued to devour her breasts while Gwendolyn found herself reaching a pinnacle of rapture she had not felt since last with him.

"Did that feel good?" Thomas murmured, gently nibbling her lips.

"Oh yes," Gwendolyn hummed happily, running her hands through his hair. She then gazed down at his penis rubbing up against her stomach. It engorged to a point where it seemed painful. She laid her head down on his shoulder and began to cry. It seemed so unfair.

Thomas felt her body quiver and sniffling in his ear, "What is wrong, Gwendolyn? Tell me…did I hurt you?"

Gwendolyn gently pulled back and kissed him freely on the lips once more. "Oh no, Thomas…it is just, you were so tender and considerate of me, and you haven't—"

"How's your strength?"

"Why?"

"Because your pleasure isn't over."

Gwendolyn giggled deep in her throat while Thomas lifted her up and then brought her down onto the bed. Vertical with him was good… horizontal with him was even better. To watch his strong aroused male body kneeling at her feet—was quite thrilling. Lightened masculine hair surrounded his robust thighs, chest, arms and infected her with lust too concentrated to ignore. "Oh God, what can I do to pleasure you?"

Thomas soaked in her curves, the plumpness of her crest, her smooth midriff and leaned down to press his lips on the base of her ankle. How many nights had he envisioned her lying on his bed? And now, here she was, naked, and wanting him, bussing her calves, her inner thighs, kissing her until his breath hovered over the triangle of bottom curls, he respired, "Say that you are mine."

Gwendolyn arched her back and bucked up her hips in anticipation of his unknown attack. "A dare?" She avowed, closing her eyes from his tongue on her sensitive flesh inside her navel.

"I dare you to resist me."

Gwendolyn gazed down at his head between her thighs and ran her fingers through his hair, tilting her own head backwards, chuckling. "Do I dare?" she cried, feeling her pleasure erupting once more.

"My sweet girl, you are mine Gwendolyn, say that you are mine... that you were always mine."

Gwendolyn felt a second arch of gratification invading through her stomach. She surrendered to the feeling and felt Thomas release his pressure, his mouth trailing towards her navel, leaving a track of moisture back up to her neck. Thomas covered her body with his and opened her entrance with his knees. Feeling the intensity of him... the power of his male dominance...laterally meeting her submission, Gwendolyn panted with expectancy.

"Are you mine, Gwendolyn?"

Gwendolyn opened up her eyes and stared into his doubt—his manhood, on the cusp of occupation. "Are you mine, Thomas?"

He met her question with a measured kiss that spiraled down to the center of her torso. Grabbing his head as he met her mania, he impelled his breadth into her...He was filling her now, and—*oh God,* as her head jerked back—he was thicker than she memorized, his aggression extremely gratifying. She maintained her clasp and felt him drive his point home, gently pulling her hair, squeezing her shoulders and hips down to meet his tempo.

Thomas cupped a breast and brought his scalding mouth down around it, kneading, licking, absorbing, and sending Gwendolyn to absolute lunacy. "I haven't touched her since your advent," he inhaled, pinching her nipple with his thumb and forefinger, "Is that what you wanted to hear?"

"Yes," she pulsated, "yes, that will do."

Thomas lifted his weight up then pulled out resting on his knees, "Then say it Gwendolyn...state what I have waited to hear."

His body left hers? *Oh God,* she wanted that indulgence back, why did he abandon her depths? Gwendolyn's arms lunged for his backside and Thomas grabbed her hands and locked them over her head, his persuasive dominance daringly coming into play.

Gwendolyn smiled inwardly; she liked how he improved very much. She felt her back arching when Thomas suddenly lunged forward and kissed her so deeply, her toes tingled and curled. Then abruptly, his mouth lefts her and he outlined the shape of her breasts with his tongue, licking and teasing her flesh, hardening their little nubs. Moaning with delight, she revealed, "You have gone to the devil."

He grinned and positioned his throbbing rod next to her thigh, "Where were we?"

Gwendolyn tilted her head back in madness, "I don't know—let my hands go so I can feel you."

"Not until you say the words."

"Now who's the tease?"

"Are you mine, Gwendolyn?" He inquired, releasing his hands to cup her hips, holding her in place to feel more of his wrath as he buried himself into her moist warmth yet again.

"I have always been yours Tommy," she expressed, meeting his sinful mouth and riveting invasion, *"Always..."*

CHAPTER 20

"*Y*a look sae peaceful, wit' a smile embraced to yar face, twas afraid to wake ya."

Gwendolyn sprung up from bed and yanked the sheet over her upper body. Thank God she was wearing her nightgown now and doesn't recall putting it back on, and when did she find her own bed? Had it all been a dream? Or a wonderful unforgettable delusion? She remembered walking on the ship, had she dreamt the bedding as well?! "Wh—what are you doing here Charles? How'd you get in here?"

Charles sat up and began to pace in front of her, "Och now, I'm a simple farm boy and dinna mind sleeping in hay wit' the horses."

"You mean to tell me you slept in the stables last evening?"

"Aye," Charles confirmed, meeting her anger.

"Why Charles? You said you would wait for me at The Quail Inn."

"Because I dinna trust the mon…Yar me lass, Gwendolyn, and no mon in his right mind wood allow his fiancée tae spend the night under the roof of another mon. Tis yar last eve in this house, yar leaving wit me now."

"I am not going anywhere Charles."

"I beg tae differ—" He exclaimed, reaching out and plopping her over his wide shoulders.

Gwendolyn punched his backside, "Let me down you big gorilla —let me down!"

Charles walked around the room and yanked up her belongings that he had already packed within his free hand. "Not till I get ya tae the carriage."

Gwendolyn began to panic and continued to hit him, "Charles McMillen, if you do not let me down right this instance, I will not marry you!"

"I will take me chances lass," he uttered, strolling down the staircase unnoticed with her still on his shoulders.

When Gwendolyn was placed in the carriage she was mortified to see that Phyllis was already inside. "Phyllis? What are you doing here?"

"I am sorry malady, but I tend to agree with Mr. McMillen," she gingerly voiced, waiving the divorce decree in front Gwendolyn's discouragement. "They were sent at dawn by messenger."

"B—but, you told me to stay here, you told me to get to know him."

"I know, I know child, I did say that. But he is no good for you. He is arrogant and disreputable and Mr. McMillen has been nothing but honorable. He is the better choice."

Gwendolyn was furious. "Why not let me decide who the better choice is?" She began to sit up only to be impelled back to her seat by the moving carriage. "We're leaving?" She asked panic-stricken.

Charles grabbed hold of her nightgown from behind; Gwendolyn had tried to escape through the window. "Aye Gwendolyn, and as soon as we get tae Kettlewell, yar gunna marry me."

"I cannot believe you are abducting me!" Gwendolyn exclaimed off the top of her lungs. I did not even get to say goodbye..." She pouted, feeling a surge of tears swelling her eyes.

Phyllis grabbed her hand, "But you did deary…"

Gwendolyn looked at her with heart-rending grief. "Phyllis, what are you talking about?"

"I wrote a goodbye letter to the Duke of Norwin."

"What!"

* * *

THOMAS ALREADY KNEW WHAT MARRIAGE WOULD BE LIKE to Gwendolyn, they were already good friends—he sought out her ideas, opinions, thoughts, humor, she was his counterpart. But last night, Gwendolyn gave Thomas a glimpse of what bedtime would entail and it only augmented his desire to be with her. They fell asleep in each other's arms and he never wanted to let her go. But just before dawn, he dressed her and carried her back to her own bed. He had to do the proper thing. Had to sever his tie with Katrina foremost, then he could continue to live a life with his wife, as it should be…as it should have been.

"Mrs. Hornebrook, has the Duchess come down for breakfast yet?" Thomas asked wide-eyed and joyful only having gotten back earlier that morning from leaving into town to speak with Katrina, but she had still been resting.

Mrs. Hornebrook had been cooking all morning, and it was nearing afternoon tea. "No sir, I have yet to see *Her Grace*. She is usually up early in the mornings. Quite odd not to see her." She then turned to Fitzwater, who entered that very moment. "Fitz, did you see *Her Grace* this morning?"

Fitzwater nodded his head, "No Madame, I have not." Thomas met their meddlesome eyes. "When you do," he declared, "Let her know I wish to speak to her at dinner. Prepare a private supper this evening Mrs. Hornebrook, there is something I wish to discuss with the Duchess."

"Very well, sir."

Fitzwater watched his employer leave on his heel before

sprinting towards Mrs. Hornebrook. "What do you think of that Madame? Was that a slip of the tongue?"

"I think our Tommy has finally seen the light," Mrs. Hornebrook rejoiced, grabbing Fitzwater and hugging the breath out of him.

An hour later, Thomas was standing by the gate to the Hale residence once more. Heart thumping too fast to figure out, he contemplated how to tell her. What was he going to say? He did not want to hurt her. Katrina had been a loyal and accommodating mistress for a period of time. How do you tell someone you do not want to marry them? Purposely break their heart. Erase all their hopes and dreams for the future with your withdrawal and second thoughts. There was definitely going to be some tears no doubt; maybe a shattered vase or two, unquestionably some name calling, maybe even some of those wonderful swear words she had picked up at the docks.

"Why Thomas, I was just at the manor coming to fetch you," Devin replied, patting his friend on the back with a fond greeting. "And here you are at my doorstep."

"Good day, friend," Thomas greeted him soberly.

"Come to see Katrina?" Devin asked, amazed. "Because if it is nothing pressing, I would like to bring you good news."

"Good news?" Thomas asked intrigued.

"The *Junia* has been found," Devin stated proudly. "She has been seen coasting off the shore of Mizen Head on her way towards Britain."

Thomas could not believe it! After all the years, all those wasted years of searching for her, the *Junia* simply drifts into port and was handed to him on a silver platter? "That's wonderful news Devin, simply wonderful!"

"More good news Thomas, the divorce decree has been completed and has been delivered to the manor with your seal and implementation," he pronounced proudly, "The wedding can go forward as planned."

Thomas felt a lump in his throat. The decree had been delivered to the manor, that's good…then he can have a private supper with Gwendolyn, tell her that he loved her and they can renew their vows. "I must speak to Katrina," he quickly mouthed, "Is she home?"

"Yes Thomas, I believe she is," Devin quickly replied, handing Thomas a letter. "Here, Mrs. Hornebrook gave this to me as I arrived. I took the liberty of receiving it."

Thomas gazed down at the letter and did not recognize the wax stamp, his heart dropped to the pit of his stomach. Gazing up at Devin one last time, he ripped open the seal.

Thomas, I do not regret our time together; in fact, I will cherish it through the end of time. I must confess that I am having second thoughts, so I am leaving for Yorkshire to see our daughter. Upon my arrival, I will write to keep you abreast of my future aspiration. Accordingly, I have taken the divorce decree with me. Gwendolyn

THOMAS LOOKED AT HIS FRIEND WITH PANIC-STRICKEN eyes, "We must get to Bristol immediately—I need to alert Fitzwater— I need to send a letter to Yorkshire."

"Yorkshire, why?" Devin asked suspicious.

"Gwendolyn has left, and I need to—" Thomas closed his mouth and searched his friends eyes, "I need to speak to your sister alone."

Devin narrowed his eyes, "I do not think so friend, we need to head out to port. The *Junia* might elude us; we need to get to her before she sets sail."

CHAPTER 21

Thomas stood on the dock's edge and focused on the haunting ship before him. On any given day, he would have been in awe of her, the *Junia* was the biggest merchant vessel of her time. Built to carry wealth from a variety of other countries, she was a supreme prize for a pirate to gain control. Compared to the Dutch flute, the 700-tonner measured 160 feet along her main deck and 34 feet at the beam. Between her flamboyant beak head and golden stern, she packed enormous potential firing power, but his father never carried cannons, he was a merchant trader, therein exposed to pirate confine. A round stern, broad-beamed and flat-bottomed, the Junia was well renowned in English waters and Thomas was utterly surprised she had berthed at this juncture.

Having alerted the magistrate beforehand, the two men inconspicuously began their stride up the floorboard. Thomas headed left, while Devin right, when the duo whipped their heads around simultaneously realizing the other was not behind—and bumped bodies. Thomas grabbed Devin's coat and pulled him aside, comically shaking a fist at him. In the corner of his eye he noticed the *Junia's* glorious sails out in full splendor being inspected by the ship hands. She was about to set sail again and Thomas gave her the respect she deserved, appreciative of her first-class grandeur. Three slender masts would soar skyward: her tiny skysails would be let loose, next would come her royals, then under those, her topgallants. Underneath the topgallants would fly her wind taut topsails and mainsails, and out puffing sideways from the tips of her yards would be tiers of studding sails. *She was magnificent...*yet upsetting. His family perished aboard this ship. The last time he set foot on her was the night he nearly died. Thomas lowered his eyes and watched the men near the quarterdeck hoisting down crates with the emblem of the Crown. He turned to look at Devin who was noticing the same crime.

"Thomas, the *Junia* is smuggling gold?" Devin asked, hushing down his voice.

"Looks that way; we must find a way to alert the magistrate from here."

"Thomas, look out!" Devin yelled, watching in horror as a sailor hit Thomas over the head with a small wooden plank.

Both knocked unconscious, the two men were tied up, gagged and sent to a cell beneath the lower deck.

When Thomas awoke, he instantly knew where he was—the magazine storeroom—only his father never used to carry canons and ammunition and this particular area was stocked full. He turned to his friend and eyed him trying to get his knots loose. He motioned for him to turn around so he can aid him with his teeth and after a few moments of restrained accomplishment, Thomas finally untied Devin's gag.

"We're moving Thomas," Devin immediately declared, tearing at Thomas' gag with his own teeth.

Thomas freed himself of the bind and spat out the restriction, "I know."

"So we are headed out to sea?"

"Seems that way."

"Katrina will be upset."

"Katrina was going to be shaken anyway," Thomas managed to say without looking Devin in the eye.

"Why?"

Thomas met Devin's hostility, "Because I was going to break my pledge."

Devin tried to get up on his knees but was unable to from the tense chains that bound him to the floor, "Why you filthy—rotten —scoundrel! I will tear your head off! Cut you down to size, you bloody bastard!"

"Seems I should have left your gag on," Thomas replied, trying to alleviate the tension.

"You compromised my sister for months, Thomas—and I have been such a fool; I should have insisted your marriage from the very beginning! I allowed your continual liaison because I knew you would do right by her! And now, this bird flies back into your life and openly flirts with you and you're willing to throw away *loyalty* for a wench you haven't seen since you were a lad?"

Thomas bowed his head in shame, "Yes," he voiced regretfully, "I did compromise your sister and I feel unwell because of it. Your sister has been a good companion and I will always care for her. But," Thomas voiced, feeling humbled at the moment, "I never allowed myself to love her."

Devin was livid, "Who said anything about love?! Why, there are countless marriages thriving without it, literally hundreds of lonely wives out there searching for comfort; case in point, Evelyn Moore for one, why I don't know where I'd be without her sharing my bed."

Thomas met Devin's anger and tried to solicit compassion, "And you would have allowed your sister to become one such lonely wife?"

Devin tried to compose himself, "Yes! No."

Thomas lowered his head, "I love her Devin…I'm in love with Gwendolyn."

Devin calmed down, and shook his head, "Nonsense Thomas, no one falls in love that fast."

"Remember when we were twenty and you were infatuated with Lady Anne of Fellows? I remember when you would have done anything to be by her side, including kissing her feet and the ground she walked on. Well, that is how I feel about Gwendolyn, only my obsession for her goes beyond the physical…I would love her even if she had no feet a' tall."

"You are breaking my heart Thomas," Devin stated mocking him.

"I have always loved her is that so hard to believe?"

Devin sat back down onto the ground and bowed his head, "Yes," he spat out angry, "no," he said instead, bobbing his head up and down. "I knew it," he replied, yanking the chains with him as he tried to stretch out his limbs. "I knew it the moment I walked into the library and saw you two together. The way you looked at her Thomas, I have never seen you look at another female that way —and I have been your partner in many a female raid."

Thomas grinned, "Yes, you have been just like a brother to me Devin, and you know me well enough to know that what I say is the truth. My intentions were worthy when I thought Gwendolyn was deceased, but now that she is alive, how can I walk away from the one person I have always dreamed of being with?"

"Never thought I'd hear another man spew sonnets of love for his lady fair."

Thomas and Devin tried to focus on the voice approaching in the darkness, gasping at the sight of a man coming into view; he was small but hefty and unaffected by their predicament.

"Sir, you are intruding on a private conversation," Devin demanded of the stranger.

"My ship," he stated in his baritone voice, sitting down on a chair just outside the steel bars.

"My ship," Thomas retorted.

"Your ship?"

"The *Junia* was stolen ten years ago, sir; and I am here to retrieve it."

The man bellowed off the top of his lungs, "And it seems yer in a very good position to accomplish the task!"

Thomas' blood began to boil.

Devin sat unfazed, "And you are?"

"Captain Hummel."

"Hummel Hobart, the notorious pirate?" Devin asked in shock.

"Everyone gets my name mixed up. It's Hobart Hummel," he corrected, puffing on his pipe.

"Last I heard, you turned privateer," Thomas included.

"Aye, the very one."

"You stole my ship Captain Hummel and when we return to Britain, I will make sure King George hangs you for the murders of my family."

He puffed on his pipe before staring straight at Thomas, "Young Hollinger?"

"And the Duke of Norwin, now I demand you let us go!"

"Heard stories yew were alive, lad, but it was not I. Oh, I was on the ship when yer family perished though, but under the direction of Captain Porter."

"Captain Porter!" Thomas yelled angry, "But I spoke to Captain Porter on his death bed. He said that the pirate Red Retropé was responsible."

Again, the bandit laughed at the simplicity of the explanation, "Aye, how noble of him to confess his crimes. Captain Porter *was* Red Retropé, his name merely spelled backwards with French stimulus."

Thomas gaped at the stranger and then closed his eyes, feeling foolish to his proven point. "He lied to me, even on his death bed, he lied."

With a chortle still in his scratchy voice, Captain Hummel said,

"He contrived his story of vengeance upon the Hollinger's because he needed usage of the vessel to smuggle trade for King Louis XVI."

"My family died for that futile obese monarch?"

"Aye."

Thomas bowed his head in disbelief. "And how is it that you have the *Junia*?" He asked suspiciously.

"Mutiny, son," he remarked ominously, "and noble diversion to gain entrance to French waters."

Thomas did not understand. "Why?"

"To retrieve me daughter."

"Daughter?" Devin asked now.

"Aye, I too hold devotion to a woman, only this beautiful creature is me one and only offspring. Seven years, I have waited for her to become free. Since that black-heart Bonaparte has been off fighting his many wars throughout Europe, I plan to take back what's mine."

"And what of the smuggling we found happening at port?"

"No smuggling on this ship, just a threat to elude questioning eyes."

"And what is to become of us?" Thomas asked sternly.

"I will use yer peerage to me advantage."

"And if we refuse?" Devin questioned harshly.

"Then suffer the same consequence as the Hollinger clan," he barked, staring Devin in the eyes.

Thomas and Devin both shot looks at one another. "When we get to France," Thomas voiced firmly, "you will surrender the *Junia*?"

"I never agreed to that...but I will agree to yer safe freedom."

"On French land!" Devin howled, flabbergasted.

"Or do yew prefer salmon?"

"What does salmon have to do with anything?"

"We're on our way to Kristiansand, lad."

"Norway! Whatever for?"

"Fish, son; have to keep up the merchant trade, then back to Le Havre."

Thomas closed his eyes and rested his head on the wall in back of him. *Three months?* It would take nearly three months up to Norway then to France back to English shores, three long months without seeing Gwendolyn. Even a minute felt like an eternity. "What do you want us to do?"

"Go to Versailles and demand yer cousin passage back to Britain."

Thomas perked up with assuredness, "And who is my supposed cousin?"

"Lady Anne of Fellows."

"Hold her Charles, hold her," Phyllis demanded, walking with him, pulling up her skirts and rushing him inside the cottage.

Mary had been playing outside when she caught sight of the carriage and ran behind to greet it. Alarmed at the sight of her mother within Charles' arms, she shrieked, "What is wrong with Mummie? Why is she like that?"

At ten years of age, Mary Hollinger was a striking child. With long black ringlets surrounding a heart shaped face, her gripping green eyes commanded immediate notice. "Hush now dear, don't you worry; your mother just needs some bed rest." Phyllis goes to her side and pats down Mary's hair, shoulders and motions for Charles to walk with Gwendolyn up the staircase. "Take her to her room Charles, lay her down on the bed, I will get Dr. Peabody."

Mary pounced on the steps behind Charles, "What is wrong with her? What is wrong with Mummie? If someone does not tell me *now*, I am going to resort to violence."

"Dinna go worrying yar little head lassie, yar mother will be fit as a fiddle in a coupla days," Charles reassured her, making his way towards Gwendolyn's room.

He laid her onto the bed and instantly knew something went terribly wrong. Gwendolyn's hair was damp from continued sweat, her tresses pasted to her face, neck and shoulders. She was burning with fever the moment they arrived back in Kettlewell. Gwendolyn could barely stand and fainted on her way out of the carriage.

Mary flew to her mother's side and held her hand, "Oh Mummie, please, please wake up, please do not die. What will I do without you? I will be all alone, please Mummie, please." Mary buried her head into her mother's breast and felt Gwendolyn's hand reach for her head.

"My darling daughter," Gwendolyn barely spoke, "Get me some water."

Mary immediately reacted and ran towards the vanity. Pouring her mother a cup of water, she ran back with it and aided the drink to Gwendolyn. "Here Mummie, now gently, there now, drink Mummie, drink."

"You do...you do look like him," Gwendolyn breathed, trying to reach out to touch Mary's cheek but fell short of doing so.

"Like who? Oh Mummie!" Mary rested her mother's head back down on the pillow and watched in horror as Gwendolyn closed her eyes and seemed to drift back to stillness. "Mr. McMillen, why is Mummie like this? Why is she so hot?"

Charles scooped off his cap and held it in front of him, "Unsure child, we all ate the same food, slept in the same inns on the way home...and yar mum, yar mum twas the only one tae come down with the fever."

"Then she is ill then? She needs a cool cloth to her head? That's what Mummie does for me when I don't feel well," Mary stated, running towards the basin again. She pulled out a nappy from within a drawer and submerged it in the water. Wringing it twice within her hands, she hurriedly went back to Gwendolyn and gently placed it across her mother's forehead. "I love you Mummie,

I am going to take care of you," Mary whispered tenderly brushing aside locks of hair that adhered to her cast.

"That's so sweet of ya Mary, yar mum loves ya so," Charles remarked, feeling guilty for being so selfish in his haste to make Gwendolyn his wife. "I shouldna taken her," he gushed, feeling his heart soften, "Shouldna left her there."

CHAPTER 22

Captain Hummel instructed his men to set his prisoners free, insisted the two men have supper with him to discuss the plan to free his daughter. Devin was released first, while Thomas was still bound and chained. As soon as his hands were free however, Devin immediately punched Thomas square in the gut.

"That was for getting me into this mess," Devin sneered, and then punched him again only this time, between his legs. "And that was for my sister." Thomas hunched over and fell to his knees; Devin counted to five and then came directly to his aid helping him back up to his feet wrapping both arms around his shoulders.

"Well warranted," Thomas heaved, trying to find his bearings.

Laughing off the top of his lungs, Captain Hummel patted the two lords on their backs as he approached. "I must say lads, I do get a kick out of watching yew two destroy yerselves." Captain Hummel shoved the two men in front of him playfully, but then Thomas and Devin turned around firm, erect and stared the Captain down. "Oh my, yew lads are tall. Six foot, three? Four?

Aye?" He questioned, shifting looks from one to the other, "Come —come, let's eat—I bet yew boys are famished."

Inside the first class dining room, Devin noted that the area was planned for meals taken in heavy seas: benches were set in the walls; bottles and glasses were held in racks. Captain Hummel had a generous meal prepared for the three, with roasted meats, hot bread and fresh fruits with an endless supply of rum and wine.

The three of them were in good spirits, until Captain Hummel shed some light on the past. Captain Hummel was no lord. After losing his wife to typhoid, he promised his love that he would take care of their only child. He wanted the best in life for his little girl, giving her everything she ever wanted on a seaman's salary. Practically raising her aboard ship, he felt Anne required more than merely sea life. She was oftentimes alone, and at eighteen, Captain Hummel decided that he would arrange a mock title for his daughter and present her properly.

Anne was a raving beauty, with dark brown hair and eyes of jade. Stealing practically every bachelor's attention her first season out, Captain Hummel knew he would have no worries for his daughter catching a husband. Several bachelors approached her, but none as smooth and debonair as Monsieur Antoine Bruneau. Captain Hummel instantly warmed up to his knowledge of the sea and Anne could not take her eyes off him. Thinking the gent was going to propose to his lovely daughter, Captain Hummel granted Monsieur Bruneau a moment alone with Anne. The scoundrel took advantage of the freedom however, and kidnapped Anne as a substitute. Captain Hummel was livid, incensed, he had never encountered a man with such devious intentions and he was once part of a notorious pirating brigade! Unable to set foot on French land due to a bounty on his head, Captain Hummel last heard that his daughter was a house servant for the Empress Josephine.

Devin could not believe what he was hearing. *What irony!* What a quirk of fate! One his way to France to free the Captains daughter only to be given free passage towards Monsieur

Bruneau's intended doom? He *would* kill him and as soon as he laid eyes on the slimy weasel, he was going to slice off his tongue, making sure the suave Frenchman would never seduce another young maiden for the rest of his wretched life.

"Have yew ever wondered lad what exactly ensued that fateful eventide?" Captain Hummel eerily asked Thomas who was in mid drink.

"Undoubtedly," Thomas quietly voiced, sipping the rest of his rum. "Yer brothers gave up such a fight. The elder one managed to untie his knots and grabbed a blade from one of the men and stabbed four men in their guts wit' it."

Thomas' eyes grew wide and so did Devin's, both men contained by incomprehension over the Captain's recollection.

"Good, glad to hear Jordan did not go willingly," Thomas haughtily stated, stabbing his own knife into the wooden table.

Captain Hummel concentrated on the vertical utensil piercing through his cherished mahogany. "None of yer brothers went willingly, lad. Only yer fathers. Guess they had to appear dignified, even at the very end."

Thomas closed his eyes and felt a rush of responsibility, the rum rapidly numbing his senses and certitude. "Yes," he agreed, taking another swallow. "Both gentry were arrogant, proud men."

"Did yew know lad, that yer mother's haggled their bodies for the lives of their two youngsters?"

Thomas sat agape. He tried to contemplate what he just heard...he might have been mistaken. "What?"

"Yer death was prevented by a proposition of sorts."

Captain Hummel could not have said anything more menacing to Thomas, he sat up straight, leaned in towards the man and was about to throttle him. "How dare you tarnish the memory of two respectable women—take that back—or I swear I will use that knife and slit your bloody throat with it!"

Captain Hummel gulped, but sat confident in his chair. "Tis the truth lad...Both women, a picture of perfection in their expensive ball gowns and refinement, most of the men had not been wit' a wench for the past several months, let alone a female as patrician as those two beauties. Captain Porter was infatuated wit' the redhead and wanted to keep her for himself. The other raven temptress traded herself for the goodwill and safekeeping of her son and his bride. Captain Porter agreed, and decided to keep yew alive and drop yew off on a deserted isle somewhere. He was just about to take the redhead down to the nearest bedding cabin when a wave of green sea rushed over the sheer, lifting and capturing both women to their deaths."

Thomas and Devin rose from their seats and lunged towards Captain Hummel. Thomas got to the man first and wrapped his hands around his throat, choking, squeezing as hard as he could. Devin came up from behind Captain Hummel and yanked at his hair, exposing his gullet for easier access. The Captain's eyes began to bug out as he tried to rip away Thomas' hands from his throat.

"Do you think he is telling the truth, Thomas?" Devin asked, grabbing the knife with his other free hand and holding it to the old man's throat.

Captain Hummel repeatedly tried to clear his gullet, "I will tell yew what happened," he strained against Thomas' grip, "If yew release yer grip and cease from pulling me hair!"

Thomas gazed down at the man; he was aging, yes, his voice the only powerful asset left in the mature buccaneer. Thomas let loose his strong grip on the man's craw, but Devin remained steady with the blade still under his chin.

"Haven't yew ever wondered how yew escaped the assassinations?" He voiced, coughing, heaving air into his lungs. "Yew was a Hollinger. One and all on board were supposed to perish."

"Gwendolyn and I were left alone," Thomas replied, gritting his teeth. "I remember coming up deck to find all hands vanished into thin air."

Thomas nodded to Devin to lower his threat and Devin

complied. The two men stood like soaring statues on either side of the Captain however, their long arms across their broad chests, rigid and ready for battle.

"As soon as Captain Porter realized what happened, he ordered the first mate to go down to the Great Cabin to retrieve the newlyweds."

Thomas' breath quickened, so far, the only person he saw that morning was...*Ralph,* the captain's first mate. "Go on."

"The first mate went down below to seize the children when another wave came over the bow and washed away a few more men. Captain Porter was distracted by the storm coming on so suddenly, he ordered the sails let down and the rest of the crew below deck."

So far, Thomas thought, he was accurate about the events that took place that day, "Continue."

"...Well, Ralph went down below and peeked in through the door. Inside, the children were asleep, resting peacefully wit' their arms around each other; broke his heart to see them so innocently unaware. He had a child of his own; it pained him to know that they would die. Instead, he closed the door, alerted them, and instructed them to stay in their cabin until he could loosen a rowboat to get them to safety. Ralph went back up deck to report to Captain Porter that the children escaped and the Captain believed him. Captain Porter was not concerned about the children; he was more concentrated on the *Junia*. The ship was a prized scale and he did not want to lose her. Ralph ran back down to the Great Cabin to find the children disappeared."

Thomas' eyes grew wide—he was flabbergasted. How did this man know everything that happened that evening? In such vivid detail, how on earth could he have known? Eyeing Captain Hummel more clearly now, he surveyed his long hair clubbed together, his extensive beard covering most of his face and neck, his clothes clean but worn. *He was familiar now...dear God,* why hadn't he seen it before? "It was you?" Thomas managed to ask before turning away from him.

Captain Hummel eyed Thomas gazing out the beveled glass. "Aye lad, me Christian name is Ralph Hobart Hummel; I use my middle name for bootlegging purposes."

Thomas eerily spoke below his normal tone, "You saved my wife, Ralph."

Captain Hummel eyed Devin who was still stiff beside him. Devin sneered at the man, but was now more concerned for his friend. "Aye... she was without help, crying and trying to hold onto the ratlines," he called to mind, turning away from Devin's intimidation and eyeing Thomas on the other side of the room now. Thomas was gazing out the beveled glass towards the ocean and he tried to solicit his compassion. "The wind was cruel that morn, brushing her easily aside. I came up behind her and grabbed her grip away from the ropes, carrying her off towards the stern ladder. We jumped onto the rowboat that was already hoisted down and quickly rolled away. We were afloat no more than a coupla hours when the waves pushed us into another British vessel."

"I—I do not know how to thank you."

"Saving me daughter will do."

CHAPTER 23

Two months identical, sixty days of waiting and wondering if Gwendolyn would get stronger but no change, she was still weak, still incoherent, still burning with fever. Gwendolyn would jerk back and forth, to and fro, and then spring from the bed to the washbasin to vomit only to fall back to bed practically unconscious. Phyllis would get excited for a split second then watch in fright as Gwendolyn would fall back to sleep.

Charles too, was very worried about her. Bless his heart; the man was just too kindhearted by far. Between herself and Charles, the two of them would alternate shifts and stand vigil at Gwendolyn's bedside, Charles in the early morning and Phyllis late at night; coming to her aid when Gwendolyn happened to stir or twitch.

"Dr. Peabody, what is your diagnosis?" Phyllis asked impatiently, pacing out in front of him.

"Some kind of extensive fever, Miss Tallyman, could be yellow fever, comes on so suddenly and consumes a person," he stated in a cold austere tone.

"Yellow feva!" Charles exclaimed, running his hand through his hair in frustration.

The doctor gave a quick look at Charles kneeling by Gwendolyn's bedside before continuing, "The fever needs to break, surround her in ice, strip her of her clothing, and make sure she is kept cool without delay. I will return in two days to see if there is any improvement."

Phyllis huffed at the sight of his departure. Country doctors! Oh what she wouldn't give to be back in London! She hated Dr. Peabody's unaffected treatment, only applying his talents to persons who were dying or bloodied. What about Gwendolyn? What is to become of her sweet charge?

"I will take the mornin' shift again Miss Tallymen."

Phyllis rushed to Gwendolyn's other side and with a cold cloth she compressed it to her temple. Surveying her body lying there, she shook her head in frustration. "Nonsense Charles, we will rotate our care, like we done before."

"Do ya think she will die?"

"Shush your mouth Charles McMillen, no one's gonna die." Charles stood over Gwendolyn like a protective parent. He wiped off her forehead with another cloth, before saying, "The child's very worried 'bout her mum."

"Clearly...as well as the both of us."

Gwendolyn began to stir, but only incoherently. "Thomas..."

Phyllis leaned in over her mouth, "What was that deary? We could not hear you."

Gwendolyn managed to move her head slightly, but then dissolved back into her condition.

Charles brought the cloth down to her shoulders, then at the top of her chest. "I'm so sorry Gwendolyn, this is all me fault. When ya well and realize what happena I hope ya find it in yar heart tae forgive me."

· · ·

THE PASSAGE TOWARDS FRANCE WAS COMFORTABLE AND yet filled with anxiety. Thomas had never been more restless. Gwendolyn was so close, nevertheless, an ocean away. He could have her now; protect her and his daughter from harm, keep her happy in return for her love for him. Oh how he hungered with anticipation of hearing those three simple words. Her physical mind-set shown clearly that night they made love. She was so attentive to his need of tangible contact, she admitted being his, but it still was not enough. Never in his life had he ached for something so critical. His dream of finally holding her in his arms was realized, however, he longed to hear the authentication. Hanging onto her every whim, he hoped to hear her gush her devotion, but instead listened to her talk about her solitude, share her experiences with his daughter after she was born; she even cried in his arms after confessing she bedded her fiancé. It stung him to hear her admission, but what could he do? He was in no position to judge; after all, the same loneliness ran though his veins as well and shed some tears of his own, releasing his past to her. This was not the end; he felt so in his heart, there was still too much to talk about, too much to share. Gwendolyn Drummond had always been his and all will be rectified from this point forward. He would make sure she was permanently owned— showering her with his love until that woman was drenched head to foot.

Two months into the ascent and they hit rough waters pushing them off course. Thomas could not believe his bad luck! He had never come across such ghastly weather, but he held absolute confidence in the *Junia*. Although most British clippers were average in the winds, the Junia had held supreme. With bursts of speed ranging from 20 to 22 knots, the Junia had less curvature from bow to stern, and a lower bulwark with a plumper waist. Bent on all canvas, her lean narrow hull would proudly enter the green sea flawlessly and run westward towards Mauritius, heading north to round the Cape of Good Hope. She could make a voyage crossing the Indian Ocean to China in about four months.

Gwendolyn's eyes finally pop open. Staring out into nowhere she took in a deep breath. Focusing on a rattling sound, she realized it was her teeth. She reached out and grabbed Phyllis who had passed out next to her. Startling her to a degree, Phyllis smiled with relief. "Lord have mercy, you are awake."

Gwendolyn gazed around her and comprehended where she was. *Her bedroom,* she realized looking down at her body, and she was *naked,* with only a thin sheet to cover her torso. She reached down and covered herself up. "What happened?"

"Some kind of fever dear, we have been so worried."

"We?"

"Charles and I."

"Oh," Gwendolyn said, realizing he was not there.

"We have been forcing you to swallow broth but now that you are awake, do you think you can eat something?"

Gwendolyn felt parched, but the thought of food made her queasy. "No, I—" she managed to say, rubbing her tummy, "Perhaps some water?"

Phyllis stood up and hobbled over to the vanity. Pouring Gwendolyn a cup, she marched back over to her side. "Here dear, now drink up, I will send up some food. Perhaps some dry toast, or protein dear, perchance some eggs?"

Gwendolyn thought about her cook's runny cuisine and darted towards the washbasin vomiting into the bowl. *Oh God,* she was so weak, so frail, so...nauseous, and felt her legs beginning to tremble. "Phyllis...how long have I been lying in bed?"

Phyllis grabbed Gwendolyn back and aided her to lie down. "Nearly ninety days dear, I have never seen anything like it."

"Three months?" Gwendolyn shot back up, reaching for her stomach instantly, feeling her inners turn against her. *Oh no... Thomas.* Thomas was to be married within the week and now it was too late. "Phyllis?" Gwendolyn carefully asked, feeling moisture at the back of her eyes, "Have you heard from the Duke?"

Phyllis nodded her head, "No dear, no word from His Grace. Why?"

Gwendolyn doubled over in bed clutching her abdomen in grief and grasped the inevitable. Thomas married that abominable girl; he made his decision and now so should she. There could be only one solution to her obvious condition…she was with child again. Gwendolyn recalled her horrible fever and nausea from Mary's expectancy, and she was experiencing similar symptoms. She had no idea if she missed her monthly courses during her unconsciousness, but she did know for certain that when she left Kettlewell, she anticipated her stream. "Did my monthly flow arrive, Phyllis?"

Phyllis arched her brows and looked curiously at her, "Why no dear, just sweat, repeated wetness from your entire body."

Gwendolyn began to fully weep now, "Why would the Lord grant such gifts if he was not going to give me the man who fathered them?"

Phyllis sat down next to Gwendolyn on the ledge of the mattress, "The man who fathered them? Do you think you are enceinte?"

"Think Phyllis? Oh, I know so! And I have been awarded my departing gift for coming in second."

Phyllis rubbed her leg and tried to console her, "Do you believe His Grace to follow through with his matrimony?"

Gwendolyn wiped away her tears; "I know Thomas…and he would not abandon me without reason. He knows he took advantage of our vulnerability and is probably afflicted with his remorse. He would never relinquish on a pledge of marriage, he is most likely," Gwendolyn paused and allowed her tears to surface and run down her cheeks, "on his way back from the West Indies on his honeymoon."

CHAPTER 24

"Why have you never mentioned her to us before, Thomas?" Devin asked, arriving alongside his friend. "And why is it that no one in London remembers your marriage?"

All morning, Thomas had watched the descent on France with unease. He wanted to get this charade over with so that he could head back to Britain to hold Gwendolyn in his arms. Thomas searched Devin's eyes for compassion before saying, "Because she was mine," he paused, "because I wanted to keep the memory of her sacred, untarnished, with no outside opinions. There were only a handful of acquaintances my father invited to the wedding supper—all quite dead now, then only family on our marriage voyage. The Hollinger's' were going to post an announcement in the papers when we returned from sea."

"Such a tidy little secret," Devin quipped, eyeing Le Havre coming into cloudless view.

"Did you know Devin, that she had her choice of husbands? That Gwendolyn was betrothed to one of us, meaning any four of us, and she chose me over my elder brother?"

"A titled heir?"

"Jordan, yes. Oh, you should have seen him, Devin; outstanding marksman, unparalleled sword-fighter, shrewd, intrepid and witty. He graduated from Pembroke too, and I always wondered why he never married. Why, there were ladies compromising themselves at our door nightly!" He laughed melancholy, "All clamoring to be seen with Jordan in a ruining circumstance."

"Sounds like a man to be envied."

Thomas gazed over at the flying, outer and inner jibs. "Yes, Devin, he was such a man. He was my hero. Until," he faded off, looking away into the distance.

"Until what?" Devin asked gingerly.

"...Until the night my father announced Gwendolyn's betrothal..."

We were asked to come into the library. My father was at the head of his desk, my mother beside him. I was the last one to arrive when I noticed my parents embracing...but that was a normal occurrence in my household, my parents were devoted to one another. I remembered gazing into my mother's eyes when she saw me coming in, her smile so warm, melted my toes. She was a beauty, with her raven tresses surrounding olive green eyes... my eyes, I realized, Jordan and I were the only siblings to have them. We looked like mother, while Philip and Andrew both took after father with dark brown hair and eyes of the same hue.

Puffing on his cigar, my father blew smoke out of his nose first before saying, "The Earl of Suffolkshire has given his daughter's hand to the Hollinger's' in exchange for trade."

My mouth flew open wide; my heart began to pound with a strange irregular ache. Gwendolyn? My Gwendolyn...was to be married?

"Father has asked me if I would do the honors," Jordan said next, "and I am pleased to announce that I will abide by his wishes," he stated convincingly. "After all, Gwendolyn is a fine-looking girl; she will keep my eyes fascinated for quite some time."

I turned to look at Jordan; he was leaning against my father's desk, his boots crossed in unison with his arms across his chest. "What does that mean?" I asked in a trembling voice.

Jordan grinned, "What it means brother is that you will have to refrain from spending so much time with her."

"Jordan," my mother voiced coming to my defense. "They could still be acquaintances; Tommy will still be part of the family."

"But **my** wife," Jordan pronounced in his usual pretentious tone. "Gwendolyn won't be allowed to spend so much free time with Tommy. She will be under my strict charge and I will have her with child without delay."

Did he just say child? That meant…him…and her…Oh, Good, God; I could not stand it…my breath escalated and my pulse beseeched serenity. Gwendolyn…and Jordan? I felt ill, my stomach began to churn and bile crept up my gorge. I wanted to slaughter him, rip him to pieces first—and then slowly kill him. I hated him. I detested that arrogant, self-righteous look on his face! He appeared confident and puffed-up pleased with himself having made such a noble sacrifice of his disreputable bachelorhood.

My father cleared his throat, his voice low and slicing through the tension. "There is still one obstacle to overcome first son, the Earl insists that his daughter have a choice in the matter," he announced in all certainty. "But we all know who she will choose, will we not?" He smiled, walking over to Jordan and patting him on his shoulder.

Her choice? Yes, why not her decision. All the girls faint at the sight of Jordan gazing their way, why not Gwendolyn as well? Jordan was the titled heir, he graduated from Pembroke and he was about to inherit a fortune!

"By the way Andrew, how is it you came upon that black eye of yours?" My father determined, walking over to his third son and raising up his chin.

"Gwendolyn's brother, Nathaniel," Andrew spat out, touching his sore eyebrow. "Cuffs-a-fist and our struggle got out of hand."

"A fist fight?" Jordan marked expertly. "You should have sent for me. I could have shown that boy a thing or two."

"Are we finished here?" Philip asked, rolling his eyes, "There is a book I'd like to close."

"Yes, but do not go very far Philip, we have to leave to Gisleham in a couple of hours," my father stated, pulling around his desk to have a seat.

"To do what?" I asked, standing to my feet.

My mother looked at me with round cautious eyes, "Why, to hear Gwendolyn's decision, Tommy."

I remember closing my eyes, but I do not remember stomping out of there. The next thing I know is running towards the door and vomiting in the nearest washbasin I could find. I fell to the floor and forced my head through my knees. I did not realize how deeply I cared for her until that very moment. The next thing I heard was the door opening and my mother coming to my aid. She knelt down beside me and I flew instantly into her arms. Her warmth and love consoled my insecurity. She caressed the side of my head and ran her fingers through my hair.

"Shush now, don't cry," she whispered against my ear.

I started babbling in between my anguish and she tried to calm me down. "Oh mother—wha—oh God—"

"What is that? I could not hear you."

"I love Gwendolyn."

My mother enclosed the space between us and continued to caress my head. "Of course you do Tommy; I can see it in your eyes when you look at her."

"You can tell? Do you think she knows?"

"That, I don't know, but I am praying she does."

"I'm gonna lose her."

"No son, do not say that."

"Gwendolyn will pick Jordan, I know she will."

"You know I love Jordan, he is my first son, but he is just a little too over-confident sometimes. Gwendolyn is yours, Tommy...she always was and no one will ever convince me otherwise."

"What does that mean 'she is mine'?"

"What it means is that you have to be brave in the next couple of hours. You have to have confidence in her choice."

"She won't choose me, I know she won't. I am her best friend, that's all I have ever been, she barely tolerates me."

I remember my mother laughing, a cute little chuckle, "Sometimes girls like to hide their true feelings. Gwendolyn likes you more than she is willing to expose."

"Do you really think so?"

"Oh, I know so."

I remembered looking into her green eyes and not being very convinced. Three hours later, we were at Gisleham and I had never been more nervous. The family greeted us, but I did not see Gwendolyn anywhere. We were then escorted to the Earl of Suffolkshire's great library and stood in line from eldest to youngest. I could not look up from fear of falling over. My eyes remained on the ground until I saw her enter through the large double doors. She appeared miserable and I wanted to soothe her despair. She acknowledged my presence for just a second but when she passed me completely my heart fell to the ground. When she headed towards Jordan first, water swarmed my eyes and my throat closed up. All sense of time stopped, I could only hear my heart breaking....

I was just about to run back to Wilderbrand when her voice came ringing loud and clear through the thick gel of silence inside my head. "...Tommy," was the only word I seem to hear.

THEN I PICK TOMMY...

After a long bit of stillness, my father cleared his throat before saying, "Are you sure, Gwendolyn?"

"Yes."

"This is for certain?" My mother asked quickly eyeing Gwendolyn's mother who already had her hand over her mouth with surprise.

"Yes," Gwendolyn said yet again.

I watched Jordan stand up straight from his leisurely position. "You pick Tommy?"

Rolling her eyes, she looked away and softly voiced, "Yes."

I blinked back my shock and my heart could calm down now; Gwendolyn picked me…Gwendolyn picked me?

I then watched Jordan amble over to Gwendolyn's side and reached for her shoulders intending on embracing her.

"May I be the first one to welcome our new sister into the family?" Jordan relinquished, locking eyes with Gwendolyn.

She appeared mesmerized by his veneer; he could always do that to a girl. He reached for her hand, but I intercepted it, purposely intertwining her fingers through mine. I stepped in front of her, obligated to protect her always, even from my own brother, who I knew deep down had nothing but the best intentions of receiving her into the family. He must have been insulted, I later realized, groomed to be the chosen one, only to find out unexpectedly, he was never in the race.

Jordan leaned back and then looked down at me, but just barely. I was amazed that I was catching up to him in height; I thought I'd never be as tall as my overshadowing brother. I watched him cock his head to one side, surrendering, "…Allow me to welcome her from afar then," he grinned devilishly, patting me on the back and bringing me in for a congratulatory hug. "The best man won now, didn't he Tommy?" He whispered at my ear, "Treat her well and know that I will always envy you."

Allowing the reality to sink in, I nodded my head in agreement then eyed in the foreground my mother hugging Gwendolyn's mother long and hard. They seemed happy, jubilant, and about to burst at the seams with organization.

I smiled down at Gwendolyn, but she did not smile back at me. She had this blank look on her face when her mother came over and yanked her daughter fast into her bosom.

"I know just the dress for you!" I heard her say then felt the immediate grunts of best wishes and thereafter was besieged by further congratulatory thumps on my back.

"I ENVY YOU TOO THOMAS," DEVIN STATED SHAKING HIS head at his friend's recollection.

"Why?"

"When we get back to Britain, you will have everything you have ever dreamed of."

"Yes, Devin, having a family is all I ever dreamt of."

"You belong with her Thomas and I will not stand in your way of your happiness."

Thomas gazed over at the ship hands about to throw anchor. "That means a lot to me friend."

Devin gazed down at the waves crashing against the hull. "I wanted what was best for my sister; I wanted to call you brother-in-law."

"I know that Devin and for that I truly apologize."

"I realize now that you would have made Katrina miserable, knowing your rightful place was with Gwendolyn," he stated, whisking around and leaning against the brim, his arms across his chest. "Anyhow, I like her."

Alarm bells went off in his head. "How much do you like her?" Thomas inquired, turning around himself and staring straight into his friend's eyes.

"I know you asked me to freeze my attempt at seducing her, but I did try, and before you take a swing at me Thomas, just to let you know, she flat out refused my advances. The chit was not even fazed by my charm, quite intimidating if you must know."

Thomas started laughing, "That's my Gwendolyn for you, unfazed by charisma."

"Well, I am still wounded from that failed effort, having never been turned down before, Gwendolyn is quite rare. I would like to remain friends with her, with your permission, of course."

Thomas raised his eyebrow, "Friends? Why?"

"I do not know exactly," Devin expressed, gazing down at the ground, "Just an unusual feeling I get when conversing with her. I just want to be able to continue our acquaintance."

Thomas gazed out towards the harbor. He trusted his male instincts and knew from past experience that Devin would never betray him when it came to family. Devin was as honorable as he was. "You will always be welcome in our home Devin."

"That means a lot to me Thomas and can I ask you one more question?"

"Certainly."

"Gwendolyn does not have a long lost sister now does she?"

CHAPTER 25

*W*atching the sunset beyond Le Havre, Thomas walked towards the sheer and tried to fathom how Gwendolyn felt when she thought he was dead. She said that she fell to the ground, weeping in her lap; even Ralph confirmed that she had been crying...did that mean she loved him? God, he wished he were certain of her feelings for him, her physical manner compelling, yet deceptive. After making love to her twice more that night, he had never been more certain of a connection. How could Gwendolyn display so much enthusiasm while being intimate with him and then run away?

Thomas continued to walk the level and found himself at the fo'c's'le deck. Standing just under the foremast, he looked out at the sunlight illuminating a triangle on the ocean's depths. Bits and pieces, he thought dejectedly. Gwendolyn had always shown her consideration for him in bits and pieces: Three times noted in the past had he felt her true feelings? Once, when they took her father's cruiser, secondly, on her fifteenth birthday, and lastly on their wedding night.

. . .

It was a 20 ft single-masted vessel, he recalled, the Earl of Suffolkshire's boat owned two bunk cabin's, a small galley and saloon for playing cards or meeting captains in and they went below deck towards her father's saloon. They were twelve that summer and Thomas will always remember it because Gwendolyn was still two inches taller than he. Thomas hated being small. Gwendolyn always encompassed this authoritative presence when he had to be the one to look up to her. She intimidated the heck out of him and Thomas was constantly trying to measure up to her superiority.

Inside, Gwendolyn wanted to show him some objects her father brought back from his recent voyage to China. He remembered being in awe of one specific trophy: a paper fan, when opened revealed a magnificent watercolor seascape of Whampoa Reach, a deep-water anchorage where ships would lie idle as they waited for the new season's tea crop. Ivory objects such as vases, flower boats, flower holders and decorated elephant tusks. Unique wonders from the other side of the world, they thought, and marveled at their intricacies...

"Can you believe this ivory is from an elephant tusk?" Gwendolyn asked, waiving the tube in front of my face. "Have you ever seen anything more beautiful?"

"No, I haven't," I said, continuing to be amazed by the elaborate artwork on the carving; tiny buildings, dwellings, trees, tiny little people, all up and down the remarkable figurine.

"I wonder why father doesn't bring any of this home to show mother," Gwendolyn supposed, fingering the flower holder. "I only found out about it myself when hearing Nathaniel comment to my father about the things he brought back from China."

"I thought you said your mother doesn't come on this boat." "She never does, why?"

"Then what is that?" I asked, pointing to what appeared to be a rather obvious corset hanging in a closet.

Gwendolyn marched over to it and yanked it off the coat rack. She wrapped it around her slender body and waist. "I don't know...maybe she does secretly. Maybe it is a secret rendezvous for my parents." She wondered

again, pulling it away from her waist and leaving it on top of a nearby bed.
"Let's go to the galley. I think there is some sugar cane my father brought
back from South America."

I followed Gwendolyn all over her father's boat that day; we were
carefree, transposed, until we found ourselves up deck to find nothing but
green sea all around us. The ropes had come loose and we drifted away from
port. Gwendolyn started to panic, which made matters worse. She had never
been on a boat before and she didn't know the first thing about sailing. But I
did. Jordan, Philip and Andrew all showed me how to sail. Why, I've known
how to sail since I was five.

I immediately went into rescue mode. Running around and unraveling the
canvas, the sails caught wind and we instantly launched forward. I grabbed
onto the rigging and maneuvered the mainsail and foresail to my advantage,
gliding us towards shore. I remembered gazing over at Gwendolyn, she was
in a huddled position and oh so frightened. But I was not the least bit scared;
I knew exactly what to do. I felt both brave and in control, and when we
reached the harbor and bumped into the pier, Gwendolyn rushed over to me
and hugged me so tight, I could barely breathe. She wrapped her arms around
my neck and cried in my shoulder for the longest time. I had never seen her so
grateful, she made me feel so valiant that day, almost superhuman...

THOMAS HAD NEVER FELT ANYTHING SO POWERFUL
subsequent to the day of her fifteenth birthday. He thought
Gwendolyn was going to introduce him to Joan, Baron Huxton's
daughter. Joan was interested in him, but he was just curious. He
approached the squealing, giggling girls and was about to say
something to Joan when in the corner of his eye, he noticed
Gwendolyn tramping away with Barry Abernathy little by little
after her. His eyes surveyed the room, she was leaving alone? His
heart began to thump in his ears and he stood motionless,
studying Gwendolyn rapidly picking up the pace. Gwendolyn was
heading towards the horse stables, unaccompanied, with Barry
briskly following behind...

. . .

I reached the hangar door in a flash, halting at the sight of Gwendolyn standing beside that bigheaded oaf, Barry Abernathy. He was one of my brother's friends, and I hated him because he thought he was the best swordsman in London. But he was not the best, Jordan was, and right away resentment entered my veins.

And then he touched her. That bastard actually touched Gwendolyn inappropriately? He was about to kiss her and all hell broke loose inside my chest.

I lunged for him and tackled Barry on his arse. His legs flew up over his head and I hit him with all my might. How dare he think he could take what was mine…if anyone was going to touch Gwendolyn improperly it was going to be me! I felt her hands about my back, but I still kept on hitting him. Gwendolyn was trying to pull me off of him and I hated her for interrupting. I wanted to murder him. Destroy him for touching her. Obliterate him for attempting to ruin her.

Before finding my stance, I cursed and spat at him before running away. Gwendolyn was traipsing after me, but I was so upset, I did not feel like talking to her just yet. She made me angry, no; I was infuriated with her for leaving without me and placing herself at risk. Just before I turned around to face her, I noticed Lady Drummond observing the both of us. With one hand over her mouth and the other on her midriff, her eyes were full of conjecture.

Gwendolyn grabbed my shoulders; I spun around to face her. Rage, ache and damage still choking me to death. "What!" I yelled at her. "I don't want to talk to you," and then it hit me. I was suddenly looking down into her shattered eyes. I was taller than her and instantly, I was filled with this overwhelming prominence.

Gwendolyn's mouth opened wide, she was about to mouth out the words…I watched her lips as they shaped. Her first word was 'I', followed by the word 'love', or so I thought. She shut her mouth tight and kept nodding her head. Before I knew it, her arms were wrapped around my shoulders and she hugged me tight. I closed my eyes from her compassionate embrace and draped my arms around her as well. Her expressive body so close to mine, sent shivers up and down my spine. It was so snug a fit, so warm; there were even portions of her I had never felt before. Her bosoms for one thing, just thinking about them pressed against my chest, jutted parts of me.

"Thank you," Gwendolyn whispered in my ear, and then she let go. Oh God she let go! My body wanted that closeness back! Her arms were free of me and I stood frozen watching her run back to Gisleham.

I then eyed her mother, she smiled at me and I stood there and stared at her loveliness. She was a beautiful woman, breath taking, and she appeared to be moved by what she had witnessed...

And then his wedding night...

They had to consummate the marriage, Thomas remembered. Had to "close the deal" per his father's instructions. Otherwise, his father would instruct Jordan to compromise Gwendolyn and the arrangement would be inescapable. Jordan would be Gwendolyn's husband...oh no, no, and no! Thomas had to transform into someone else that night; had to be aggressive in order to make a stubborn girl like Gwendolyn completely cower down. He gave her direction, although a strict order, "you have to do what I say." It was not so hard to do; in fact, it felt quite natural, to be assertive, to be so bold, and Gwendolyn seemed to recoil almost immediately, changing her serious tune...

"Now, I'm going to kiss you," I claimed next, watching her lie still, unprepared. Gwendolyn chose me, and I was going to make damn sure she was stuck with me.

"You are?"

She seemed surprised, but I didn't care, I was on a mission and kissing her first rather than violating her body seemed the proper thing to do and more correct.

Lying on my side, I reached over and cradled her face within the palm of my hand. Rubbing my thumb across her mouth first, I soaked in the reality. She actually let me touch her and my heart expanded with glee. I then leaned into her lure and gently kissed her pucker. Her lips were nice, soft, and gently pressed against mine. I remembered thinking why we never tried this before. We were both certainly at that age where curiosity was our ruler and we could have easily begun this pleasant contact long before our forced matrimony.

She then wrapped her arms about my back and the affect satisfied my need for her approval, her simple caresses caused my lower regions to come alive. She began to explore my shoulders and skin, which made matters intensify. Did she realize what she was doing to me? I could not believe she was actually curious about my body and I began to freely kiss her... everywhere and anywhere. And, good Lord, I could not get enough of her... her delicate touches were making my body do crazy things. I was beginning to think I was going too fast for her, but as soon as I opened up her mouth with my tongue, hers was there to caress back. And, Oh God, the taste of her! She was so sweet, all around supple and my body craved to get even closer. I wanted her naked now and began yanking off her nightgown. Gwendolyn twitched only slightly then helped me take the garment down.

My hands had a mind of their own, come to think of it. Gwendolyn allowed me to explore her unclothed, which was something I thought she would never allow me to do. Up her neck, down her lower back to her buttocks. She was so velvety-soft, so yielding and even allowed me to handle the parts of her that intrigued me the most. Never in my wildest dreams could I have imagined myself being drawn to that part of her anatomy, but I was, and I could not stop touching her breasts. But then I felt her hesitate, which made me stop, as I watched with round eyes her hand reaching up to mine and guiding it back down to her skin. I traced my finger around her nipple and was swelled with emotion.

"Oh God," I whispered, kissing her lips ever so softly, "You are so beautiful Gwendolyn, so sweet, my sweet, sweet girl." Every inch of her was satisfying my senses when I suddenly felt her fingers running through my hair. My male instincts took power and I kissed her intently before doing what my brother said to do. Gwendolyn continued to kiss me back...and, oh God, her wanting me that much, set my plan into action and I entered her quickly. I felt her wince beneath me and I closed my eyes expecting her to retaliate, but she didn't? But I apologized just in case, "I'm sorry...so sorry."

And she said nothing. Just continued to close her eyes and lie there, looking every bit of beautiful...even more so now underneath me, so dear. This was it, my body could not take much more and raw passion exploded. It came on so sudden...could not seem to stop it...when a shuddering release erupted and spread through my body that nearly paralyzed me. I was out of breath; I had never felt anything like that before. Gwendolyn meant everything to me and I could not wait to tell her how much I loved her.

Her arms remained in the center of my posterior, gently caressing my flesh with her fingertips. Savoring the sweet taste of her skin, I closed my eyes in bliss, as she reached up and cupped the back of my head.

I pulled away from her nestle and asked, "Did it continue to hurt?"

"No," she blushed, caressing the sides of my face.

I smiled freely, "Want to do it again?"

She giggled, and then closed her eyes. "I was just thinking the same thing," I heard her say. I then thought about the next three weeks and looked forward to each and every moment spent within her arms. If she wanted, we could stay in bed our whole trip. She brushed back hair that mottled my face and my heart appeared to stop. She was just about to say something, the words I have waited to hear, but cried instead. Tears bunged at her eyes and dripped down the sides of her face. Alarmed, I began wiping the wetness away.

"What is wrong Gwendolyn, tell me," I asked, kissing her tears away.

Gwendolyn wavered and looked deep into my eyes. There it was again... my heart stopped a second time. It was in her eyes, I could feel it, sense it, it was there—I knew it was there! I bent forward and kissed her with all the affection I was feeling at the moment and reopened the passion I felt before. Little did I know, that would be the last time I got to touch her and the memory of this night replayed in my mind over and over wishing it were repeated, but knowing it could never be...

CHAPTER 26

Standing on the dock, on solid ground, Thomas surveyed the many clipper ships anchored at Le Havre, 170 foot, massive beauties. Measuring 33 feet in breadth with a 19 foot depth, the 907 ton ships had jutting stems with a razor-sharp bow that flared out in concave curves. Capable of packing 1,100 tons of cargo, the ship's hulls were full-bodied with a rounded turn of the bilge. Concentrating on that darn red, white and blue American flag waiving in the breeze up above him, Thomas shook his head in defeat. *He had to start building larger ships,* he realized. The bloody Yankees were gaining the lead.

Thomas and Devin were both hesitant to be in France, just a few years prior, the British signed the Treaty of Amiens, thus setting the terms of peace which included the withdrawal of British troops from several colonial territories recently occupied. The peace between France and Britain was uneasy and short-lived. The monarchies of Europe were reluctant to recognize a republic as they feared the ideas of the revolution might be exported to them. In 1805, Britain convinced Austria and Russia to join a Third Coalition against France. Napoleon knew the

French fleet could not defeat the Royal Navy and tried to lure it away from the English Channel in the optimism a Spanish or French fleet could take control of the Channel long enough for French armies to cross and invade England. However, because Austria and Russia had prepared an invasion of France, he had to change his plans and turn his attention to his own country. The newly formed Grande Armée secretly marched to Germany and on October 20, 1805, it surprised the Austrians at Ulm, but the next day Britain's victory at the Battle of Trafalgar meant the Royal Navy gained control of the seas. A year later, Bonaparte would wage economic war with an attempt to enforce a European commercial boycott of Britain calling it the "Continental System". It had little success.

Devin and Thomas immediately transformed into the roles they were about to play. Being well known throughout the ports of France already it was easy to ask questions without bringing on suspicion. Through their many contacts within the maritime realm, the men learned that Anne had been Bruneau's mistress for years but was then discarded for a prettier face. Monsieur Bruneau was a distant cousin to Empress Josephine and Anne had been prepared for one of the Empress' confidants and had been very well guarded.

The Palace of Versailles was a royal chateau, a symbol of the system of absolute monarchy. From 1682, when King Louis XIV moved from Paris until the royal family was forced to return to the capital in 1789, the court of Versailles was the center of political power in France. When Thomas and Devin arrived at the Palace of Versailles, they were detoured by yet another obstacle. Napoleon never stayed there, neither did the Empress and her court and the two lords were then directed to Fontainebleau.

Thomas then met with Captain Andrassy, a chatty man who held high rank in Napoleon's legion. Through him, Thomas learned that there were rumors that Napoleon was in need of an heir and it became apparent that if he were killed, the French Empire would collapse. Through all the chaos of the most major elemental necessity, Napoleon decided to divorce Josephine and she in turn, fled to her chateau at Malmaison.

The Chateau de Malmaison was a country house just about eight miles west of central Paris. Josephine bought the manor house for herself and her husband when he was fighting the Egyptian Campaign. Malmaison was a run-down estate that encompassed nearly 150 acres of woods and meadows. Bonaparte expressed fury at Josephine for purchasing such an expensive house with the money she had expected him to bring back from the campaign. The house, for which she had spent well over 300,000 francs, needed extensive renovations and she spent a fortune doing so. Josephine built a heated orangery large enough for 300 pineapple plants and animals of all sorts were allowed to roam free among the grounds; and, when it was done, Josephine was in the company of kangaroos, black swans, zebras, sheep, gazelles, ostriches, a seal, antelopes and llamas to name a few. After the divorce, Josephine received Malmaison in her own right and remained there until her death in 1814.

Anne was not with Josephine at Malmaison, she was being held back to prepare for the new Empress, Austrian Archduchess, Marie Louise. Thomas and Devin were then sent back to the Palace at Versailles and to the Tuileries palace to meet with the Grand Marshal of the Palace, General Duroc.

General Geraud Duroc, Duke of Friuli, was an agreeable fellow in terms of reputation. He was responsible for the measures taken to secure Napoleon's personal safety, whether in France or on his campaigns and he directed the minutest details of the imperial household. He looked upon Thomas' peerage as an honor to be acquainted with him. He was well aware of the Hollinger Commerce Company and their many vessels created for Britain and the Royal Navy and wanted to strike a deal with its Chief Officer to set up berth in France. Business was business, and with all the rumors floating around that the French would soon flee to British shores, Thomas decided it would be beneficial to his thriving corporation. General Duroc confessed that he was sensitive to Bruneau's mistresses, but was completely unaware that Anne had been stolen from her family. Admirable as he was, General Duroc commanded Anne's release immediately and the two actors entered the French Parliament awaiting Anne's freedom.

"JORDAN!"

Thomas whipped his head around to greet the Yank who apparently thought he was his older sibling. They were standing in an open corridor, lavishly decorated in marble, gold and oddly enough, Roman statutes. As not to bring any further attention to them, General Duroc asked His Grace if he could await Anne's release amongst the other foreigners in the Compensation Room.

"No, you are mistaken," Thomas nodded, continuing to stare at the man coming near.

The Yank extended out his hand for shaking, "Yes, I'm sorry, but you two are related, correct?"

Thomas surveyed the man cautiously, too relaxed by far, he wore a long green coat over an open shirt, exposing his neck and chest. His boots were worn, but expensive. His belt housed a magnificent holster with, no doubt, an exquisite sword. "Yes, a brother, and you are?"

"Captain Whitlock," he pronounced, lowering his voice. "Tim, to my friends, I own my own cargo ship. I was on a voyage to Sri Lanka with your brother."

Thomas raised his eyebrow. The chap could come in handy. "Were you now?"

"How's that brother of yours? Betcha he's married now with a gaggle of kids, ain't he?"

Thomas' smiled dropped, "No Tim," he said despondent, "My brother is deceased."

Tim could not believe what he was hearing, "Dead? Jesus, what happened? That guy was invincible!"

"Yes," Thomas relayed, "I agree. Murdered...at sea, ten years ago."

Tim stood agape, "Ten years? Unbelievable...I'm so sorry," he apologized, shaking his head and being summoned over for payment. "Excuse me," he stated, walking away from the two lords.

Devin and Thomas both eyed the Yank standing at the payment window. Thomas wanted to continue speaking with the man about his brother, but then they heard their names being formerly announced into the span.

The twosome stood arrogant and confident within the French Parliament. Without blinking, their buoyancy and eminent aristocracy was bestowed release of the Captain's daughter without further delay. Anne appeared a few moments later. *She could have easily passed for a sister,* Thomas thought, as she glided towards the two landed gentry. Black hair, eyes as green as emeralds, still as thin, but not as beautiful as she once was; an evident scar from the tip of her temple down to her chin screamed mistreatment. She stood motionless now, staring at the Englishmen before her.

"Lord Hollinger?" She questioned, immediately recognizing and remembering his solid attractive façade. She would identify him anywhere; clapping eyes on him several years ago in her first and only season, practically following him around the ball that night like a puppy. She was spellbound, a loss for words, she never expected her father to send him to her rescue.

Thomas stepped into her, "Why cousin, I am so glad to see that you were treated well."

Anne's heart began to pound and gazed at the members of Parliament. "Why yes," she lied, "...I told you in my letters that I was treated well."

"Yes, yes you did, and I have a surprise," Thomas remarked, clearing way for a view of a lively Devin. "Your betrothed."

"My betrothed?" Anne blinked with the humorous shock. She immediately recognized him as well. "Lord Hale?"

"My sweet," he played along, grabbing her into his arms and tasting her. *Oh, sweet, sweet justice…and the irony!*

General Duroc had been standing a few feet away from Anne in case there was a problem and raised his eyebrows at the absurd flaunt, "Take her, we are quite done with her antics."

Thomas bowed to the man. "Good day, General Duroc, you should be hearing my decision soon," and the two men, along with Anne in tow all began their wade through a grove of French cavalier stuck-up noses, when they heard…

"NOT YET."

Thomas turned around and eyed a flamboyant French aristocrat standing isolated. An exotically handsome man with long black ringlets surrounding his sun-tanned face, the man was dressed in his flashy red silks and gold ringed fingers and stood proud and arrogant, narrowing his blue eyes on Anne.

"And who are you?" Thomas inquired, curious.

"Antoine Bruneau," Devin voiced with distaste.

Anne immediately closed space between Thomas and herself, she was afraid of Antoine, scared of what he might do. Antoine was a callous lover, oftentimes beating and tying her up naked for days. She instinctively wrapped her hand around Thomas' elbow and squeezed it tight.

Knowing this female reaction coming from fear, Thomas placed his protective hand over hers and leaned into Devin. "I take it you two are already acquainted?"

Devin grabbed Anne to him and pushed her behind his back. "She's mine Antoine and I am taking her back."

"You haven't asked permission."

Devin lurched towards Captain Whitlock and borrowed his sword. Swinging around him, he met Antoine's sword that was already at attack and pointed towards his chest. "Is this permission enough?"

"Oui."

"Duel!" Members of the Parliament shouted, all encircling the two men on the brink of murder. Tables were scooted aside, chairs were lifted and rugs were rolled up, people all around created a ring just to make room for the two heated opponents.

Thomas ran towards his friend, "You do not have to do this, Devin. This was not part of the deal."

"No friend, but I must, I really must," Devin eerily stated, maintaining constricted meditation on the dastardly rat. "My honor is at stake, or should I say my sister's honor."

Thomas raised his eyebrows and knew exactly what he was implying. Everything fell into place. Katrina's ease the first time they were together, her continued acceptance of their liaison. Antoine Bruneau had been Katrina's first lover?

Antoine Bruneau, illegitimate son to Empress Josephine's second cousin was not the least bit surprised to see Lord Devin Hale again. His sister was indeed, a tasty morsel. Even if Monsieur Hale insisted under gunpoint above a pot of boiling oil, he would have never married the *fille*.

Anne ran to Thomas immediately and wrapped her frightened arms around his waist. "Lord Hale does not have to defend my honor, what is he doing?"

Thomas nearly laughed aloud; it was so blatantly obvious that the girl wanted to touch him. Anne began to run her fingers up the small of his back in her failed attempt at seducing him. He unhooked her grip and pulled her aside. "He is so in love with you Anne, never got over you," Thomas joked, watching Devin expertly match every position of Antoine's sword fight.

Devin winced, and then tripped slightly when he overheard Thomas' ridiculous proclamation. Lunging for the man, he shoved his sword towards Antoine's shoulder. "I must confess," Devin announced craftily, "That I once held the record at Pembroke for the most victories," he assuredly passed on, clipping Antoine's shoulder and watching it turn red. "Awe, that felt good, I rather like seeing you bleed."

Antoine was embarrassed; no one had ever nipped him before! He ran towards Devin and whipped his sword towards his challenger's head and tried to behead him. Devin fought him off quite skillfully; breeching his strain with both strong arms, crisscrossing his sword into Antoine's other shoulder, making him lose blood there as well.

Gasps were heard throughout the great hall, there were even some claps and cheers. Antoine Bruneau was not as popular as he so thought. With his left hand up in the air, Devin's right sliced the atmosphere towards his competitor. Competitor, hah! The man was an amateur, Devin found out, as he continued to markup Antoine's sweet and sour face.

Anne attempted another seduction, as Thomas stood near her again. His body was so enticing; she could not help but lust after the man. "You married now Lord Hollinger?"

Thomas gazed away from the continued sword fight and down at Anne, "Yes, how did you guess?"

"Lucky woman, your wife."

Thomas grinned, "I am the lucky one, Anne."

"So she has your heart?" Anne asked with her own twitter patting. "No other woman can entice you to her bed?" She asked, wide-eyed, fingering the crest of her exposed bosom.

Thomas eyed her hand for a moment, and then looked way. "No other, Anne. The lady owns my *desire* as well."

CHAPTER 27

The end of each day had been the hardest for Gwendolyn. With every sunrise, there was hope and expectation that Thomas would be filling her doorway and whisking her away to Wilderbrand to be with him. But with every sunset, came despair, and Gwendolyn quickly withdrew her confidence. Determining it was best not to tell Mary that her father was alive, Gwendolyn chose silence as well, and each day hurt her like a stake through her heart.

She wished he would come to his senses and realize he had made a mistake. She was so sure on that night that they made love that Thomas was hers forever. Pleasing her every time they touched, wrapping her arms around his chest and gaining reassurance that she was in her rightful place; talking to him in between kisses, sharing further experiences about Mary. He was so perceptive to what she desired, he responded ultimately, each and every time. One moment in particular, he was lying on his side with his elbow bent, holding up his head with his hand. He looked absolutely wonderful in that lazy pose; she just had to collide with him once more and kissed him. She leaned into him, touching his chest and he grabbed her head and kissed her deeply. Her hands roamed his sinewy backside and he covered her body with his, thrusting his hardness into her warmth. She had never felt anything so perfect, all sense of time, vanished. So overwhelmed with emotion, she began to release tears of joy and he softly kissed the moisture away from her face. She should have confessed her love for him right then and there but did not want to be susceptible to his rejection. Only now does she understand that his finesse included simulating reciprocal fondness. What a fool she was for thinking that they could resume being a genuine family. He must have concluded that they could never be. Trying to hypothesize the excuses he had lined up in his head...He was pledged to another woman...he was intoxicated that evening and was not thinking straight. But his intimacy did not indicate the latter, he was so earnest in his compassion for her...*and oh God,* she was utterly in love with the man and he fled with complete utter silence?

That was the worst, really, not hearing from him at all. She felt she deserved some kind of an explanation. But where were the letters? Their friendship merited some sort of clarification. What was he thinking? How could he live with himself? Hold his head up high and know that he took advantage of their familiarity and still recite his vows? What was she to him now? No longer his friend, he said he could not continue mutual esteem without touching her, so he chooses absence? Not his mistress by reason of the two duration's she was with him, she had still been his wife. His wife? Huh! Even that covenant was not sacred enough; he still found a way to complete his pledge to Katrina. *It must her,* Gwendolyn realized. The serpent incarnate with blonde hair and blue eyes, keeping her tight grip on the reigns of her husband's whereabouts. Having a taut hand in everything he did, said and went. Gwendolyn learned firsthand what kind of controlling person Katrina was. She never did let Thomas out of her sight during the whole extent Gwendolyn was there and she had even been a victim to her venom. Thomas must have confessed his final affair with Gwendolyn, and therefore, knowing Katrina's personality, must have assigned him strict limitations.

But what Gwendolyn was most unhappy about was the fact that Thomas would never be able to see his children. When she thought him passed, Gwendolyn used to speak to the heavens and imagine him listening, she would ask him if he had seen what his daughter did that day and sometimes when a peculiar gust of wind would blow through her hair, she believed she received his answer.

She was being punished, she figured; reprimanded finally for ignoring him time after time, treating him harshly when they were younger. She used to love to tease him, challenge him, argue with him and even run away from him. How dare she think by treating him so unfairly would be rewarded? She would take it all back though, every single minute of it if she could have a second chance. But she did have a second chance and there would be no third. But stubborn as she was, Gwendolyn believed it was not over between them, she felt so in her heart. But where were those letters? Tommy Hollinger used to be her shadow, her tail, his surfacing had always been counted on, taken for granted; for God's sake the boy was always following her! *Oh God... he was always following her!* Why couldn't the man be pursuing her now?

Six months expectant, Gwendolyn hobbled along the dirt path towards St. Paul Church. She passed several villagers on their way towards town and they all stopped by to say hello. Gwendolyn greeted the passersby with a friendly nod and then waved goodbye. Some of the advantages of being away from the upper classes and living in the country were that no one judged you. Her Great-Aunt was very well loved within the community, and therefore, any respect that was lingering with her passing was now bestowed to her niece. Phyllis later spread that Charles had fled to London to demand Gwendolyn's hand in matrimony, they were still seen together in town; they must have gone through with the marriage for no one raised an eyebrow to her condition—it was a normal course.

Finally reaching the churchyard, Gwendolyn ambled over to the cemetery. Her grandparents, Great-Aunt and Uncle were buried there, along with a monument constructed for the family members who perished at sea. And, over to the left of that headstone, a special gravestone for Gwendolyn to visit when she felt lonely as she did so now.

Gwendolyn was amazed to see a dozen long-stemmed red roses next to her mother's nameplate. *Baron Huxton,* she realized and the thought of him loving her mother to this day brought a smile to her face. "At least someone does not mind traveling."

Brushing away some fallen leaves from a nearby oak, Gwendolyn stared down at the tombstone.

IN MEMORIAL
THOMAS ALBERT HOLLINGER, III 1782 – 1798

GWENDOLYN FELT A RUSH OF SENTIMENT ENTER HER throat; tears spurted through her eyes instantly, not really departed, but still the same heartache. "...Where are you? What has happened to you? You were once the most benevolent, unselfish boy I knew. *This man...*this man that you have become, is so unlike you, I do not understand. Help me to understand..."

Gwendolyn buried her head in her hands and began to cry. Her unborn child kicked the side of her womb, which made her chuckle through tears, "Even your descendant wants to hear your excuse."

Gwendolyn stood back up from her knees and cleared her nose into her apron. "No more crying, Gwendolyn...no more sadness... you have children to raise. He will come around one day...you know so in your heart. One year, two, five years, ten, it was all the same. You will see Thomas Hollinger again. They'll have an argument one day, and he will act mutinous...he will head to Yorkshire." Wiping the dust away from her hands, she brushed back her hair. "There is still faith in his appearance...for now he is mortal and occupying the living."

When Gwendolyn got back into town, the community was already a buzz. Every three years fairs were held in the village: one of which was a hiring fair where men came from Westmorland to be hired for labor in the limestone mines. However, the weather had been horrible lately; torrential rains, high winds and muddied roads had blocked all inward bound transportation, the town's people were so unnerved, every season when the leaves turned orange the village would also celebrate the commencement of fall. A town banquet had been preplanned for months and was now underway.

Gwendolyn, Charles, Phyllis, Mary and a few other villagers were laughing and discussing the beautiful weather when along came an elegant wagon heading up the road. Everyone stopped to gape, as its two massive labor horses pulled along its glorious entrance. When it stopped right in front of Gwendolyn and the others, Gwendolyn's heart began to pound.

"Mummie, who is it?" Mary asked, holding her mother's hand.

"I don't know," Gwendolyn gulped. It was not a human carriage, she realized, it was a wagon full of cargo.

"I am looking for Lady Hollinger," the coachman stated for all to hear. He got down from his high perch and gazed around at all the onlookers. "Anyone here know where I can find Lady Hollinger?"

Hollinger? Why would anyone address her formally? Hoping that no one caught the slip, Gwendolyn raised her hand finally, "I will receive it," she voiced, pulling away from the others.

"Lady Hollinger?"

Gwendolyn agreed by nodding her head.

"Please sign here malady," the coachman asked, handing her a receipt. When she handed it back to him, he surveyed her obvious condition. "Is there anyone here that can help me bring down a crate?"

Gwendolyn gazed around her for Charles and waived him down. Charles came rushing over and strides towards the coachman. The two men marched to the side of the wagon and the coachman opened up the interior. Inside, was a wooden crate about four feet wide in dimension? Charles grabbed hold of one end, while the strong coachman gathered together the other. Both men walked the crate to Gwendolyn's side and plopped it down with a great big thud.

The coachman then grabbed his ax and broke open the chain that surrounded the box; he pulled the chain down and then with the ax again pulled apart the nails that held it together. With authority, he puffed up and shouted, "Who is Mary?"

Mary's eyes lit up with glee, "I'm Mary!"

The coachman greeted her with a wink, "You have the honors, malady," he uttered, handing her a sizable iron key.

Mary ran over to the crate and several of the other children followed her. Inside the crate was a brown weathered trunk, with metal handles and golden knobs bordering its majestic scarlet painted entry.

"Oh, a treasure chest!" Mary exclaimed for all to hear.

Gwendolyn covered her mouth and barely contained her happiness for her daughter. She watched with round eyes as several other villagers gathered round Mary, all-clamoring to see what could be inside the beautiful carved chest.

Mary took the key and unlocked it. Opening it slowly, she gasped from its contents. Inside the luxurious purple velour lined trunk were one of kind riches from all over the world. A beautiful porcelain doll with green eyes and black hair cascading down the sides of her shape from Italy...Several outfits to change the doll in...along with a buggy to push her outdoors... A telescope to see the stars up close with from China...and magnifying glasses to view the bugs underneath from Egypt... Numerous original dresses, all of which were made of fine expensive silks imported from the Orient, Africa and Brazil...Slippers and hair ribbons to match...ivory brushes and combs. A separate hatbox was hidden in a corner with two envelopes attached under the tie; one addressed to Mary, the other, to Gwendolyn.

Mary pushed aside the letter to her mother and ripped open the envelope addressed to her and began to read it out loud.

My Dearest Mary,

To a precocious, fun-loving and curious little girl. Even though we haven't met yet, I feel we are formerly acquainted. Having missed so many birthdays, I hope these gifts greet you with happiness and joy, as I felt tranquility sending them to you. Take care of the larger present, he needs special attention only you can provide.

Always in my heart, Father

"Father? But I don't have a father—Mummie?" Mary shouted off the top of her lungs for everyone to hear.

Gwendolyn rushed to her daughters' side and tried to change the subject. A crimson thrash surged up her neck and she hoped to God no one noticed. "Let's see what is in the brown box, shall we? Open it darling, you know how mother hates mysteries!"

Mary untied the string and ripped open the carton. Inside was more paper followed by the finest silk she had ever seen. Mary's green eyes flew open wide at the sight of burgundy velvet, boots, hat, and rider's crop. "Oh Mummie," she gushed, "have you ever seen anything so beautiful before?"

Gwendolyn leaned down in amazement. "No darling, I haven't," she simply said, reaching down to feel the silky textile.

"It is sort of a silly present though, such a fancy dress to ride on a pony."

Gwendolyn began to laugh, and so did others who gathered around to take a look at the outfit.

Mary held the jacket up to her body and admired the smoothness of the fabric. Within trying it on, she discovered a lump in one of its pockets. Out of the pocket, she noticed a carrot. "What is this—?"

Gwendolyn eyed her daughter's surprised look. "What is it?" "A carrot," Mary called out, showing everyone her discovery.

"For the larger present," the coachman stated who waited in the wings until the girl opened the box, per his instructions. The man hobbled over to the enclosed wagon and opened up the two doors in the rear. He motioned for Mary to come take a look, and all the other children ran over with her.

Mary stood mesmerized for a moment, and then reached in the pocket for the carrot. Gwendolyn stood immobilized and watched in utter shock as the magnificent black steed she remembered Katrina riding on so long ago came trotting out of the enclosure. The villagers gasped in revelation as the horse followed Mary who continued to hold its enticement. She petted the horses raven mane and ravished its existence.

"Oh Mummie," Mary cried, a loss for words for the very first time. "I have seen something more beautiful. He is gorgeous Mummie, simply gorgeous!"

Gwendolyn stood crying and eyed Phyllis who was also in shock. "What a grand present to give his daughter," Phyllis uttered sorrowfully, "you see, he has not forsaken his obligations."

Gwendolyn wiped away her tears, "He should have delivered them himself." She stated, pulling up her skirts and running towards her cottage to have a good cry.

CHAPTER 28

*A*fter Captain Hummel secretly undermined the original plan to meet Thomas and Devin at Le Havre, he took Anne and the *Junia* and headed off to Gibraltar instead. The two lords were forced to stay in France another week to wait for the *Endeavor*, a merchant ship under the employ of the Hollinger Commerce Company.

The *Endeavor* was on its way back in from the West Indies. While fearful Cape Horn consumed many ships and crew without a trace in violent southern seas, the ultimate graveyard of ships was 8,000 miles northeast in Britain's granite-fanged Scilly Isles and the headlands of Cornwall. Lying 25 miles off Land's End, the 50 islets of the Scillies covered only 50 square miles, the Scillies divided the Bristol Channel from the English Channel, endangering all ships trying to find their way home. The *Endeavor* nearly met her doom; the menacing tides, gloomy fogs, diabolical gales and monstrous seas mislead her compass, nearly losing her existence upon the reefs.

It would be another week until the *Endeavor* would reach English refuge and Thomas could not wait that long. After nearly drinking himself into oblivion with French red wine, Thomas was never happier to see a Yank.

Inebriated, and on the verge of lunacy from further inconsiderateness, Thomas thumped towards Captain Whitlock. "Captain—Captain— Captain!"

Captain Whitlock turned to look at Thomas staggering towards him. "Well, hey, if it isn't the look-alike...what is your name again? Lord something?"

"Thomas...call me *Thomas*, ole friend, ole buddy of mine," Thomas joked around, patting the man on his chest, whipping his other arm around his neck.

"Thomas, right," Tim replied, rolling his eyes away from his forwardness. "What can I do for you?"

Thomas gulped, and then his hands found Tim's shoulders. "Please tell me you are on your way to London."

Tim's eyes lit up. "How did' ya know? On my way there in two days, in fact. Just have to finish up some business here. Need to reload my cargo, then I'm off to Bristol."

"Outstanding!" Thomas shouted, walloping Devin out of a lip lock with a barmaid.

All during the voyage towards Bristol, Thomas anticipated every angle. Katrina was abandoned at the altar. He never held the chance of speaking with her beforehand, and he was sure that she was furious. Then Gwendolyn and her puzzling note. She wrote she was having second thoughts? It did not make any sense. Her physical feelings were hard to ignore...showing him her mindset... did that mean she was in love with him? Each time she clung to him, touched his chest and wrapped her arms around his shoulders in affection his heart expanded with joy. Fulfilling his fantasy of her yielding to his every suggestion, she responded to him unlike no other, and he relished in the fact that she admitted being his. Was it all a mirage? Or a final farewell? He should have told her that evening that he loved her, that was stupid, stupid, stupid of him not to say anything, but he was so hungry to hear her say it first.

He finally snared what he longed for, Gwendolyn's absolute focus, only to have it yanked away by her reconsideration? Was she really going back to that overgrown simpleton? How could Gwendolyn so easily accept his body and then receive intimacy of that buffoon?

"Cannot thank you enough, Tim," Thomas expressed, shaking hands with Captain Whitlock. "Anything you need, do not hesitate to ask." Thomas added, gazing towards the pier, expecting to see her face. *Where was she? Where was Gwendolyn?*

Devin then extended his hand out to the Captain himself, "Thanks for the use of the sword," he laughed, combing his hair with his other hand. "Monsieur Bruneau looks nice with his new scarred face, wouldn't you agree?"

The three men all expressed amusement when Thomas gazed over at his ships in the harbor. "You need help with your cargo Tim?"

"Help? Why yes, I am oftentimes overloaded. But with one ship—"

"Surely you could use an extra hand."

"Sure can, but I can't afford to purchase another boat."

"Then take your pick," Thomas waived, extending his hand over his brigade of vessels.

Tim stood agape and eyed all the many crafts with the *"HCC"* flag raised up her masts.

DEVIN AND THOMAS WERE BARELY WALKING DOWN THE pier when they were harried by endless questions: "Where were you?"

"What happened?"

"What took you so bloody long?"

Thomas had a few of his own for Mrs. Hornebrook and Fitzwater when he met Katrina's eyes. She was not angry, rather the contrary, she looked scared. He watched her give her brother a welcoming hug, then observed her drawing near.

"May I have a word?"

"Certainly," Thomas announced, motioning for her brother to linger alone, he then noticed Henry arriving alongside Devin, shaking his hand.

Katrina had to spurt out what she was going to say before she lost her nerve. "Thomas, let me begin by telling you that I was terribly upset when you abandoned me on our wedding day. The pain from the embarrassment will brand me evermore."

"I know—"

"Let me finish, Thomas," she said, wiping away a tear. "I meant what I said when I told you that I cared for you. But a woman like me has goals and I could not be kept in suspension forever. Not once have I heard you speak of your devotion to me, and yet, I believed it would come with our nuptials. I am no martyr Thomas, I am a social climber and I am sorry to say that I used you to gain status in the *ton*."

Thomas laughed and fingered the lining in his hat. *What a relief,* she was letting him down? "A social climber?" He quipped with a sneer, "Why, I knew that the first day I met you," he paused, having had a better word for it, like *snob*. "But that inspiration did not scare me away, love," he voiced, lowering his intonation. "Why, I exercised you as well. No hard feelings, we had fun, did we not?"

Katrina was beet red. Her dismissal was not going according to plan, instead of him afflicted with remorse; it was she who was suddenly feeling grief jabbing at her heart. "I married Henry."

Thomas did not seem the least bit surprised, he knew her too well and Katrina had been spoiled to the core. If she did not get what she wanted immediately, she had to lash out and try to harm him instead. He turned around and judged her new husband. Henry stood defeated and lowered his eyes. "Did you now?" Thomas cracked, turning back around to meet Katrina's resentment. "Does he make a fine husband?"

"Yes," Katrina added with a stiff upper lip. "Henry is a good man."

Thomas lowered his voice to a charming timbre, "Does he finish you as well?"

Katrina stared at his lips and felt her own separating. *No,* she thought, but she would never admit to that. Henry was a pleasant lover, while Thomas was sinfully carnal. Still allured by his engaging glare, she said, "Yes, we are enceinte."

Thomas perked up immediately, "Why, that's wonderful! Congratulations!" He presented, whirling around and walking towards Devin and Henry. "I could not be happier," he remarked, patting Henry on the back. "Congratulations, ole boy, I guess this means you'll be asking for an increase in pay?"

Henry laughed and stood erect now. "I must say Thomas; you are taking this news very well."

Thomas had news of his own to share, if only...*if only he knew her reply?* He had expected to see Gwendolyn here receiving him with open arms, but she was nowhere in sight. Thomas gazed around the threesome and spotted Mrs. Hornebrook with Fitzwater. "Mrs. Hornebrook, has any letters been delivered to the manor?"

"Letters, Your Grace?" Mrs. Hornebrook questioned back. "Just the usual mail, social invitations, tax statements, invoices and receipts."

Thomas stood grave, he then looked at Fitzwater. "Have you seen or heard from her Fitzwater?"

Fitzwater knew exactly whom he was speaking of. "No, sir," he answered feeling melancholy for his employer.

"You did get my note, is that correct? Regarding the delivery of the gifts?" Thomas asked dejected.

"Yes, sir and they were promptly sent," Mrs. Hornebrook lied, feeling his anguish with each realization. She did not have the heart to tell him that they were barely sent three weeks ago due to bad weather.

"When?" Thomas quietly asked, bowing his head, taking off his hat.

"Four months ago, sir." Fitzwater confirmed, wavering also.

Thomas then closed his eyes. *Four months…*with no reply? What does he have to do to make her love him? Why does she keep treating him this way? What was wrong with her? Runs away when he gets too close, some kind of panicky reaction when emotions get excessively comfortable. He loved her more than ever before only to have his heart crushed once again. What cruelty! What pain! Worse than the floggings he used to receive when he had stolen food. Amplified torment knowing she did it deliberately. Used his flesh and then discarded what she couldn't fit into a traveling case. What a fool he was, what a complete and utter fool to hang onto such a small expectation that they'd finally be a real family. All that hope and probability blown to smithereens! *She must have married her Scotsmen,* he realized; must be kept under harsh boundaries to not utter another word. Oh God in heaven, Gwendolyn had made her choice, and now…so should he.

Thomas pulled away from his servants and headed off to be alone, not recognizing his friends attempt to call him over, or Katrina's shattered reconsideration.

Katrina watched him trudge away and her heart fell to the ground. "Thomas!" She shrieked, spinning Devin's head around towards her fright.

Devin immediately rushed to her side and grabbed his sister by the shoulders. "Stop it, Katrina, stop it. Your husband is barely two feet away, and here his wife is crying after another man? Show some restraint, will you?"

Katrina buried her face into her brother's shoulder and continued to watch Thomas melt through the crowd. Her heart was shattering in an earth-crushing whack. Tears began to fall from her eyes, as she shut them tense realizing she could no longer see him clearly.

CHAPTER 29

"*W*hy willna ya marry me, Gwendolyn?" Charles asked, dropping the flowers to his side. "The townspeople all believe we are already married. I do not wish to pretend, I want ya tae be by me side."

Gwendolyn remained in a lying position on a lounge in her parlor, a knitted shawl across her torso and legs. She was not feeling well that morning and decided to stay in seclusion. "You are a wonderful man Charles, and I do not want to hurt you."

"Why wood marrying me, torment me?"

"Because it would not be fair...because you would be sharing a life with a woman whose heart belonged to another."

"Did ya ever love me, Gwendolyn?"

Gwendolyn stared at Charles' genuineness. For so many years he had been her savior, rescuing her from a pit of gloominess. Each day would get easier and easier to adjust; it was like she was living another life – a dream life. Neighbors were close by and friendly. Everyone knew everyone and when someone was rumored to be sick, Charles was the first of the neighbors to volunteer his hands to work in the fields. She loved that about him. He showered her with happiness and she had been nothing but grateful. He was a kind, gentle man and she hated hurting him. "No."

"But ya let me—"

"Yes—I know, I do not regret that, not one little bit. I will always care for you Charles McMillen. You have brought nothing but joy and happiness into my life, you are a dear man and I consider you a dear friend, you've given me comfort when I needed comforting, humor when I needed to laugh...but I have always loved Mary's father."

Charles shifted with anger and possessiveness. "Blasted noble, the next time I lay eyes on the mon, I will tear him limb from limb."

"No Charles, no one is going to tear anyone's arms off."

"But Gwendolyn, the babe needs a fatha," Charles conveyed, scratching his chest, "If he willna take responsibility, then I will. I always thought I'd be a good fatha."

"Yes, yes you will be...someday, Charles. You are such a good man; I do not deserve a friend like you."

Charles stared at his former fiancée. He recalled when he first laid eyes on her; she was like a gem in a pile of corn. Poised and exquisite, this was no farm girl. She hypnotized him with her confidence, her knowledge of the sea, and her quick wit. He welcomed her flirtatious moods and looked forward to the days when he could hold her in his arms throughout the night. But alas, it was not to happen, his future bleak and filled with solitude once more. Friendship was all she was offering. Closeness he would greet with open arms if she would keep her word.

"If I canna have ya as me wife, Gwendolyn, then I will settle for yar kinship," Charles let go disappointed, "Anythin' ya need, ya can call on me."

"Thank you Charles."

He slowly walked over to a table and placed the flowers gently on top. He was just about to exit and caught the door deciding to test her pledge. "If ya feeling better tamorra', will ya accompany me on a journey?"

"Where you off to?"

"Scarborough Harbor."

"What business do you have at port?"

"Och now," he said scratching his head now, "Seems I am not tae only male having problems with the female persuasion."

Gwendolyn laughed, "What happened?"

Her amusement always seemed to melt his heart. She was still his friend, thank God. "Me damn bulls willna mate with me heifers. Had tae acquire male bovine from a friend of mine in Shrewsbury. Four steer heading by way of transport ship."

Gwendolyn thought about it. "I don't know Charles; fish smell makes me queasy regardless."

"Och now, com'on Gwendolyn, ya' been pinned up in yar cottage for nearly a month now. Mary can even come along. She would enjoy a change in scenery. Ya know the lass always liked the ocean."

"Yes," Gwendolyn cast down, "Yes...she always has."

THE FOLLOWING MORNING, CHARLES WAS SEEN scratching his head in bewilderment. With Gwendolyn and Mary by his side, he was beyond perplexed.

Charles surveyed the hefty steers and shook his head, "They look identical tae me others!"

The seamen all laughed at the Scotsman's density. "They've got his stink on'em," one sailor spat out. "The bull is rejecting the heifers 'cause they're familiar," another sailor joined in.

Gwendolyn covered her daughter's innocence as Mary stood fixated, her mouth open wide from the chap's candid narration.

"Charles?"

"Aye, Gwendolyn?" He asked, turning to eye Gwendolyn with her hands over her daughter's ears.

"Mary and I will be walking the merchants. Meet us in about an hour? Do you think you will be done by then?"

Charles gazed around him and at the bulls. "Plenty 'nough time, Gwendolyn, have a good time. Dinna purchase everything ya see. Make sure tae barter the price. Dinna accept face value."

Gwendolyn huffed and dragged Mary away by her hand.

* * *

THOMAS FELT KATRINA'S EYES UPON HIM, BUT HE DID not care. The *Junia* had been found deserted, floating near the coast of Scarborough Harbor, that's all he had time to think about. *Business, finances, ships.* No women had entered his mind. No women...well, maybe *one.* The only one who always seemed to occupy his thoughts when he allowed her entrance.

Thomas set eyes on Devin and his friend gave him a half smirk considering the circumstances. Devin tried, he really did to try and cheer him up. He even took him to Bristol for a night of cards, drinking, and Devin was hopeful, wenching. Two bar maids, nice looking brunettes in fact, decided to give the two gents their sole attention that evening, and sat in the men's laps the whole entire evening. Thomas acted like he was enjoying himself, but deep down inside, Devin knew he was miserable. Thomas even lifted the female off his lap and set her aside several times just so that he could straighten out his waistcoat. Who cared about his bloody clothes why wasn't he feeling amorous with the curvy, soft female bouncing on his lap? What was it going to take to get his friend's mind off his woes?

Rowing away from the *Junia*, Thomas now eyed Katrina. She was sitting next to her husband with Devin on the other side. She looked unhappy, but so was he. Even if she were available he would never go back to her. After spending time with Gwendolyn, no woman would ever measure up to her level. *Gwendolyn was perfection,* he realized. All his life, he searched for her equivalent, probing through the handful of women he allowed into his life. With Mrs. Putnam, it was her brazenness like Gwendolyn's, which kept him intrigued. With Mrs. Carmichael, it was her sense of adventure, similar to Gwendolyn's, that kept him coming around for so many years. Then, it was Lady Krausman, her youthfulness and humor parallel to Gwendolyn's that caused him to spend so much time with her. Then Katrina, his harbor of comfort, her gracefulness constantly compared to the one-woman... hell and damnation, the only female he simply could not get out of his head.

Thomas turned to Cornwall who was sitting beside him. "Is it ready, Cornwall?"

"Yes sir," Cornwall stated, ready to give the signal.

From mast, bow and stern, Thomas had ordered the *Junia* burned in the harbor. Thomas does not want that ship, he hated that vessel. Detested it with a passion, knowing what murders took place aboard that ship. Gazing up towards the bow, the ghosts of his family could be seen clearly atop her crest: his mother, father and all three brothers, waiving to him farewell. *Oh, how he missed them!* So many memories dashed in and out of his head, he could hardly keep up. It was all so long ago...in a different lifetime...in a distant memory. His father's solid authority... his mother's loving embrace...his brother's watchful eyes. Closing on his grief, Thomas finally nodded his head and lowered his gaze.

Edmund gave the signal for the men to fire up the gunpowder and the barrels of ammunition exploded instantly in a mighty explosion. Suppressed memories flashed before Thomas as he absorbed the brilliant mushroom of orange flames plaguing the sky. Bittersweet memories, he thought dejectedly, like the day Jordan showed him how to steer the *Junia* and how to read her knot speed. The first time he saw her royals spread out gloriously in the wind, and the last time her topsails blew violently in the rainstorm. Jolly times, when Andrew and Philip took him fishing and they caught a tiger shark. Philip had straddled the poor fish while Andrew punched it in its mouth to stop it from flopping around. The night when his father and mother took him aside just before the wedding and told him how proud they were of him; his father giving him a hug, his mother kissing his cheek. And then, ultimately, the sunset ceremony that joined him to a commitment that captured his very soul.

Thomas watched it burn through tear-filled eyes and finally felt released from the anchored guilt from being the only one who survived. His family should be alive, not he, in fact, he felt so lifeless lately; he could barely find the energy to breathe.

They reach the pier finally and descend. Turning around, they watch the *Junia* gather up in flames. Dressed in coats from the chilled sea air, Thomas, Devin, Henry and Katrina were mesmerized by the sight before them. A crowd had gathered around them; merchants from every country came together to watch the spectacle. A cloud of black dust erupted in the sky as the drums of bombs continued to blow up the craft.

* * *

"WHAT WAS THAT NOISE?" MARY ASKED, PULLING HER mother in the direction of where the booming sound came from.

"Slow down child, you do not want to get mother sick again, do you?"

Gwendolyn and Mary both stopover at the sight of the awe-inspiring plume of smoke being hurled into the air.

"What is happening, Mummie?" Mary asked, trying to peek through the hordes of onlookers.

Gwendolyn concentrated on the noteworthy scene before her. "Someone has ordered expulsion of a ship," she said, watching the vessel now engulfed in flames. It was slowly disintegrating right before her eyes; the masts cracked in two like twigs, then fell into the ocean one by one.

Mary turned away from the exhibition and eyed a group of

gentleman chatting. Pointing to one of them, she asked, "Who is that Mummie?"

"Who is who?" Gwendolyn asked, looking down at her daughter.

"That man over there," Mary stated, pointing towards the group of men. "The tall man, holding his hat in his hands, he looks like the man in the portrait you have hanging on our staircase."

Gwendolyn could not move…he was just several feet away. Seeing Thomas anew after all these months, her feet planted firmly to the ground.

Thomas was in mid-conversation with one of the dock men talking about the removal when he did a double take and noticed her standing there with a young girl. He turned around and walked towards them, meeting eyes with Gwendolyn.

"Hullo there."

"Hullo yourself," Gwendolyn smiled, squeezing Mary's hand in hers.

"See Mummie, he does look like the portrait you have hanging in the staircase," Mary exclaimed, bringing exclusive attention down to her curiosity.

Thomas knelt down and stared into her eyes. Gwendolyn was right; Mary did take after the Hollinger family. Wavy black hair, dark eyelashes surrounding olive green eyes, she was a miniature version of his own mother. "Hello Mary," Thomas managed to say, soaking in her existence. "You are the vision of your grandmother."

"How do you know my name? Did you know my grandmother?"

"Yes—I," he said tongue-tied, standing up, but continuing to gaze down at her.

Gwendolyn then kneeled down to Mary's eye level. "Remember that present you received, the early birthday gift?"

"The treasure chest, and my horse, Whinny?"

Thomas laughed, "I like that name."

"Yes darling, *Whinny*. Well, remember the note that came along with it? It was sent by a person claiming to be your father." Gwendolyn then stood back up and met Thomas' unsmiling stare. "This is your father, Mary...His Grace, Lord Thomas Hollinger, the Duke of Norwin."

Mary's eyes grew big as saucers, "Really Mummie? But you said that my father died at sea before I was born."

Gwendolyn gulped and tried to blink back her tears, "Yes darling, I did say that. But I was wrong, your father is alive...and by the looks of him, he wants to know you."

Thomas grinned and then met eyes with Mary again, "Do I attain your permission?"

Mary leaned into her mother's skirt, "Yes, I guess so. Can he come to my birthday party? Can I show him off?"

Thomas rolled his eyes only to close them. His daughter had a morbid sense of humor, just like her mother.

Gwendolyn tried to swallow her laughter, "Mary! It is not proper—"

"But he is my father!" Mary exclaimed with innocent eyes. "No one would have to know Mummie, he could be there in disguise and we could introduce him as our cousin," she pleaded; unaware of the similar justification conjured up before. She turned to look at Thomas once more, "Please say that you can attend, sir?"

"Thomas? Are you ready to go?" Devin voiced behind him, not realizing that Gwendolyn and a young girl were standing near.

Thomas turned around and eyed Devin and Katrina walking up with Henry slowly behind. When he turned back to speak to Gwendolyn, Gwendolyn turned pale and got her confirmation of their union.

Thomas once asked her if she could remain amiable, well here was the test of self-control. Standing there looking at him, dressed in those darn boots, that long sable Carrick of his, and his wonderful stylishness that made him look so heavenly, took every bit of will power she had remaining not to run into his arms with his wife next to him. *And, oh God, could it be?* Katrina was with child? She even cupped her hand underneath her womb to show her swelling. Oh, why did he marry her? Where was Gwendolyn's romantic happy ending? Oh how could she have been so stupid? She should have never let him go that wonderful night they made love. She should have expressed all that she was feeling; she should have shouted it out from the rooftops of Wilderbrand!

"I would not miss it, love," Thomas articulated to Mary, feeling pressure on all sides. He noticed another familiar face, Charles McMillen, who came up beside Gwendolyn all of a sudden.

"Is something amiss?" Charles asked, looking at Thomas while he asked.

Thomas immediately backed away when he got his validation that yes indeed Gwendolyn married her Scotsmen. He knew he could not do it and he could not be amicable now. Seeing her standing compact with him...and she was with child? *Oh, hell...* imagining her accepting his touch thrashed him down with repetitive blows. Someone please, just put him out of his misery. Someone please just shoot him already! Thomas' eyes wandered from one place to another until they finally set on Gwendolyn. His obsession tried to solicit her selfishness. *Why, Gwendolyn why?* Why pick him? Why not me? Swallowing the rest of his emotion, Thomas let go, "Yes, we were discussing birthdays. When do you expect me?"

"In four months," Gwendolyn replied, feeling her heart swell up inside her chest. "...Mary's birthday is in four months' time."

"Splendid," he quickly ended, looking over his shoulder noticing Katrina and Henry looking oddly at him. "Nice to see you again Gwendolyn, and..." he paused to bend down to whisper to Mary, "It was very nice to finally meet you Mary."

"It was my pleasure, sir," Mary said, continuing to hold her mother's hand.

Thomas could not look at Gwendolyn anymore when his heart was about to rupture. He would look like a dunderhead quivering at her feet in public display with her husband next to her. He tediously turned around and walked towards his friends. He was just about to make a mad dash for the pier and dive off the deep end when he heard the child's voice ring after him from behind.

"Father!" Mary yelled, letting go her mother's hand and running towards Thomas and jumping into his open arms.

Thomas grabbed his daughter and picked her up from her bottom. Practically hugging the life out of her little body, he held her firm, burying his head in the side of her neck.

"I love you Father," Mary exclaimed whimpering. "You promise you'll come in four months' time?"

What a wonderful child, he thought...so open, honest, and unregulated with her true feelings. "I promise, love," Thomas honestly uttered, feeling moisture at the back of his eyes. Unconsciously, his eyes fluttered towards Gwendolyn one last time. She had her hand over her mouth and was shedding tears. Charles was at her side, trying to console her with both his hands resting on her shoulders. Thomas could not take the sight of her with him any longer and released his daughter instantly. "I promise Mary, I will see you in four months..."

CHAPTER 30

*S*he knew he was coming and she was prepared for their arrival. Thomas promised his daughter, and Gwendolyn knew he would never break that pledge, never disappoint Mary if a bond were to remain. She only met him once and already Mary could not stop asking questions about him. Curious about her father now, she asked Gwendolyn how they met, why they broke apart, and if they were still friends.

Yes…were they friends? Once the best of friends, now unable to prevail due to outside influences. Yes, he married her…Thomas married Katrina. Imagining him holding her, kissing her with his body propelled Gwendolyn into hyperventilation each and every time she thought about it. The tender way he caressed her after making love, the forceful way he took her in his arms and left her breathless and longing for more. Katrina had won, she secured Thomas' attention and Gwendolyn had no other choice but to ingest the defeat.

Gwendolyn had never been tenser. Thomas now was considered to be her children's creator. No longer a friend, but a past paramour and she did not know how to handle a visitation from a former lover and his wife. Not his mistress...Thomas took care of his mistresses, isn't that what Mrs. Carmichael affirmed? Then what was she? Not a friend, not a mistress, but a mistake. How to deal with the fact that the man arriving today was not hers to own, and yet, she had two children by him?

Nathaniel was born in the middle of the night and Phyllis had been by her side all day long awaiting the infant's arrival. Identical to Mary's birth, Nathaniel entered this world with Gwendolyn crying into his diminutive flesh. So much anguish, not enough ease to be truly happy with his ingress. Mary, bless her heart, was elated and could not stop holding him. Where did he come from? How did her mother have a baby? It would be the three of them from now on and Gwendolyn had to settle with the certitude that Thomas would only be a guest in her home in the future. He would be welcome; she would make sure of it. They had been through too much anguish from losing their own families; Gwendolyn would never deny him familiarity of his own flesh and blood. Katrina would just have to be one understanding wife. Thomas had other children who needed him as well. And maybe... just maybe, they could mend the damaged friendship they once shared. Gwendolyn would hail his alliance again, she would...she would have to. If she could not have him as her husband, she would settle for his friendship. Isn't that what she had promised Charles?

Oh God, how did she allow this to happen? That was stupid, stupid, stupid of her not to express what she had felt that night in his arms! She made a horrible decision of not telling him that she loved him. She did not want to ruin the atmosphere by expressing her devotion in fear of his rejection. Being cast aside was the worst feeling and being second choice was evenly insulting. Once upon a time, he was hers, she was first, and she had him in the palm of her hand, only to destroy their bond by continuous unwise suppression. When the timing was right—maybe even today—she would ask to speak to him alone and tell him about his son.

Choking back her tears, Gwendolyn sat down on the edge of the bed and stared at the boy in the bassinet next to her. Running her thumb across his head of hair, Gwendolyn allowed the tears to fall from her eyes. *Thomas will acknowledge his heir,* Gwendolyn thought, even if it turned ugly and Katrina would demand her child be his heritable successor, Gwendolyn would still show a good fight. Theirs was an unusual circumstance. Theirs had begun with too much history to disregard. Theirs was a special accident...and, just like her mother, Gwendolyn would journey through life loving someone else's husband.

* * *

The long ride to Yorkshire was serviceable for Thomas. He not only experienced the beautiful countryside on the way towards Kettlewell, he was also able to mend his broken spirit. The past few months were tedious to say the least, arriving to this point was nerve-wracking and getting over her was slow. The one he loved...loved someone else and he just couldn't bear the separation. All he craved for was an answer, just to hear her explain her selection. Their close history warranted an explanation. This time was a catastrophe of emotions because she was alive and she discarded him willingly. She played her part perfectly, showing him interest, loving him through the night only to take some other path and live with another man? What did he contain that Thomas lacked? Was she not impressed by the success of her father's company or the wealth he managed to maintain? She would rather live in squalor with her livestock breeder, than be by his side in riches and comfort?

Thomas threw himself into work, trying to erase those images of her and him inside his head and occasionally it would ease, most of the time, it would not. Nighttime was the worst and closing his eyes was sheer torture. Rolling up into a ball, clinging to his pillows, his blankets, wishing she were there lying beside him. He would wake up listless, tired, sickened by the sun bringing on a new day, and then eventually, ending his monotonous evenings.

One eventide, Thomas was so distraught, the breaking point to a juncture of no return when Mrs. Hornebrook found him on his hands and knees in his bedroom, dripping wet and sobbing. He had purposefully sat outside in the storm and tried to get himself sick. He was shivering and drenched and Mrs. Hornebrook aided him to his bed.

"She...she does not want me," he cried, "why doesn't she want me?"

Mrs. Hornebrook pulled off his saturated coat, cravat and boots. Picking up his legs, she tucked him under the heated blankets. "Shush now...no more nonsense, let's get you warm," she said sympathetically, rubbing his cold hands and wiping off the dankness from around his forehead and face. "Now, just hold onto me, I am going to use my body to get you warm."

Thomas closed his eyes and experienced instant comfort from within her motherly embrace. She showed him love and compassion, and his heart cried out for even more. He had to speak to someone and his housekeeper's presence served her purpose well. "I do not want live without her. Just let me die... leave me be...let me just end it."

Mrs. Hornebrook tsked at him, "Shush now...you are sputtering nonsense. Now, Your Grace—*Thomas* now, I have known you since you were a born and I have never seen you in so much torment."

Thomas laid his head on her bosom and continued to cry, "But I do not understand it, she was mine...she was always mine, she came back into my life for a reason, only this time, she does not want me?"

"Shush now, you are still shivering, now try and calm down, let me tell you a story," she voiced tenderly, running her fingers through his dampened hair. "I once knew a girl...my best friend in fact, worked with her for many, many years. I watched her cry in her room as you are doing now. For years, she was in love with the lord of the manor and every time he would go out for the evening, she would run to her room and have a good cry. He was a disreputable rogue and occasionally dallied with her fondness. I wasn't surprised when she fled to the country to give birth to his son. The lord was so troubled when he found out that she had abandoned his estate, he could not eat, and he definitely could not sleep and finally chased after her. As soon as she saw him at her door she expressed her devotion, and wouldn't you know it, the lord returned her affections and Millicent was married the following day."

"My mother," Thomas voiced quietly. "...And father."

"Yes son, your mother and father. They loved you so. You were their baby; your mother's sweet little boy and she showered you with affection. You remind me so much of her and I promised her I would look after you when she was away, and that's just what I am going to do. You mustn't give up hope, Thomas. There is a greater reason behind all this anguish."

"But my hands are tied, Mrs. Hornebrook...there is nothing more than I can do. This time she did not choose me."

Mrs. Hornebrook continued massaging his shoulders. "I believe in my heart Thomas, that she is still yours. No one, not even Satan himself would ever make me believe otherwise. That girl loves you. You were created just for her, and vice versa. She was always next to you, even when you were toddlers. Why, I remember when she used to make sure to push everyone aside, her brother and yours, just to make room for you at family picnics. She was always making sure you were right beside her. Why, I don't think Gwendolyn felt comfortable without you in the room."

She was right, he realized. Thomas leaned up and stopped crying. He instantly recalled his own mother saying nearly the same thing to him. "If she was so attentive back when, then why is she so evasive now? Why did she marry that farmer?"

"That I do not know, but you can ask her," she remarked

simply. "I know it is highly inappropriate for you to be seen together with your former wife, but I say buck convention. You were invited to your daughter's birthday celebration and I think that's a wonderful opportunity for you to shed some light on your doubt. You two have always been friends, and links you shall remain."

"Mary," he conveyed, "...yes, we still have that connection."

"Be strong Thomas, you have to be convincing in your happiness for her. I am sure she will explain her choice if you ask her."

"Yes, you are absolutely right. She would...I know she would."

"See now, you are chills have ceased. Now, let's get you some more blankets and I will go warm up some tea and broth for you to eat."

Thomas watched her walk around the bed before saying, "You are a good friend, Mrs. Hornebrook...and...and, I love you."

Mrs. Hornebrook bit down on her lower lip and fought back her tears. "Oh I know, child...I know."

* * *

AFTER STOPPING AT A NEARBY WATERING HOLE TO SOAK his horses, Thomas had asked for the location of the McMillen farm. Some of the villagers knew exactly what he was looking for; most of them had not. When one villager spoke up unannounced, she offered Thomas information he did not quite count on.

"Gwendolyn does not reside at the McMillen farm," the woman spoke with evident assurance. "They live at Crestwood Square, in the Drummond cottage, up the hill...keep following the path, and you'll see it, atop the bluff."

Thomas thanked the woman and handed her a shilling. She was so elated by his gesture, she nearly fainted.

I have to be convincing in my happiness for her, Thomas thought while winding along the dirt path towards Gwendolyn's home. This was Gwendolyn's choice. The only role he would play in her life from now on would be the sketch of father. It would be a routine he was willing to perform in order to stay involved in his daughter's life. His daughter, his seedling...unexpected to be known as someone's parent. He was so careful in the past not to father any children out of wedlock, he never wanted offspring by any other woman, but with Gwendolyn, he wanted several. On that night he made love to her he tried to get her pregnant. Oh, he knew it was self-seeking, knew it was manipulative, but he did not care. Staying inside her longer than need be, he wanted her without end. All that concerned him was that Gwendolyn was his, under his charge, heavy with child once more. She would have no option, no decision to make; her fate would be mapped out for her. She would have to remain his wife, stay with him indefinitely. However, his undertaking failed; there would be no second chance. With Mrs. Hornebrook's reminder, there was opportunity now where there once was none, through their daughter. He could remain on pleasant terms with Gwendolyn in order to see his child. He was determined to know his descendant. Mary was not illegitimate; therefore, she did not deserve to be swept under the rug like most of the bastard children of England and Mary would grow up with dignity and purpose, pride and his future legal heir; her children would secure his title and he would never deny her that.

As soon as he arrived at Gwendolyn's home, his heart began to thump. Outside, across the lawn, children were laughing, jumping and playing. There were chairs and blankets sprawled out over the grasses, tables with food, pastries and drink. He eyed Phyllis first; who had been serving biscuits at the buffet.

"How are you Miss Tallymen?" Thomas asked arriving on foot around the many guests.

"Oh Your Grace, I am so very glad you decided to attend," Phyllis gushed, grabbing the back of her husband's shirt. "But I am no longer Miss Tallymen; it is Mrs. Archwald...Mrs. Stewart Archwald."

"Nice to make your acquaintance, Your Grace," Stewart said, with a courtly bow.

"Father! Father! You came! You came!" Mary screamed, running towards him and jumping into his arms.

"I promised you I would come, love...and I never break a pledge," Thomas said, receiving his daughter's welcoming hug.

"These are my friends," Mary exclaimed, "and this is my Father!" She hollered excitedly.

"Nice to meet you all," Thomas freely smiled, bowing to all the youngsters.

"Father, this is my best friend, Marcus," Mary gushed, yanking the boy's shirt from within the circle.

Thomas was nearly knocked down with shock. *A boy?* Her best friend was...a lad? "Nice to meet you, Marcus."

"The pleasure's all mine, sir," Marcus claimed, bowing as well.

Thomas then nodded to all her many friends staring up at him. "Where is Whinny?" He asked, gazing around him.

"He is over there," Mary stated, pointing at the corral. "Why?"

"Because I have a present for him."

"A present? Why, it's *my* birthday."

"Yes, I know, it's your present too."

Thomas whistled and *Cherish* comes trotting over next to him. She is a magnificent buff Arabian and by her side is a tiny foal. Black mane and tail, the filly is the spitting image of its dam. "It's a girl...and she's yours."

Mary's eyes flew open wide and all the other children gasped in awe. Mary runs towards the colt and grabs its neck pulling it into her for a hug. "Oh she is beautiful Father, thank you, thank you so very much," Mary spurted, "I cannot wait to show mother."

Thomas ran his fingers nervously through his hair, "By the way, where is your mother?"

Mary does not bother to look at him and continued to gush at the foal. "She went back to the cottage."

CHAPTER 31

Gwendolyn was in the kitchen putting the last of the frosting onto the birthday cake. Alone, and talking to herself, she went to wipe the bottom of the wax paper and stuck a finger of frosting into her mouth. "Oh darling...mother made you a wonderful cake," she voiced, gently picking up the block and placing it onto a tray to take outside.

In the corner of the kitchen, Nathaniel started to whine and Gwendolyn turned around to get him. "My—my, what big lungs you have deary...mother is coming...mother is coming." She bent over the baby's cradle and picked up her son. Within hearing his mother's comforting voice, the baby started to wail even louder. Calming down her son, cuddling his head and tiny body to her breast, Gwendolyn stood quietly shushing the baby and spun around to gape into questioning green eyes.

Thomas leaned over and took a peek at the bundle of joy. "Boy or girl?"

Gwendolyn could not breathe...she couldn't even speak; seeing Thomas authentically dashing, hurled her heart to the pit of her stomach. "Boy," she exhaled, peeping down at the baby.

"Congratulations," he gave to her dismally.

Cradling the baby within her arms, Gwendolyn tried to regain composure. "Th—thank you."

"Nice home," he said despondent, putting down his hat and eyeing the décor. He walked around the open area; it was a woman's touch with feminine furnishings, where were her husband's possessions? He then closed his eyes. *You have to be convincing in your happiness for her.* If this was going to work, you have to display your acceptance of her choice. Only Thomas' heartrending stare almost gave his heartbreak away. He stood there like an idiot, gaping at her with that farmer's baby in her arms. A child—he wished to God—was his. She looked beautiful, absolutely glowing and he wanted so much to hold her in his arms. But he knew he could not and therefore would not. It was not right; this whole situation was off the mark. His words were stuck inside his throat, everything he was feeling displayed by way of his pitiful worship of her. His heart pounded fierce, he wanted to ask her how, when and why, but the only words that seemed to form on his lips were, "...H—How are you?"

Gwendolyn soaked in his sadness, he was miserable; she could tell the moment he gave her his best wishes. It was how he said it —it was in his tone. She could always tell when there was something wrong with him and he looked as if he were about to cry! She wanted to console his despair, wrap her arms around his shoulders and hug him near to her heart. What was wrong with him? What on earth happened? "We are doing well...we are all doing well."

Be convincing will you! He petitioned for her compassion by staring at her some more but it was no use, he had to settle for her friendship and his anxiety was overwhelming. Maybe things were better left unsaid? No, he had to find the nerve to ask her.

"May I...may I ask you something?"

"Yes, of course, what?" Gwendolyn then blinked out of her haze. Something was not quite right. Why was he so sad? Why did he seem so lost? What was so wrong? Something was misplaced... someone was missing. She looked beyond him before saying, "Where is Katrina?"

Thomas swallowed his anguish and looked at her strangely, "Katrina?" He asked surprised now, "Why, she is...she is back with Henry, where else would she be?"

"Henry?" Gwendolyn asked taken-back, "Why is she with him?"

Thomas shook his head and realized that the two of them were on different spectrums. "Because he is her husband, that's why."

"What!" Gwendolyn bellowed, scaring the baby within her arms again. Her son began to wail.

Poking his finger in his ear and jiggling it, Thomas pronounced, "Oh my—he is a loud little thing."

"You have no idea," Gwendolyn returned, trying to shush the baby down. "...So you did not marry her?" She asked wide-eyed, holding her son's head up to her neck, shushing him continuously.

Thomas glanced away and eyed the furniture again. How was he ever going to get that courage back to ask her why she married her farmer? "We did not marry," he let go hopeless, turning around then closing his eyes in frustration.

Gwendolyn looked at his backside with round eyes. "But...but, I thought you *wanted* to marry her...I expected to see you, but, well since I had not heard from you, I thought you had found a way to proceed with the matrimony. Only seeing you together at Scarborough did I get my confirmation."

Thomas tilted towards Gwendolyn and his heart pounded oddly at the sight of her eyes beginning to water. All his festering incertitude vanished. "I explained everything to you in the letter Gwendolyn."

"What letter?" Gwendolyn asked while kissing her son's forehead. He was finally calm, and babbled within her grasp.

What letter?!

Thomas' heart began to thump in his ears now. "The one that

was addressed to you with the gift I sent for Mary. It was placed under the string with Mary's note, did you not read it?"

Gwendolyn then realized what he was speaking of. "Inside the treasure chest? Are you sure? With Mary's enthusiasm—*oh no*— she pulled so many things out of the trunk at once, it must have fallen back in."

Thomas began to panic, "Good God Gwendolyn, so you did not read the letter? And your marriage—*and his son*—could have been prevented!"

"My marriage? And...his son?"

"By Mr. McMillen."

Gwendolyn closed her mouth and began to walk into another room. Thomas watched her tramp away and began to follow her from room to room searching for something. It was such an awkward hunt; he noted continuously, she was not able to move many things, what with the baby still in her arms. Bending down with one fluid hand she shuffled through papers, making a horrible mess and he watched her do this several times; in the parlor...and out the sitting room, in the sewing room...and out the dining area. When he finally had enough of her inelegance, he blurted out, "Slow down, you are going to drop the infant."

Gwendolyn spun around and offered Thomas the baby. "Here, you hold him. I need to find that letter."

Thomas reluctantly took the baby and uneasily held him out in front of him. His heart began to break just holding that farmer's child within his hands. But then the babe looked up at him and with ample green eyes the son's mirror image impaired him like a thunderbolt. Through choked emotion, Thomas carefully peeled back the blanket that draped over his head and ran his thumb over the infant's black hair. Instantly closing his eyes, he brought the boy lovingly into his chest. His answer was here...He had it all along...His prayers were fulfilled and through tear filled eyes, he observed Gwendolyn pull out the letter from the bottom of the treasure trunk and began ripping it open. "Gwen—"

"Not yet Thomas—" she snapped cutting him off and then it hit her. Here...all along, was the response to all her endless perplexity, the reasons why he stayed away, the motivation to all her insanity. But somehow, as she gazed up to look at Thomas now smiling down at his son, what she desired to know did not seem all that important compared to what she suspected needed to be revealed. "I could not marry him," Gwendolyn set free, clearing her nose into her skirts. "I could not marry one man when I was in love with another." Gwendolyn then pulled off her soiled apron and bunched it up into a ball. "I love you Thomas," she whimpered freely, "I don't think I have ever told you that. I love you, Lord Thomas Albert Hollinger, III. I have loved you since you rescued us on that day we drifted away from port. Loved you even more when you saved me from a tarnishing situation on my fifteenth birthday...fell head over heels for you on our wedding night...and, Heaven help me now... my heart is bursting with love for you at this very moment. I love you, love you, and love you Thomas...are you listening to me?"

Nathaniel's tiny hand had wrapped around his father's index finger and Thomas bent over and kissed his little forehead. Upon closing his eyes, he continued to caress the baby's head with his cheek and softly voiced, "Read the letter Gwendolyn."

Gwendolyn found a seat and tore the letter open immediately.

MY DARLING GWENDOLYN,

I hope this letter reaches you before your joining to Mr. McMillen. I had the messenger send my gifts prematurely, in anticipation that it will arrive on time.

My sweet, sweet girl...I have been in love with you since the day you helped me back to the manor with my broken arm. Our persistent friendship only a vantage to the affection I held for you. No second thoughts here Gwendolyn, you are the first thing I think of at daybreak, and my last attention upon nightfall. Too many years have been spent apart from the one person who always eased a smile to my lips. Seeing you again made me realize how much I need you and without you to share my life with, then I might as well have drowned.

My pledge to Katrina will no longer be official once you have read this. I am calling off the wedding because I am without end your devoted husband. I love you, love you and love you Gwendolyn. Come back to Wilderbrand, bring our daughter and wake up in my arms.

I wait with bated breath upon hearing your reply.

Yours Evermore, Thomas

P. S. The horse's name is "Desire", but Mary can change it if she so pleases.

GWENDOLYN DROPPED THE LETTER TO THE FLOOR AND buried her face within her hands, crying from jubilant release, she allowed her tears to happily drop down the sides of her cheeks. "I love you too, Thomas."

Thomas did not bother to look her way and continued to make funny faces at the baby. "I know…"

"You know?"

Thomas mouthed out the words "I know" to the baby and his son gurgled at him as he smiled.

Gwendolyn walked over to them and shook her head at Thomas' obvious self-assuredness; "His name is Nathaniel by the way…after my brother."

Thomas persisted on with his entertaining; his son reacting to his father's every comical expression. "Nice name, I like it."

"But his ordained name is Lord Nathaniel Kenneth Hollinger… Earl of Suffolkshire, Marques Hollinger and Viscount of Wilderbrand."

Thomas grinned into the baby, "I know…those are my eyes looking up at me."

Gwendolyn gave up and began to smile; she stepped into Thomas and placed her hand on his back. Looking down at her bubbling boy, she expressed, "Your father is such an arrogant man, Nattie."

"And this arrogant man is—*profoundly*—in love with his mother," Thomas adoringly expressed, meeting her teary eyes, leaning over to give Gwendolyn a gentle kiss on her lips, increasingly ardent and tenderly yielded.

They pulled apart and stared at one another, bringing forth-longer tears. Gwendolyn then wrapped her arms around his neck and buried her face into his throat and sniveled, "Where were you?"

Thomas lowered his head and kissed Gwendolyn on the side of her neck. "Devin and I were detained, marooned actually, in France...where were you?"

Gwendolyn continued to capture his intoxicating essence from his incredible warmth against her body, "...Waiting for you to wake up and realize that you were still obsessed."

"Who's obsessed?" Thomas joked, pulling away from her nuzzle and gazing down at his son and nodding at him.

Gwendolyn touched his face with her hand and then wiped away a tear that rolled down his cheek. "We are," she could barely say through stifled sentiment. She leaned in to kiss his soft lips once more, squeezing him tightly to her breast as she did so.

"Mummie! Mummie!" Mary stomped in, yelling, "Father is here! Father is here—" She cut off, watching her mother and father kissing. Thomas broke away from Gwendolyn and eyed Mary's approximation. "Come here, love...go and stand by your mother."

"What are you doing Thomas?" Gwendolyn asked, holding the baby now with one hand and then grabbing Mary's with the other. In total stupefaction, she watched Thomas get down on one's knees before the three of them.

Phyllis and Stewart came in from around the corner and then Marcus, a few more villagers, followed by a startled Charles.

"Good, I have witnesses," Thomas settled, looking over at all the inquiring perception.

With a smile pasted to her face, Gwendolyn forthwith realized what was about to happen. "Thomas, there is no need—"

"Shush Gwendolyn, but there is," he suspended her. "Now, I am taking control of this meandering ship so allow me my address."

Gwendolyn bit down on her lower lip to keep from laughing, "But Thomas—"

"Gwendolyn—*please,*" he cut her off, "...when we were married the first time, we did not have a choice in the matter. Now, we do," he voiced quietly and serious now. "And I...Lord Thomas Albert Hollinger, III, 5th Duke of Norwin and Earl of Wilderbrand, want to take care of you and my family...I am in love with you Lady Gwendolyn of Suffolkshire and I would be honored...no *euphoric,* if you would become my wife once again."

The biggest smile appeared on Mary as she looked up at her mother who was in tears. Mary wrapped her arms around her waist and gave her mother a hug. "What is your answer, Mummie?"

Gwendolyn cleared her cheeks, before saying, "But Thomas, we are already married."

Thomas frowned, "What?"

Gwendolyn reached out and touched his chin; "I never sent the papers back."

"The divorce decree?"

"Yes," she confessed. "I still have them. I *never* signed them. If you wanted to marry that malevolent girl, then you would have to answer to *me* first."

Thomas stood back up again and puffed up with open-mouthed wonder, "Another trick, Gwendolyn?"

"A challenge Thomas."

Thomas grinned, "Challenge?"

"A dare to love."

"Still married then, eh?" Thomas accepted happily, "Then we must renew our vows, tomorrow, today...no now!"

"Now?" Gwendolyn asked astonished.

Thomas hushed down and whispered in her ear, "Gwen love, I wish to be present at the birth of our next child we conceive, so unless you want to continue to be my brood mare, I say most definitely now."

Gwendolyn's mouth flew open wide from the obvious insinuation and innuendo in his stare, "In front of all of these people? You would drag me away? You wouldn't dare."

"Try me."

FIVE WINTERS LATER

WILDERBRAND CASTLE

*L*ying down, Gwendolyn was upstairs in the master bedroom with a thermometer sticking out of her mouth. Looking up at the doctor, she watched him as he recorded her examination. She gazed outside her window and awaited her husband's arrival. Amazing, how five years could come and go so fast, they were practically a blur. She was in love with him…he was in love with her…and Gwendolyn could not help but still miss him every second he was not around.

They did get remarried in a modest chapel in Kettlewell. With little fanfare, her second wedding ceremony to Thomas was one she would never forget. Even though just a few people were in attendance, the ceremony was both beautiful and poignant, and Gwendolyn swore she caught a glimpse of her mother in the shadows of a doorway. And when the Monsignor pronounced that Gwendolyn and Thomas were man and wife, Gwendolyn threw herself into his embrace, wrapped her arms underneath his arms and they remained intertwined and cried in each other's neckline for nearly half an hour. Mary had to finally rip her parents apart and remind them that it was still her birthday and she had presents to open.

Since Gwendolyn never had a real honeymoon, Thomas whisked her off to Egypt to view the pyramids, to Africa to encounter obscured wildlife and to South America to sample the best melon and passion fruit she ever tasted. They kept her Great-Aunt's cottage for the summertime and decided not to sell Gisleham Manor and restore it back to its original splendor; concluding to give it to Mary for a wedding present, when she was old enough to marry of course.

Moving into Wilderbrand was also an experience. She had never managed a household that expansive before, but she was up to the challenge. Thomas insisted that she hire a governess for the children as well, but Gwendolyn was adamant. She was used to raising her children without any help, but after Thomas told her that they were expected to make appearances and would be attending many social events as the Duke and Duchess of Norwin, Gwendolyn gave in.

Their Graces, the Duke and Duchess of Norwin, she would probably never be so incredulous over that title. To be known officially as the "Duchess of Norwin", oh heavens, so much prestige and adulation walked hand-in-hand with nobility. She remembered the first time she heard that heading being announced when they were at a social function; everyone who's everyone was in attendance, even his Royal Highness. When Gwendolyn and Thomas were formerly introduced all eyes turned to them and a sea of gasps was heard throughout the great ballroom. Everyone knew that Thomas was about to get married, but not to Gwendolyn. Did the Duke of Norwin really marry his mistress? There were rumors flying around town about his latest exploit, but then a handful of elder guests knew the real truth, and that was what started the world of chitchat: "Of course she looks familiar!" "Remember the Drummond's of Suffolkshire?" "Lady Mary Drummond?" "Gwendolyn was the daughter of the Earl of

Suffolkshire." "Yes, the Earl that perished at sea." "So tragic, the whole family, lost." "Lovely couple, we wish them all the best."

As the doctor took the thermometer out of her mouth, Gwendolyn pinpointed a vase in the corner of the room filled with pink roses. Pink always reminded her of one person—*Katrina*.

After learning that Katrina married Henry and gave birth to a daughter, Gwendolyn thought that would be the end to her larking about. But no, Katrina made sure she was still in Thomas' area of interest. She would visit Henry on a daily basis, making sure she bumped into Thomas every chance she got. It was over, he would remind her, he married Gwendolyn, they were extremely happy, but she never got the point. Thomas was so sick of her following him around that he gave her an ultimatum. Either she terminated her harassment or he would send Henry to America to assist him with his new venture being developed there. Katrina Barton was further distressed, she could not believe that Thomas was no longer interested. Katrina was so far gone, she even showed up unannounced at dinner one evening, crying and begging to see Thomas. Gwendolyn should have been bothered, but she just felt sorry for her. Thomas had no other choice but to send Henry to America, and last Gwendolyn heard, Henry was doing well with the new **HCC** in New York and Katrina gave birth to another daughter.

And the best part of all of this would be Amy, Henry's sister. She finally found the man of her dreams...Charles McMillen. Oh yes, Gwendolyn was totally surprised when she heard too. Disappointed that the bulls he purchased in Scarborough failed, Charles went to Manchester to purchase two additional males. Once there, he met and fell in love with a beautiful brunette. Both utterly surprised with their mutual acquaintances, they married three months later and now have two sets of twins.

Gwendolyn continued to stare out the window and watched the sun go down. Thomas would be home soon and she could not wait to talk to him. They were going to have a family supper that evening, with no guests; guests, meaning, no Devin Hale. Oh, Gwendolyn loved Devin, how could she not? He was Thomas' surrogate brother after all. He shared the same interests as her husband, even the same humor. *Devin was a good man*, Gwendolyn realized, she just wished he would find himself a wife. Gwendolyn loved to toy with him occasionally, telling him that if he was not careful he may just wake up in love. But he was still a rake though, breaking hearts throughout London, but he always found the time to come by and visit with the children. She could always tell the misguided men apart from the selfish ones, by way of their interest in the little things, like children. Devin loved playing with the boys; Gwendolyn could always find him in the nursery playing blocks with them, he even spent time with Mary, showing her tricks on horseback and how to fight with a sword. Oh Gwendolyn raised her eyebrow over that little hobby, but figured; maybe Mary would need to know one day and allowed her lessons. He was not really upset about his sister either, figured it was time to concentrate on her husband and new family and what better opportunity to have Katrina an ocean away from temptation.

Married life was wonderful. The first time she experienced waking up in her husband's arms was the last time Gwendolyn ever cried. Releasing tears of joy was like diving into their shared lake, inspirational and invigorating. No more looking back, only looking forward; each day, a new beginning to create new memories to share with her forever best friend.

* * *

THOMAS FINALLY ARRIVED AT SUNSET FROM A HARD DAY at work. Devin stayed late as well and the both of them tried to figure out how to keep up with the American's. Seems they were building huge clipper ships, *Windjammers*, the Yanks were calling them, and they were even challenging Britain to some kind of race. Up the China coast and back, who could make it the quickest?

Well, Thomas was absolutely up for the challenge and he and Devin began devising a plan for their expected victory.

After taking off his Carrick, Thomas roamed around from room to room searching for his wife. Usually, Gwendolyn was at the door receiving him with wide-open arms, but on this night, she was not? He was wounded—he had not felt that sort of pang in his heart for quite some time.

In the library, Thomas noticed Fitzwater restocking his cigars in his cedar box on top of his desk. "Fitzwater, where is the Duchess?"

"I believe she is upstairs, sir."

"Upstairs? Why?"

"The doctor is examining her."

"The doctor!" Thomas exclaimed. "Is she ill? Why didn't anyone send for me?" Thomas immediately stormed out of the room and ran up the staircase. Mrs. Hornebrook was on her way down, "What is wrong with her? Why didn't anyone send me a note?"

Mrs. Hornebrook caressed his cheek, "Calm down Your Grace, it is not that kind of sickness."

Thomas searched her kind eyes and realized what she was trying to imply. "Oh…I see, well, thank you Mrs. Hornebrook."

"You are very welcome, sir. And I am so happy for you," she smiled, while walking down the staircase. "So much laughter in this dwelling now, it is such a warm feeling."

Thomas stood idle watching Mrs. Hornebrook mumbling to herself and then preceded up the stairs. When he reached the main bedroom, Dr. Lynch was by Gwendolyn's bedside.

"Oh Thomas, you are finally home!" Gwendolyn replied, smiling with glee upon seeing him.

The doctor turned to look at Gwendolyn one last time before he left, "Now remember what I said Duchess, the time frame, it must be followed accordingly."

Thomas shook hands with the doctor right before his exit and then slowly emerged towards the bed. "What is wrong, love? What does he mean by time frame?"

Gwendolyn blushed and patted the empty spot next to her by the bed. "Come...come sit by me."

Thomas immediately rushed to her side but instead of sitting calmly by the edge like she asked, he grabbed her into his arms and squeezed her tight. "Are we going to have another baby?"

Gwendolyn wrapped her arms around his shoulders and held him tight. "Yes."

"Are you all right, love? Any fever? Is the baby all right?"

Gwendolyn pulled apart from him and melted at the sight of his concerned stare. "Yes, darling, everything is fine. He just wants me to stay in bed for a while, that's all."

"You do not seem to get so sick when you are immobile, love, maybe that's sound advice. I will have Fitzwater send out the proper letters and cancel all future engagements for the next few months."

"Yes," she added, looking down at her lap.

"Something else is wrong, I can feel it," Thomas asked panicky. "Tell me."

"Well, he says...that it is unnatural for a woman my age to keep having children...that...that after this one, the doctor suggested that we..." she paused, trying to find the right words, "Discontinue from having them."

"Discontinue? You mean...stop?"

"Yes."

"You mean you and I...everything...bring to a halt?"

"Yes."

Refrain from touching his own wife? The woman who sometimes brought him to his knees by her beauty from across a room? Thomas' whole body went on the defensive. "You are only thirty-one Gwendolyn, why my mother was thirty-five when she had me!"

"Really? How do you know that?"

"My father was a notorious rake, don't you know?" He sailed on, "My mother was a servant in his household; Jordan was illegitimate the first few months of his life. She was in her mid-twenties when my father married her."

"I never knew that," Gwendolyn pronounced in awe, watching Thomas fidgeting in his seat.

"See, you learn something new every day," he quipped, leaning into her and kissing her on the forehead. "Oh bloody hell...I won't be able to follow through with it Gwendolyn; is Dr. Lynch suggesting that we do not touch? If I cannot hold you in my arms...I will go mad!"

Gwendolyn caressed his cheek, "The same goes for me too. Why, just looking at you makes me want to pounce on you."

Thomas grinned and then kissed her softly on her lips. Kissing her once was never enough. Oh God, he knew this going to happen. Five children later and he could not stop handling her. His lips found their way to her neck and Gwendolyn arched her throat up to receive him.

"It is no wonder I'm with child again," Gwendolyn gushed, closing her eyes from his mouth nibbling on her ear. "My husband is an insufferable insatiable man."

Quickly, his passion for her inflamed and they were immediately in each other's arms. He was hotly bussing her mouth; kneading her breasts through her bodice when the rumbling sounds of stomping rounded down the hallway...then towards the door...then through the door...then pounce...on top of the bed!

Thomas and Gwendolyn split apart and were besieged by mayhem. Thomas just barely opened up his arms to receive Millicent, their three year old daughter who jumped into his open embrace.

"Did sister put that crown of duck feathers in your hair?" He asked, kissing her forehead. Grey-green eyes and dark cherry hair, she looked exactly like Gwendolyn's mother. Nodding in agreement, she laid her head down on her father's chest and stuck her thumb in her mouth.

Gwendolyn tapped Thomas on the shoulder and shook her head at him, "Do not let her do that, her teeth will get crooked."

Thomas gently pulled out her thumb then ran his fingers through Millicent's soft curls then eyed the raven beauty making her regal entrance.

Mary came through the door holding Philip, barely a year, followed on her heel, Nathaniel, five and Jordan, four years of age.

"Father, Jordy keeps sticking his tongue out at me," Nathaniel glowered, crossing his arms into his chest.

"No, I won't, Nattie, stop whying," Jordan spat back at him.

"Yes, you do, like this," Nathaniel displayed, sticking his own tongue down to his chin.

Briskly coming to the rescue, Thomas stepped in between the two little boys, "Now men, we do not act like savages in this household, we are gents of fashion. Now, go back to the nursery and get ready for bed. I will be there in a moment to tuck you in."

Gwendolyn rolled her eyes and got out of bed. "Oh Thomas, really, they're too young to understand that low tone of voice of yours when you are trying to get your point across."

"What low tone of voice?"

"That one," she stated, pointing to his throat and then leaning into to him for a softhearted kiss.

Mary now ambled over and plopped her body onto a chair near the both of them. With a heavy sigh, she watched her two brothers' stick their tongues out at each other once again before darting out of the room.

Thomas drew Millicent into him and kissed the back of her head before setting her down as well. She too, shot off and out of the room in a jiffy.

Gwendolyn walked over to her daughter's side and knelt at the base of her legs. At sixteen, Mary Hollinger was, by far, an unparalleled stunning young maiden. With her father's coloring, she inherited her mother's façade and many young bachelors who asked about her daily eagerly anticipated her come-out.

Taking Philip from within her arms, Gwendolyn wrapped her finger around one of Mary's long ebony tresses and curled her thumb around the ringlet and inquired, "What's the matter, love? You are wearing that look when you have lost a horse race."

Mary suddenly buried her face within her hands. "Oh Mummie — Father, I've clapped eyes on someone and he acts like it does not matter!"

Thomas quickly met eyes with Gwendolyn, "She is sixteen Gwendolyn, do something!"

She watched him pace the floor out in front of them. "Thomas, stop panicking, we were young too. I think you were six when you fell in love with me."

"So."

"So," Gwendolyn retorted giving him a condescending smirk and caressing her daughter's back. "Why do you think he does not care, Mary? What does he do, or does not do when around you?"

"Like the other day, he was with a group of friends and I was with a group of friends and normally when I gaze at him, he is staring at me. He makes my legs go weak with his big brown eyes. Only this last time when I looked at him, he pretended not to notice."

Thomas took Philip away from Gwendolyn and laid him down on the bed. Instantly, the toddler rolled over onto his stomach and began to flap his legs and arms like a fish out of water. "The other day? Why Mary, we were at his majesty's family affair, which boy are you interested in?"

Mary suddenly met eyes with her father. "Lord George Fitzclarence, Earl of Munster."

"Fitzclarence! Of the Royal Family?" Gwendolyn shrieked, scaring her son on the bed.

The little guy looked up at Thomas with huge brown eyes,

about to cry. "I know them. I do," Thomas voiced, picking up the baby, cradling him in his arms and trying to compose him.

"Why, isn't he at least twenty? Oh Thomas, this must be genuine. What do we do?" Gwendolyn asked, searching her daughter's eyes for gravity.

"Oh now you want my advice, well, King George is quite mad I have heard I bet I could barter the union. I have business dealings with the Royal Navy."

Gwendolyn tsked at him, "Oh no you are not! My daughter will be married for love, not through arrangement. If Lord Fitzclarence cares for Mary, then he will have to show purpose. I refuse to force my daughter—"

"Our daughter, Gwendolyn," Thomas proudly interrupted her.

"Our daughter, marry through orchestration."

Mary crossed her arms in front of her, "I agree with Mummie."

"You do?" Thomas asked suspiciously, arching a black brow.

"Yes, I do not want George's forced attention; I want to know if his affection will be returned."

Gwendolyn grinned and continued to rub Mary's back. "Everyone does," she relayed, getting back up on her feet, only to feel extremely queasy. Holding her hand over her mouth, Gwendolyn darted to the washbasin to vomit.

Mary sprung from her seat and replied, *"Oh no, not again."*

Thomas stepped over to Gwendolyn and assisted her back to bed. Picking up his little one carefully, he laid his son back down onto his mother's chest. Philip had fallen asleep. "Your mother and I love each other, Mary…children are the result of such a love."

Mary rolled her eyes, "I seem to have the only parents in London who seem to exhibit their devotion. None of my friends have parents who still procreate."

Thomas stood beside Gwendolyn and brushed away hair that mottled her face. When Gwendolyn glanced up at him, he traced his finger alongside her chin. Rallying her attention, he related,

"And they won't stop having them until Heaven replenishes their family. Right, Gwendolyn?"

Gwendolyn blinked back her tears, "I was thinking the very same thing."

Their eyes lock and hold.

"I love you," he whispered to her.

"I know," she whispered back smiling.

Thomas grinned into her jesting then swiftly turned around to address his daughter. He walked over to her sternly, but then reached for her embrace. Mary warmed up to him instantly and ran into his arms. "Now love, about you and Lord Fitzclarence..."

Continued...

ABOUT TRISHA

With over 50 books to her credit, prolific romance author Trisha Fuentes also owns Ardent Artist Books, a thriving independent press she launched in 2008 that now houses over 100 titles.

Ardent Artist Books expanded significantly in 2020 by welcoming best-selling authors Savannah Kole and Aubrey Tate. Trisha's recent writing features fun, fast-paced, and steamy romances with witty heroines finding their gorgeous, sexy heroes quickly. These romances always lead to a satisfying Happily Ever After with a dash of sweet angst in both historical and modern settings.

Rejoice, Romance Reader...

Official Website
trishafuentes.com

instagram.com/authortrish
amazon.com/Trisha-Fuentes/e/B002BME1MI
facebook.com/booksbyTrish
youtube.com/theardentartist

ALSO BY TRISHA FUENTES

❀❀ Modern Romance ❀❀

A Sacrifice Play

Faded Dreams

Never Say Forever

The Price of Everything

One Weekend One Mistake

* * *

❀❀ Historical ❀❀

The Anzan Heir

Magnet & Steele

The Relentless Rogue

One Starry Night

In The Moonlight With You

Captivating the Captain

The Merry Widow

Unrequited Love

The Summer Romance of the Duke

A Dare Maid in Vain

A Marriage of Mismatch

The Spoiled Duke

A Season of Second Chances

Propriety and Passion

A Countess by Arrangement

When Fates Collide

The Rake's Honor

When May Met December

The Viscount's Gamble

❀❀❀ **Series Books** ❀❀❀

HOLLINGER

Dare To Love - Book 1

A Matchless Match - Book 2

Arrogance & Conceit - Book 3

Impropriety - Book 4

SERVICE • DAUGHTER

The Steward's Daughter - Book 1

The Cook's Daughter - Book 2

The Curator's Daughter - Book 3

THUNDERBOLT

The Surprise Heir - Book 1

A Dance of Deception - Book 2

Win the Heart of a Duchess- Book 3

OBSESSION

Unsuitable Obsession - Part One

Broken Obsession - Part Two

ESCAPE

Swept Away - Book 1

Fire & Rescue - Book 2

The Domain King - Book 3

AGE • GAP • ROMANCE

Whispers of Yesterday - Book 1

His Encore, Her Ecstasy - Book 2

Against the Wind - Book 3

❧

SERIAL • ROMANCE

The Rekindled Flame - Book 1

The Power of Two - Book 2

Facing the Past - Book 3

Taking a Chance - Book 4

Choosing the Future - Book 5

❧

↪**Full Paperback**

https://bit.ly/3XbNK2e

www.ingramcontent.com/pod-product-compliance
Lightning Source LLC
Chambersburg PA
CBHW030630110726
47901CB00002B/392